# The Devil's Guide
## To Managing Difficult People

### ROBYN BENNIS

D0188125

To those who go on.

# 1

I met the devil at a Motel 6, poolside.

"Call me Dee," she said, with a disarming crinkle of her nose.

She didn't have horns and hooves. She didn't radiate waves of evil. I couldn't hear the echoing screams of the damned behind her voice. If I felt revulsion toward her, it was because she fit so well into a two-piece bathing suit.

"You look like you could use a friend."

I should have run, but here's the thing: if you ever met the devil—and knowing the assholes you hang out with, you might have—she looks like any other traveler.

We talked, as travelers do, exchanging vacuous comments about the weather and the latest movies—all the usual stuff you say to people you meet on a business trip. We didn't talk politics, we didn't talk religion, and she never mentioned her line of work. Only the last struck me as unusual.

I went back to my room, thinking I'd never see Dee again. But when I checked out the next morning, she was in line behind me. After settling my bill, I hustled to grab a taxi before she could suggest sharing one, because I'd used up all my vacuous conversation the day before.

Naturally, I ran into her less than an hour later, in the security line at Tampa International. We had nothing left to talk about, so I suffered an uncomfortable silence all the way to the body scanner. Worse, every time I glanced at her, she was smiling hopefully at me, as if she expected me to start in on a topic.

I didn't. Awkward as the situation was, getting friendly would only come to more pain in the long run. On the other side of security, I grabbed my bag, said I was late for my flight, and rushed to the gate.

I arrived to empty chairs and an airplane that wasn't scheduled to take off for over an hour. When I looked back, I saw Dee glancing from her ticket to my gate and making a straight line toward it.

*Fuck.*

I ducked into the nearest concourse store and pretended interest in racks full of flip-flops and sunglasses. I couldn't handle another hour of meaningless silence, and the only alternative was forming a personal connection—which is behavior I barely tolerate from my friends, let alone strangers.

I snuck from store to store along the concourse, until I reached an out-of-the-way gate and sat down there. Just in case Dee happened to wander over and see me, I made a phone call. That's the kind of thing military strategists call "defense in depth." Always have a backup plan, even if it involves calling up a sex line and talking to the operator as if you were old friends. The charge to your credit card will sting just once, while the emotional distance you create between you and some rando will last for the rest of your life.

It was my lucky day, because I didn't need the sex line this time. I called David, a guy I was…dating? I'd gone on a date with him the week before, anyway. The point is, I saved $4.95 a minute.

"Hey there," he said, picking up.

"Hey," I answered.

"What are you up to?"

"Waiting at the airport."

It may occur to you that this is exactly the sort of vacuous conversation I was trying to avoid with Dee, but with David it felt comfortable and warm. It's all about context, you know?

"Your mom lives around there, doesn't she?" he asked.

"Yeah, but I didn't get a chance to see her."

We chatted about this and that, until I heard my flight number over the intercom, and I could hardly believe it. I looked at the time. I'd spent almost an hour on the phone, talking about nothing.

"They're calling my group," I said.

"I should let you go, then. Hey, do you want to do something tonight? Maybe a movie?"

My first reflex was to say yes—to say it repeatedly and exuberantly—but that reflex was checked by a mountain of reasons to say no. I settled on "I dunno. I'm probably going to be tired as hell. Flying does that to me." I know this is shitty, but I was hoping he'd talk me up to a yes.

Sadly, he had too much respect for my stated preferences. He made a cute, disappointed little "Aww" sound and said, "Okay. Maybe sometime this week?"

"Yeah. That would be nice."

I slipped into my boarding line, kept my head low, and made it all the way to my seat before I saw Dee again, shuffling down the narrow aisle, sandwiched between a sunburned teenager and a sunken-eyed man dressed in business casual. I gave her a professional head-bob, and she returned a giddy smile. She waved her ticket at me, shouting across ten rows, "Hey, Jordan, look! We're seat buddies!"

There was no stopping it now. We were stuck together until I got off in Atlanta to catch my connecting flight to Boston. By that time, I'd either be dead of boredom, or Dee and I would be exchanging phone numbers, friending each other on Facebook, and promising to always keep in touch.

*Fuck.*

As the line of travelers moved along, bringing her inexorably closer, I played the eye-contact game. You know how it works: you're stuck facing someone you barely know and you have to calculate the most polite frequency and duration with which to make eye contact. Too little and you're rude. Too much and you're a creep.

I like to aim a smidge on the side of rude, because there are asymmetrical risks involved, but Dee chose full-throttle weirdo. Every time I glanced at her, she was staring back at me, her perfect teeth showing through a perfect smile. This behavior admitted only two possibilities: she had a bizarre obsession with me, or she was anxious because she was planning to blow up the plane.

When she sat down, she hugged me and said in the most cheerful tones, "I hope there isn't a movie, so we can talk through the whole flight." Oh, God, why couldn't she be planning to blow up the plane?

"That'll be great," I said, as I looked through my purse for sleeping pills. I found one in its foil blister package, and another lying loose in a corner, covered in tissue lint and a light dusting of face powder. I glanced up to see Dee smiling like a lunatic, and decided to take both of them. I can handle two sleeping pills as long as I don't take them with alcohol.

"What are those?" she asked.

"Vitamins," I answered, without a second thought.

"Here, wash them down with this." She held out a plastic cup filled to the rim with a pale red drink and one lonely ice cube.

I examined it. "Where did you get that?" I hadn't seen her bringing it on the plane and there had been no drink service. We weren't even in the air.

"I nabbed it from someone in business class," she said. "It's just cranberry juice."

If I'd had more time to think, I would have refused. I would have refused, refrained from taking my sleeping pills, and spent the rest of the flight with my keys in my hand, in case I needed a weapon in a hurry.

But I didn't have time to think, and concluded without thought that cooperation was the safest option. I put both pills in my mouth and took a sip. "Well," she said, as the beverage hit my tongue, "cranberry juice and a shitload of vodka."

Robyn Bennis

Grey Goose, I think, or possibly Svedka. Definitely a winter wheat variety. I could smell it before it hit my lips, and there was a half-second window in which I could have refused, but my natural instincts were at cross-purposes to rationality. Once I started, Dee tipped the cup up so I had to either drink or let it spill. So, I drank it down, sleeping pills and all.

Dee took the cup back, set it on the floor, and used her foot to push it under the seat in front of her. Then she looked down into my still-open purse and asked, loud enough for the whole fucking plane to hear, "Hey, you have any spare tampons?"

"Uhh..."

"I don't need one. I'm just curious."

You know that lost, helpless feeling you get when things are happening faster than you can process them? That's what I had.

"Oh, Jordan! You're a hoot!" she said with frenetic energy, even though I'd just been sitting there, staring blankly back at her. She gave me another hug—one of those long, tight, rocking-back-and-forth hugs that are typically shared only between close family and lovers. When it was over, I could have told her if she had a breast lump. Before I could give her the clinical report, she said, "We have to promise to be friends forever."

My vodka and doxylamine cocktail was already kicking in, so I just smiled and nodded as I slipped into slumber.

When I next rose to lucidity, Dee was still in the seat next to me.

Well, that's not quite accurate. She was about three quarters in the seat next to me, sleeping with her head nestled against my shoulder and one hand on my lap. This circumstance became all the more unnerving when I realized that I wasn't aboard the same airplane I fell asleep on.

I don't know exactly what this says about my priorities, but my most immediate fear was that I was on the wrong connecting flight. Only after several seconds had passed did it occur to me that I might have been roofied. No, wait, that wasn't quite right. I'd actually roofied myself, hadn't I? I didn't know what the legal implications were, but I was pretty sure the resulting criminal trial would inspire an episode of *Law and Order.*

"Excuse me," I said, using my free hand to tap the guy sitting in front of me. "Where is this plane going?"

He twisted around in his seat and said, "It's going straight up your big fat ass, you retard."

So, it *was* going to Boston, thank God. But why was Dee on it?

She opened her eyes and said softly, "Hey, you."

Why, oh why, couldn't she have been there to blow up the plane? "So, uh, you're on this flight, too?" I asked.

She smiled as she stretched. "I changed my flight when I saw you needed help. You don't have a very high tolerance for alcohol, do you? That one drink knocked you right out."

What a disaster. Someone changes their flight for you, and that's an automatic, lifelong friendship right there. You can't wriggle out of that shit.

I thanked her profusely for her help—because what the hell else could I do?—and we chatted through the flight, until finally I happened to ask, "So, what's your profession, anyway?"

"Oh, haven't I mentioned?" She smiled the most amiable, peaceable little smile, and said, "I'm the devil."

"I see," I said, laughing it off. "How does that pay?"

"Pretty well," she said, quite seriously. "I mean, I'm the devil."

## 2

The devil followed me home. I even paid her subway fare.

But I wasn't about to let someone who thinks she's Beelzebub into my apartment. At my front door, I beamed my best smile and said, "I just can't thank you enough for what you've done. Here, let me get you a rideshare back to the airport."

Dee frowned. "I don't know. I feel like you still need my help, Jordan."

I wore the same friendly smile you might use on a dangerous dog. "No, I'm good. Thank you again."

She scrunched her lips and turned her eyes to the side, as if struggling to understand. I took the opportunity to turn away and look for my phone.

"Where the hell," I began, and turned back to see Dee holding it.

"Hey, who's this guy that's all over your Instagram?" she asked, as she scrolled through photos from my date with David. "At a movie. Then dinner. Then an arcade. Aw, that's cute. Then doing shots. Oh, and look at the timestamps. Big gap from 9 pm to 10:30 pm." She waggled her eyebrows. "Girl, you must have banged hardcore."

I reached out to take the phone. She handed it back, wearing a pout. The pout only intensified and was joined by widening puppy-dog eyes as I slipped inside my apartment. I kept the door open a crack but made sure my body was blocking it. I spoke through the gap. "Thank you! I'll hail a ride for you. Should be here in a few minutes."

I shut the door and, quiet as possible, set the dead bolt.

Inside, the landline was ringing. I went to the kitchen and disconnected the cord from the wall. I'd been meaning to get rid of that thing, anyway. Nothing but telemarketers and pushy relatives, right?

"Hope that wasn't an important call." Dee's voice came from the living room, inside the apartment.

My heart stopped, then made up for the oversight by beating fast and hard. I could feel my skin heat. I *had* set the deadbolt, right? I knew I'd set the deadbolt. I was one hundred percent sure I'd set the deadbolt. Yet here was her voice, coming from the living room.

I cautiously stuck my head around the kitchen door.

She was sitting on the couch. She had a bag of chips open in one hand and a beer in the other. My chips. My beer. From my kitchen. The kitchen I was in. The kitchen she couldn't possibly have accessed without me seeing. She held the beer between her legs, dug into the cushions for the remote control, and turned on the television.

I reached behind me to open the cutlery drawer. "So, uh, how did you get in here?" My voice trembled, cutting in and out like a sheep's.

"I'm the devil," she said, her eyes on the television as she clicked from channel to channel. "Didn't I mention that before? I'm pretty sure I mentioned that. Oh, look, Maury's on!"

I slid a long, sharp boning knife out of the drawer. With my other hand, I reached for the telephone, before I remembered that I'd just disconnected it. I went for my cell instead.

"Who ya calling?" Dee asked, but not from the living room. Her voice came from just behind my ear, so close I could feel her breath rustling my hair.

I whipped around, felt the cell phone fly from my hand, saw it break into a dozen pieces against the fridge, heard my own desperate scream echo off the walls.

Before I even knew what I was doing, I'd stuck the knife into her belly.

We looked down at the bloody handle together, both of us more surprised than frightened. Without a word, she wrapped her hands around mine, clutching tight as blood oozed over our fingers. I stepped back, let go, wrenched free of her grip.

I took another step back, then another. A wave of cold dread hit me, radiating outward from my core, rather than inward from the air. My skin, though suddenly wet with sweat, was uncomfortably hot. It felt like it was tightening, squeezing into my organs.

I backed away until I was through the kitchen door and flat against the living room wall. I closed my eyes so hard it hurt, then opened them as wide as I could, as if the entire situation were a broken laptop that could be fixed by turning it off and on again. When that failed, my mind raced with ideas to undo this. Not to deal with it, mind you, to *undo* it. To unstab the woman bleeding to death in my kitchen.

Dee's eyes drifted to mine as she fell across the countertop. She shot me a somber, accusing look as her knees buckled. "Out, out, brief candle," she said, struggling to hold onto the counter. "Life's but a walking shadow, a poor player that struts and frets his hour upon the stage, and then is heard no more." She lost her grip and fell to the tiles, leaving a trail of blood down the front of my dishwasher. "It is a tale told by an idiot." The blood came faster. Half the kitchen floor was covered in a red, curdling puddle. "Full of sound and fury." She lay her head against the tile, her fingers relaxing from around the knife handle. "Signifying nothing." Her arms and legs went limp, but at the last moment, she perked up and asked, "Hey, do you have any domestic IPA? That beer in the fridge is shit." And then she went still, her vacant eyes still fixed on mine.

I was just as vacant-eyed and nearly as still. My mouth hung open so long that my tongue ached from the dryness. Dee's blood had spread nearly to the living room carpet before I could think clearly. I looked at the shattered pieces of my cell phone, like little islands in a sea of crimson, wondering if you're supposed to dial 911 when somebody's already dead. And if not 911, then what? Is there a special number?

"She looks so peaceful," Dee said, right beside me.

I screamed louder than before, and if I'd still had the knife in my hand, I think I would have stabbed her again.

"Geez, you're jumpy today." Dee—living, breathing, unbloodied Dee—stepped on tiptoes into the pool of blood in the kitchen and stood over her own limp, duplicate body. The two were identical in every respect, except for the pallor and the knife sticking out of one of them. "Oh, a boning knife!" the living version of Dee said, examining the corpse. "Good call. A lot of people go for the chef's knife, because it looks scarier, but the boning knife drives deeper with less force. You know, with your instincts and experience, you could kill people professionally."

My eyes whipped between the two Dees, one dead and one alive. "But...how?" I stammered.

"Oh, I know some guys. I'll hook you up."

"HOW ARE YOU ALIVE?"

She scrunched her nose. "Oh, that. I feel like I've already mentioned I'm the devil?" She opened the fridge and looked over the shelves. "Seriously, is this the only beer you have?"

"You're the devil?"

She glanced up from the fridge and gave me the sort of look reserved for idiots.

"Why would the devil be in my kitchen?"

"I'm here to help you," she said, popping the top off a beer with her fingernails. "I feel like I already said that, too. I can't tell if I'm having déjà vu or if you're just very, very stupid."

"I...I...I don't need help with anything," I said, with ironic desperation.

The devil gave me another surprised look. "You have more murdered corpses in your kitchen than you have palatable beverages, and you expect me to believe you don't need my help?" She walked into the living room, brushing past me and leaving bloody footprints on the carpet.

"You...you'll help me with this?" Again, you may think me a moron for asking the devil for help, but give me a break here. It was my first brutal murder.

"Absolutely I will," the devil said, leaning back on the couch and putting her bloody shoes up on the ottoman. "First, you better answer the door."

"What?" There was a knock, which made me jump again. I looked at Dee and asked, "What should I say?"

"Hmmm," she said, seeming to think. "Tell them you didn't just totally murder someone."

At the time, that almost seemed like a good idea, but I was just clearheaded enough not to say it. I set the security chain, positioned myself to hide the blood on my clothes, and opened the door.

It was my upstairs neighbor. "I've told you about the noise," she said, trying to peer through the narrow opening. "I'm not your mom, but I wish you would keep it down."

Ha! Not my mom. Yeah, because if she was my mom, she'd be on three of every drug and wouldn't give a shit how much noise I made—or who I brutally murdered, for that matter.

I didn't say that, of course, because my upstairs neighbor isn't exactly a bad person. She's just a sheltered, judgmental twentysomething who'd never lived in an apartment before moving to the city. She told me her name when she moved in, but I forgot it immediately.

Her eyes narrowed as she noticed that I was hiding myself from the neck down. "Why don't you open the door? Are you naked? Do you have a man in there?"

"No, she doesn't!" Dee called out.

My neighbor's jaw tightened with a mix of revulsion and giddy anticipation, until she seemed to remember she wasn't living in a town where you could shun someone for being gay. She held onto her revulsion but replaced the anticipation with chagrin.

Under ordinary circumstances, I suppose I would have told her the screams she heard were me fucking a lady, in the hope she'd be sufficiently disgusted to leave me alone. I wasn't thinking clearly, though, so I casually rested my hand against the door frame and said, "Oh, no, it wasn't that. A mouse startled me."

"A mouse?" she asked, her eyes drifting to my hand.

Only then did I remember that my fingers were covered in blood. "Don't worry. I killed it with a boning knife." I've always heard you should wrap a lie in the truth. It might have even worked, if my tremulous, sheep-bleating voice hadn't picked that exact moment to return.

"That's a lot of blood for one mouse," she said.

"M-might have been a rat," I said. "B-b-big sucker. I put it down the garbage disposal. Thanks for checking on me."

I closed the door and slumped against it, sliding down to the floor. I could hear her lingering on the other side for a minute, and felt every single second as an eternity of cold dread. Then she went upstairs. I didn't hear her calling the police. Then again, wouldn't she keep her voice down, if that's what she was doing?

"Hey, could you run after her and see if she has any good beer?" Dee called from the living room.

# 3

The upstairs neighbor did not call the police, though an hour of agonized wondering passed before I was sure of it.

It took me all afternoon and half the night to clean up the mess. Every time I thought I'd gotten the last of the blood, I noticed more—another puddle under the fridge or a clot stuck in the grout. It's funny, because you never realize how sticky blood is until you have an entire person's worth seeping into your grout. And all it takes is a microscopic splatter to get the victim's DNA. I know. I watch crime shows.

Dee's help consisted of tracking blood through the rest of the apartment and, when I walked to the supermarket to get bleach and cling wrap, telling me which brands of beer to pick up. When I returned without any beer, she clucked her tongue and said, "You know, the people at the store are going to remember someone who went in and bought nothing but murder clean-up supplies."

I was too frightened to answer back. I was pretty well convinced that she was the devil by that point. Even if she wasn't—even if she hadn't displayed an abundance of evil and supernatural powers—it's pretty distressing to have someone hanging around your first murder scene. It has a tendency to put you on edge, you know?

It was well into evening before I worked up the nerve to say, "Hey, this whole helping-me project you keep talking about? Were you planning to do it at any point?" Probably not the best approach when you're speaking to the devil, but between adrenaline withdrawal and hours kneeling in blood, I was feeling a tad nihilistic.

"I had planned to," Dee said from the couch, where she was playing a Super Mario game, "but then I realized I'm the victim in all this."

I was half a second from asking her how she figured she was the victim, when I remembered murdering her. So, I asked in a teensy, tiny, polite little voice, "Can you maybe help me move the body?"

"To where?" the devil asked.

*Shit.* I knew I'd overlooked something. I began working the problem over in my mind.

"You're trying to remember how they get rid of bodies on TV, aren't you?" the devil asked.

"No!" Well, yes, actually. I'd already ruled out burying it in the backyard, because they always find backyard graveyards about fifteen years later, and because I didn't have a backyard. I couldn't dissolve it in acid and flush it down the drain, because I didn't trust the ancient pipes in my apartment building—we aren't even supposed to put coffee grounds down there.

That left burial in the woods. The problem was, I didn't have a car. I had a Zipcar membership, but the nearest lot was three blocks away and I couldn't work out a way to drag the body that far without being seen. I was beginning to despair for a solution and on the verge of tears.

It took me five minutes to realize I could drive the car around to my apartment and load the body there. Call me a moron, but let's see how clearly you think the next time you murder someone.

I reserved a hatchback online and got to work encasing the body in cling wrap. Oh, and here's a lifehack for the next time you stab someone in the belly and you're encasing the body in cling wrap: start at the middle and work your way outward. If you start wrapping at either end, you're basically just squeezing a big bag of watery shit with a hole in it. For related reasons, you really want to wrap the body up *before* you've scrubbed the area down with bleach, because otherwise, you'll have to repeat that step.

"Sorry about that," the devil said, stepping over the shitty mess on her way to the fridge. "I had one of those fifteen-dollar sandwiches on the plane and I don't think it agreed with me. How come you don't have any ice cream?"

It was at this point that my fatigue caught up with me. I sat back on my heels, the sponge drooping in my gloved fingers. "Why are you here?" I asked.

The devil peered deeper into the freezer. "Well, I came in looking for ice cream, but now I'm kind of eyeing those waffles. You think it's too late for a waffle?"

I no longer had the energy to be exasperated or terrified. "I'm not going to sell my soul to you."

She pulled her head out of the freezer and laughed. "Don't flatter yourself. I'm not here to buy your crummy soul. I'm here to help you."

I tried my best to be diplomatic—polite but firm. "Well, I feel very helped. You've definitely helped me. Thank you. Now please leave me alone."

I braced myself, expecting her to burn me to cinders right then and there. Instead, she stuck a box of waffles under her armpit, closed the freezer door, and ruffled my hair on her way to the toaster. "Oh, Jordan" was all she said, her voice lilting.

While the devil toasted and consumed a late-night waffle, I finished cleaning. The body was ready to move now. I just had to pick up the car.

"Where you going?" she asked when I passed her in the living room.

"To get rid of the body in my fucking kitchen."

She looked a little offended that I was cursing. "Jordan," she said, "that's silly. Just put the liquids down the toilet and the solids down the garbage disposal, a few little pieces per day."

"A few little pieces per day? What the hell do I do in the meantime?"

She looked at me, baffled. "I just told you."

I was still wary of contradicting her, but it seemed she had no immediate plans to incinerate me, so I answered frankly. "I can't have pieces of a body in my apartment! It'll smell like my mom's house. People will notice that."

"What people?" she asked with a snort.

"I entertain!" As soon as I said it, it struck me that I'd just yelled at the devil. But she still didn't incinerate me, so I was emboldened to continue. "I have Gabby and Michael over. Maybe David will come by sometime."

"So what?" Dee asked. "Get rid of the skull first, skin the corpse, and put the rest in the freezer. Tell them it's venison."

"If I tell them it's venison, Michael will want to take some home."

"Even better! You can get rid of half the evidence in one swoop."

"That's not happening. I am not giving my friend human flesh and telling him it's venison."

She shrugged. "Okay, then. Drive safe." She waved a waffle at me, dripping syrup on the couch cushion.

I fetched the car and parked it out front. When I went back in to get the body, Dee was engrossed in a television show about ancient aliens. I rolled the body up in my only rug and dragged it out to the car. Now, I'm not exactly what you'd call an athletic person, but I think I set a land speed record for the fifty-meter dash that night, despite dragging a hundred pounds of tastefully carpeted corpse on the ground behind me.

I stuffed it through the hatchback door and glanced along the street, from window to residential window, to see if anyone had been watching. It looked like I'd pulled it off without being observed, but my heart still pounded and my head felt like it was about to pop from the pressure inside. Even in the chill fall air, I was dripping with sweat. I took a moment to catch my breath, then went into the apartment to get a few extra things.

When I came back outside, the devil was in the driver's seat, buckling herself in.

I took a moment to compose myself, then tapped on the window. The devil rolled it down. "No" was all I said. I was maybe getting a little cocky from not being incinerated.

Dee smiled. "Jordan, you can trust me."

"You're the devil."

She put her hands on the wheel. "Exactly. So, I'm driving, unless you want to run and fetch another car."

The thought had crossed my mind, but I was already getting wise to her. "Is this some kind of metaphor?" I asked. "Are you trying to tell me that you're taking over my life, and I might as well be a passenger in it from now on?"

"Oh, Jordan" was all she said as she reached out to ruffle my hair again.

I stepped back, out of the way of her hand. I know how pathetic this sounds, but in that moment, not having my hair ruffled, to say nothing of not being burned alive in a pillar of hellfire, felt like a real victory.

She revved the engine, as if in warning, and I went around to the passenger side. I buckled in as fast as I could, because I already knew what was coming.

Sure enough, Dee peeled out, or came as close to peeling out as you can in a three-door subcompact. She blew through the stop sign at the end of the road and skidded out onto Mt. Auburn Street, which was blessedly deserted at that time of night. In the back, the body slid across the cargo area and thumped against the side of the car.

"I think we should find some woods near Lincoln," I said, for all the good it would do.

The devil took both hands off the wheel to adjust her short red hair in the mirror. "And you were planning to go straight there and back?" she asked, as the car veered across the center line. "Because that won't look suspicious at all on the GPS records."

Even as I clutched the seat, I had to ask, "These things have GPS?"

She put one hand on the wheel, just in time to avoid a head-on collision with a tree. She shook her head at me and said, "Sweetie, a little advice? You sound smarter when you don't talk." And with that, she slammed the brakes, leaving four dashed trails of rubber on the road behind us, spaced to the pulsing of the antilock brakes.

My head rocked forward and whipped back. We came to a screeching halt in front of a liquor store.

"Mind the car, will you?" she asked as she got out. She must have seen the look on my face, because she added, "We wouldn't have to make these stops if you'd jot down a list when you go to the grocery store."

The moment she disappeared inside, I saw flashing red and blue lights illuminate the street and heard a single whoop from a siren. I looked back to see a police cruiser two blocks away and coming up fast.

So, this was it. I was going to prison. Do you think they have free Wi-Fi in prison? Probably not, right?

The cruiser was a block away now, blasting out another siren whoop as it flew through an intersection. Now half a block. Now it was just a few car lengths away, lights illuminating the subcompact's interior in alternating flashes of blue and red.

But it wasn't slowing down. It flew by, going so fast it made the car rock. Another blast of the siren and it was through the next intersection. It disappeared around a bend in the road.

I breathed.

The devil returned with two bottles, already opened, and handed one to me.

"I'm not sure I should be drinking right now."

She rolled her eyes as she started the car. "If you haven't finished that beer by the time we get to the river, I'm not helping you dig." She gulped from the other bottle and stomped on the gas.

I was worried about having an open container in the car, until I realized how truly ridiculous that was under the circumstances. I downed a third of the bottle in one long pull. "I don't usually drink IPA," I said.

"How can you call yourself a hipster and not drink IPA?"

"I don't call myself a hipster."

She looked me up and down. I was, admittedly, wearing a tatty old pair of jeans and a plaid button-up shirt that was two sizes too big, but that's just because I like to be comfortable when I'm flying. "Was that supposed to be ironic?" she asked.

"This isn't the way to Lincoln."

"Of course it isn't. You know how suspicious that would look? No one from Somerville would ever go to Lincoln, except to bury a body. You're going to the movies in Framingham. Did you bring the knife you murdered me with?"

"It's in the back."

"Get it," she said, her eyes forward.

I stared at her a while, not sure whether she was trying to help or just messing with me. Either way, I wasn't up to taking a stand, so I twisted in my seat and retrieved the knife.

"Roll down your window," she said.

I complied.

We were coming up on the Charles River. "Toss it. Now!"

I threw it just as we rolled onto the bridge, and momentum took it out to the middle of the black water. I turned to Dee, and with a touch of bleat returning to my voice, I asked, "Why are you being so helpful all of a sudden?" Whatever it was, it made me more nervous than when she was sabotaging me.

"Maybe I just get stupid when I'm drinking." She looked at my bottle. "Didn't I tell you to finish that? I wish you'd take your projects more seriously."

I would have finished it if she hadn't blindsided me with that knife thing, and with suddenly being all helpful and shit. Anyway, I only had one digging implement, if my old frying pan even counts.

Halfway to Framingham, somewhere around Wellesley, Dee stopped at a green light. This was especially odd, since up to then, she hadn't bothered to stop at the red ones. I looked out at the empty intersection, surrounded by woods. "It's, uh, it's green," I said.

"No," she said, "you distinctly remember it being red. It was definitely red, and you definitely didn't jump out and unload a body while you were stopped here, at this definitely red light." She turned to me. "That was a hint."

I ran around the car, popped the hatch, and dragged the body out—rug and all.

"Don't forget your frying shovel," Dee said, over her shoulder.

As soon as I had my hand on it, she drove off so fast the hatch swung closed, narrowly missing my wrist. As the taillights receded in the distance, I looked around. It was just me, my frying pan, and a dead body out in the middle of the woods—or as close as you get to the middle of the woods in eastern Massachusetts. I didn't know which way to go. The woods couldn't go back very far, and in the darkness, I might end up burying the body in some nosy asshole's backyard.

"That way," said a voice behind me. I should have been expecting it, but I jumped anyway. I turned and there was Dee, pointing north with her free hand—the one that didn't have a beer in it.

Like a moron, I stammered and asked, "Where's the car?"

"Heading toward Framingham."

"But how," I began, before she cut me off.

"Okay, this time I'm, like, a hundred percent sure I already told you I'm the devil."

"Right," I said. It's amazing how quickly you adapt to these things and start accepting the impossible. It's like your mind knows it has to tuck and roll.

As soon as I began dragging the body, Dee started in with her critique. "Carry it on your back, unless you want to leave a trail so obvious, any moron could follow it." As I tried and failed to lift the body, she shook her head. "It's sad, really. You have the raw talent for a career in the murderous arts, but you just don't apply yourself."

It took me a few tries, but I eventually got the thing over my shoulders and was slogging my way through the woods. Dee walked along beside me, whistling merrily between sips of IPA. We must have walked half a mile, and I thought I would die of heat exhaustion, when a wind kicked up. At first, it was a blessed relief, but as it chilled my dripping sweat, I thought I'd go the other way and die of hypothermia.

Finally, Dee said, "Here's good. Anywhere in the past few hundred yards would have been fine, actually. I don't know why you carried it so far."

This time, it wasn't fear of being incinerated that kept me from shooting her a baleful stare. It was simple exhaustion. I dropped the body and caught my breath before I got to digging. I chopped at the stony, root-laden New England ground with a goddamn frying pan, while the devil looked on and made demeaning comments about my fitness, my preparedness, and my unflattering attire. In two hours of digging, I managed to make a hole three feet deep and barely wide enough for the body. I stuffed it in, covered it up, and scattered leaves over the site.

"See, wasn't that easy?" Dee asked.

"Want me to say a few words over your grave?" I asked, turning toward her. "You understand they'll be mostly curse words, of course." Tuck and roll, baby. Tuck and roll.

She didn't answer.

I turned all the way around and saw that she wasn't there. She'd simply disappeared, leaving nothing but a fine, ash-like substance suspended in the air, illuminated by lines of green light shining through the trees from the intersection.

I cleaned the dirt off my clothes as best I could, then made my way back. The car was waiting for me, stopped at the light, with no one in it.

I counted my blessings and drove home.

# 4

The alarm clock went off an hour after I got to bed—which is not to say "to sleep." I rose cautiously and crept through the apartment, peeking around corners and doors. Dee was gone, but her legacy lived on in the form of a disheveled living room and a fridge with all the waffles and half the beer missing—beer she didn't even like.

I'd taken a shower before getting into bed, and now I took another. I scrubbed my hands until they hurt, thankful that Dee wasn't around to quote *Macbeth* at me.

I snuck into Social Services half an hour late and quietly settled into my cubicle. To be honest, this was nothing new. In an average week, I'm late for work about three days out of five, and I usually sneak out early. I'd blame it all on being burnt out, except that "no longer gives a shit" is so much closer to the truth. I became a social worker expecting to love my job, change lives for the better, and make very little money. I was right about the last one.

On my most productive days, I might help some poor mother finally get the health insurance her kids have needed and been entitled to for years. Hurray. On my less productive days, I read hundred-page reports and inscrutable guidance documents until the words run together. This particular Monday, I spent the morning trying to fix the cellphone I'd dropped when Dee startled me.

I had all the little bits in a plastic baggie, like a hundred-piece jigsaw puzzle. I laid them out, separated the electronics—mostly intact, thank goodness—from the outer case, and wiped them all clean with an alcohol-dampened cotton swab. I fit the bits back together as best I could with hands that were still trembling from the night before, belying the impression of normality and calm I thought I'd been successfully projecting.

Still, I think I did a half-decent job of joining the pieces with scotch tape from the supply closet, though a few bits were inevitably missing—lost forever in some unseen niche of my kitchen. I filled those gaps with poster tack and covered it with a double layer of tape. There were several hairline cracks in the LCD screen that threatened to split it apart, so I strengthened them with instant glue.

I hit the power button and, against all odds, my plucky little Frankenphone came to life. The screen was distorted and the vibrate function had a habit of shaking the jigsaw pieces into a slightly different configuration, but it was otherwise functional. I broke for a celebratory lunch and, when I got back, turned my attention to the important business of thinning out my voice mails.

"Jordan, this is Simon—" *Bleep.*

"Jordan, we need to—" *Bleep.*

"You can't keep—" *Bleep.*

"Damn it, I'm your—" *Bleep.*

Delete. Delete. Delete. You can't let random stuff pile up in your inbox, you know. It makes your life untidy.

Near the end of the list, there was a message from my friend Gabby, asking if I wanted to get drinks after work. I texted back, *Hell es,* because the Y button on the virtual keyboard occupied a spot on the screen that was more glue than pixels now.

*Is that Spanish?* she texted back. *Hell es otras personas?*

I love Gabby. Plus, she projected a sense of cool control that I desperately needed in my life at that moment.

I spent the balance of my work day placing high school dropouts into a six-week vocational program that was supposed to train them for jobs in the tech sector—a sector that won't hire a janitor without a four-year degree. Most of my energy was dedicated to moderating their expectations without blurting out the truth: "This program will do absolutely nothing to help you find work. In fact, it'll hurt your chances, because you'll be stuck in a classroom for the next six weeks. But make sure you attend every day, even if it means turning down a job interview, or your kids will be kicked off transitional aid for having the bad judgement to choose you as a parent."

Perhaps you can see why I hated my life, even before I went and murdered the devil.

By 4:53 pm I was on an elevator going down, standing shoulder to shoulder with all the other disillusioned government drones who'd left work early. By twenty after five, I was in a bar off Central Square in Cambridge. I'd just snagged a table when Gabby came in. I waved her over.

Gabby looks like she belongs in front of a blackboard, carrying a pointer stick and whacking kids on the knuckles for bad penmanship. Then she talks, and out comes the easygoing, slightly hoarse voice of a farm girl.

"You drinking IPAs now?" she asked, picking up my bottle and examining the label.

I started to make an excuse for deviating from my usual, but she cut me off.

"It's okay," she said, "I won't tell shitty beer you're cheating on it. Michael's coming too. Keep an eye out for him." No sooner had she said it than he appeared, and we waved him over.

Michael, unlike Gabby, looks exactly like he sounds, and awkwardness is his superpower. You could hear him on tape, then pick him out of a photo lineup. He's tall and lean, and looks uncomfortable in any situation. I have this great picture of him, where he looks like a marionette puppet with his strings tangled. I took it while he was breaking the Boston University ROTC record for the two-mile run.

I've known them both since college. We all moved to Boston from different places, and all stayed after graduating. In Michael's case, he didn't even move off campus. He's still in the middle of a postdoc in demography. "Michael, what is demography?" I asked as he approached the table. I'd been meaning to ask for years.

He froze in the middle of sitting down, his eyes shining like a deer in the headlights. After a few seconds of tortured silence, he said, "Well, I'm not sure anyone really knows."

"Is that why you've been studying it for fifteen years? To find out?"

"No," Gabby said, "it's because he's afraid of the real world."

Michael clutched his chest, as if he'd just been punched in the heart, then turned a chair around backward and sat down, long legs splayed around the backrest in a manner that might have looked cool if he was anyone else.

Gabby leaned over the table and we both leaned in to meet her. "A little birdy told me something," she whispered.

We waited, but she wouldn't say anything more until Michael asked, "What?"

"It said worms are delicious and shiny things are awesome." She leaned back. "Turns out birds are shallow, and they don't gossip as much as people think. But then later, someone told me Jordan and David are dating."

"Huh," Michael said, thinking it over. "Who's David?"

"You know him," Gabby said.

"Not dating," I said. I wanted to shut this down before the speculation ran rampant. "It was just one date."

"I'm confused. Where do I know him from?" Michael asked.

"Everywhere. You've met him, like, a million times."

I laughed nervously. "I'm not even sure it was really a date, you know?"

Michael made a face. "I don't think I know him. The only David I know is Agent Dave."

Gabby made a face back. "Yeah. Jordan and him are dating."

"No" was all Michael said.

"Yes!" Gabby replied.

He stared back at her like she'd shaken his entire worldview. After a long silence, he said, "I wouldn't have expected that."

"It's not as strange as it seems. They've been circling each other for years, like a couple of horny wolves."

"Fucking hell," I said. "Was there a documentary about this on PBS that I missed?"

Gabby shot me a sly smile. "Come on, Jordan. It's obvious. He's been looking to take you to the bone zone since he broke up with Madeline. And then, all of a sudden, out of nowhere, as if to take advantage of this short window of opportunity, you break up with What's-His-Name?"

"Josh," I said, with a bit of disgust in my voice. "And I wouldn't even call it a breakup, because I wouldn't even say we were dating. He just started telling people we were dating, and for a while there, I was too polite to correct him."

Michael looked at me, impressed but still skeptical. "And now you're dating Agent Dave. The actual Agent Dave? I'm still not sure we're talking about the same guy."

"He's not a secret agent," I said. "He's in biotech."

"But that's exactly what he'd have to say," Michael said, tapping his temple, "if he was a secret agent. Right?"

"Michael has a point," Gabby said. "All the signs are there: effortless style, a closet full of evening wear, denial that he's a secret agent. Odds are, he's recovered at least one stolen rocket formula just while we've been talking."

"I'm not even sure if we're dating!"

"Well, go on another date with him, and then you'll be sure," Gabby said. "Only, be prepared to get swept up in an international intrigue after dinner."

"I'm not sure if it's a good time for this sort of thing." I took a swig from my beer and examined the label minutely, as if it might contain personalized instructions for getting me out of this conversation.

"Yeah," Gabby said, "you may not be ready to kill the Russian vixen sent to seduce and assassinate him."

Michael alone seemed to notice my distress. He reached over and put his hand on mine. "Hey, is everything all right?"

And now Gabby picked up on it too. "Did Agent Dave say something to hurt you?" she asked. "Because, just say the word, and I will throw acid in that pretty face of his. From a special acid-shooting pen, if that's what it takes."

"It doesn't have anything to do with David," I said, still studying the IPA's ingredient list.

"So, what is it?" Gabby asked.

I've always been able to tell Gabby and Michael anything. Absolutely anything.

"It's nothing."

Okay, almost anything.

They didn't buy it, of course, but I stuck to my guns and, after a round of drinks, the matter was forgotten. Turns out beer really was the solution to my problems. That's an important lesson they should really teach kids in school.

"Should we order food?" I asked. "They have great soups here."

"Soup isn't a food," Gabby said.

Michael rolled his eyes. "Oh, no, not the soup thing."

"What?" she asked. "Foods are solid. Soup, at best, is a beverage with ideas above its station."

Michael shook his head at me. "You just had to suggest soup. You had better hope those acid-shooting pens don't come two to a pack."

I held up my hands. "Don't blame me. I didn't know about the soup thing."

Gabby was about to say something, but Michael cut her off. "She's been radicalized, Jordan. She's a soup racist now."

"I should have seen the signs," I said. "I mean, none of her friends are soup."

"You know what?" Gabby asked. "Go ahead and order soup if you want to. Keep fooling yourselves."

"I think I'll just get the buffalo wings," I said. "It seems like the safer choice."

"Well, I, for one, will not be cowed," Michael said. "As a loyal Bostonian, I will be enjoying this fine establishment's lobster bisque, which the menu informs me is 'famous.'"

We ordered and caught up until the food came. While I dug into chicken wings and Gabby crumbled crackers on vegan chili, Michael slurped loudly at his bisque while staring pointedly at Gabby.

She leaned over and whispered, "You're sipping a lie."

"And you don't have enough local pride," Michael replied.

"Yeah," I said. "Didn't you know Boston invented blender seafood? You have Boston to thank when you go to any of the great cities in the world where they make seafood in a blender—a list that includes Boston and...probably Bangor, right?"

"Yeah," Michael said, and slurped twice. "I've been to Bangor." *Slurp.* "They have good bisque there." *Slurp.*

"I hate you guys so much."

I just grinned. "Seriously, though, what is this about? Did soup hurt you?"

Gabby wrung her hands and said, "You remember how I was going to lease the ground floor of my building so they could put a coffee shop in?"

I nodded.

"Well, we signed the lease. Then, a week later, I go downstairs and see a big sign in the window. COMING SOON: THE SOUP PALACE."

"Oh, fuck," I said. "Will they at least have an espresso bar?"

"No," she said. "I made sure to ask before I called a lawyer."

I laughed softly until I realized she wasn't joking. "Shit, man! You lawyered up over *soup?*"

"It's not just about the soup. We had an oral contract. I wouldn't have leased the place to that asshole if I'd known he was going to put a soup place there. He said he was opening a coffee shop. I've always wanted to live upstairs from an independent coffee shop. Can you imagine it? Waking up to the smell of roasting beans, going downstairs for a soy latte in the winter without even stepping outside? That's like a dream for me, Jordan."

"When you put it like that, it sounds perfectly rational to hire a lawyer. Over soup."

"Is he, like, a soup lawyer specifically?" Michael asked. "Or does he litigate other side dishes? Because I feel like I might have a legal case against places that serve soggy french-fries. You know, pain and suffering."

Gabby was noticeably silent.

"No way," Michael said. "He's an actual soup lawyer?"

"*Kind of.*" Gabby sighed. "He's been involved in several cases that involved soup, and he won them all. I think it's maybe become a joke at his law firm."

"Or maybe he just hates soup?"

"No, no, he's been on the defense side a few times." Gabby held her hands up to stop us before we could speculate wildly about the nature of that defense. "Like, health codes and stuff."

I swallowed the last of my beer. "Another?" I asked Gabby. She nodded. "Another?" I asked Michael. He held his hand over his mug and shook his head.

I rose and went to the bar, pushing my way through a gaggle of dudebros gathered to watch *Monday Night Football*. I had my drinks and was just turning back to the table when the TV cut away from the game for a news update. I hardly noticed it, until the image changed to a very familiar traffic light.

*Shit.*

*Shit shit shit shit shit.*

Behind the bar, festooned on a ninety-inch screen in glorious 4K HDR, a reporter was standing in a cordoned-off intersection, pointing into the woods. The closed captions told the rest of the story. "...this small community rocked by a brutal murder, as the body of an as-yet-unidentified young woman is found wrapped in a carpet, buried in the woods."

The image cut back to the reporter in the news studio, who went on. "More details of this grisly murder at eleven. And then, at 11:05, could your dog be suffering from seasonal affective disorder? We'll give you five warning signs that your pooch may have...the winter blues."

I stood there, a beer in each hand, while the screen cut to a car commercial. "Oh, God."

A voice came from behind me and said, "Guess again."

# 5

I turned and she was there. She pantomimed doffing a cap.

"Oh, God," I said, again.

She shook her head, playing at disappointment. "You already said that one. You have one guess left."

The dudebros were staring, so I shifted both beers to one hand, grabbed her by the arm, and pulled her into a corner. You probably shouldn't do that to the devil, but I was running on hot wings, IPA, and panic. "What the hell are you doing here?" I asked through my teeth.

She frowned. "I feel like I've already answered that."

"You're here to punish me, aren't you? You're here to torment me for my sins."

She studied me for a moment, quite seriously, then broke into snorting laughter. "Conceited much? Your sins, as marvelous and noteworthy as they may seem to you, just aren't that interesting. Jordan, I already said I'm here to help you."

"Like you helped get rid of that body?"

She wasn't abashed in the slightest. She only said, "That was a side project which, I admit, could have gone better." Her eyes went to the bottles in my hands. She took one from my yielding fingers and clinked it against the other. "Cheers."

"I'm going to go to jail!"

She shook her head. "Only if you're a moron." She looked me up and down. "Oh, right. But hey, I can hook you up in prison. If you knew how many jailbirds owe the devil a favor, you'd be…well, completely unsurprised."

I looked around the bar, half-expecting to see the police already coming for me.

"Relax!" the devil said. "There's nothing connecting you to the body.

25

Unless you were stupid enough to bury that tacky throw rug with it."

I just stared.

"Ah," the devil said.

"I'm going to jail forever."

The devil scoffed. "Not forever, sweetie. Just until you die. And considering what you eat, that can't be too much longer." She put a comforting hand on my shoulder and motioned to Mike and Gabby's table. "Hey, your much cooler friends are trying to get your attention."

I shuffled over to them, head low and shoulders slumped. I put Gabby's beer in front of her, crumpled into my chair, and collapsed with my head resting on the table.

"Subtle," Dee said, right behind me.

I tossed my hand up, waving it vaguely in Dee's direction. "This is the devil," I said. "Call her Dee. Dee, meet Gabby and Michael."

My eyes were staring into empty space, but I imagine that Gabby and Michael traded significant glances. "I don't get it," Gabby said.

My eyes focused and I saw Michael looking around. "Like, your hand is the devil? Or are we doing shadow puppets? Because I can do a great dog."

"Anyone can do a dog," Gabby said.

"Yeah, but this is a *great* dog."

I pointed. "No, this is the devil. Here." Dee smiled and curtseyed.

Michael frowned. "The devil doesn't...talk to you, does he?"

"I only wish I could get her to shut up."

"I resent that," Dee said. "I lavish you with my wit and wisdom, and this is how you show your appreciation? You're lucky I'm a forgiving sort."

"See what I mean?" I asked, and let my head fall against the table again.

After a long, uncomfortable silence, Gabby finally asked, "Does the devil ever...tell you to hurt people?"

I shook my head, pressed as it was against the table top. "No. I think she's here to torture me for my sins, but mostly she just makes nasty comments about my fashion sense."

"I do not!" Dee said. I could hear her gulping down a mouthful of beer. "Though, now that you mention it, those pants make your ass look like a pot roast."

I let out a long, tortured sigh.

"Is this because of that news report on canine seasonal affective disorder?" Michael asked. "Is that what's got you feeling this way?"

I looked up. "What?"

"We saw you watching it at the bar," Gabby said. "You looked worried."

"I know how you feel," Michael said. "My sister's Pekinese has C-SAD. Between December and January, the poor guy hardly gets out of his little bed."

"No, no, it's the devil." I hooked a thumb over my shoulder. "Well, I guess you can't tell she's the devil. Dee? Tell them you're the devil."

"I'm the devil," Dee said. "Hold on, I have my ID somewhere."

I looked at Mike and Gabby expectantly.

They both leaned in, and Gabby asked, "Who are you talking to?"

Dee let out a torrent of giddy laughter. I think she'd been holding it in for a while.

I let my head fall against the table again, buried it under my arms, and said, "Oh, God, nobody else can see you, can they?" And yeah, I know. You figured that out like, right away, and I didn't. Congratulations. You're very smart. Fuck you. You weren't there.

The laughter trailed off. "Yeah, they can't see me if I don't want them to." Dee said, breathless. She took a big swig from her beer bottle, which, apparently, they also couldn't see. "I would have told you earlier, if not for the fact that it was hilarious."

Okay, I know what you're thinking now. You figure Dee wasn't real at all. You figure she was a hallucination born of my anxiety, which is why she disappeared when I got rid of the body and only reappeared when it was found again, right?

Okay, I have two answers to that. One, that would mean I murdered some innocent woman in my kitchen, and how the fuck could you think that? You barely even know me. Two, did a hallucination eat my fucking waffles? Because hallucinations don't do that.

I could hear Gabby and Mike whispering above my head.

"How much has she had?"

"Just this, but don't IPAs have more alcohol?"

"Do you think maybe she started drinking before she got here?"

"Maybe she's on K. Didn't someone in our freshman dorm overdose on K and see the devil?"

"No, no. He saw Shiva."

"Yeah, but Shiva's, like, the Indian devil, right?"

"No, he isn't."

"Let's check Wikipedia."

I jerked my head up and said, "I'm not on K! I don't even know what that is!"

Michael narrowed his eyes. "So...how do you know you're not on it?"

Dee snorted and said, "I like the way he thinks. Is he single?"

"I think I should go home," I said, tired and beaten and hopeless.

Within seconds, Mike and Gabby were on either side of me, helping me up even though I didn't need it. Seriously, they're like, tied for first in the category of nicest person in the world. I adore them. They were by my side all the way home and even offered to stay the night, which would have been a comfort. I only refused because I had some things I needed to say to Dee.

# 6

When we got home, Dee went into the living room first thing. I heard her flop on the couch, but I waited by the door until I heard Gabby and Michael walk away. Once they were well out of earshot, I wheeled around and stormed toward her, screaming as I went.

"Just where the hell do you get off? You have no right, no right! I don't give a damn who the hell you are, you have no right to come into my life and wreck the place! I want you out. I want you out tonight!"

I loomed over her, voice growing louder, as she settled into the cushions.

"Don't get comfy, bitch, because you're leaving! And if you don't want to go, then you might as well incinerate me right now, because there is no way in hell I'm going to let you screw things up for me any worse than you already have. So? So? What's it gonna be? You gonna kill me, bitch? You gonna burn me in a pillar of flame?"

Dee was completely calm and phlegmatic. The woman could have taught a class on phlegmatism.

"What, nothing?" I shouted. "No fiery death? No retribution against the insolent mortal? Nothing to back up that unending torrent of insult that comes from your mouth? Then get out! Get out! Get out of my life! Get out!"

I honestly don't remember when I started kicking her. It might have been earlier, but it was only now that I realized I was doing it. I kicked at her shins and knees, so hard it hurt my foot. She didn't react—not even a flinch.

"Why me? Why me? Why did it have to be me? Aren't there bigger sinners in the world? Aren't there murderers, rapists, people who fart in elevators? Why don't you go bother some of them, fuck up their lives, make them look crazy in front of their friends, *eat all their fucking waffles?*" I can't

28

explain why the waffles, out of everything, bugged me so much. They just did, okay?

And now I was punching her. These weren't light punches, either. I was putting my weight and all my frustration into them, pummeling her with a flurry of hooks, crosses, and haymakers. I'm not even sure which of those is which, but I'm sure I used them all. I'd been pretty scrappy as a teenager—I had to be—and in that moment, I think I could have given a heavyweight boxer a run for his money.

I still screamed at her, now with far too much rage to form coherent sentences. I threw every curse I knew, including a few I'd picked up in sophomore French and thought I'd forgotten. I'm not even sure how long it went on. I was locked in a strange, hypnotic dissociation where my actions and thoughts seemed to be in separate worlds. Some corner of my brain was warning that if I kept this up much longer, I'd have another body to dispose of and I still wouldn't be rid of the devil, but it wasn't that realization which finally stopped me. It was simple, overwhelming exhaustion. If I could have, I'd have gone on hitting her until every bone in her face was reduced to pulp, or my arms fell off.

But she wasn't a pulp. She wasn't even bruised, hadn't suffered so much as a split lip or a swollen ear. She looked exactly as she always did, and as cheerful as ever. As my shaking legs gave out and I fell to my knees, she reached out to playfully tweak my nose, and said in a singsong voice, "Somebody's a grumpy bunny."

You know in movies, when the hysterical love interest gets irrationally mad at the hero and starts hitting him? And he just lets her do it, because his jaw is so chiseled it can only be hurt by man-punches? And then she starts crying, and he comforts her, and then afterward they have sex?

That's pretty much what happened with me and Dee. Except for the sex part.

I slumped against the sofa, pulled my knees against my chest, and had a good, long cry. Dee crawled down, sat beside me on the floor, and put both arms around me. I didn't stop her, and told myself it was because I was just too tired to push her away. But really it was because, God help me, who else could I go to with this problem? If I'd spilled it to Gabby and Michael, they'd have me committed.

I didn't cry for as long as I thought I would. I never do. And when I was finished, Dee wiped away my tears and helped me blow my nose—with what I later realized was a pair of my own panties, stolen from my underwear drawer. "You want to talk about what's bothering you?" she asked. "Because no one's ever attacked me like that unless they were quoting scripture."

I buried my face between my knees. "I don't want to talk about it."

I was expecting some argument, but she only sighed and said, "Fair enough. But if you ever do want to talk about it, I'll be right there. And I'll be right there in the intervening period, too. If you want to take that as another incentive to get it off your chest, you're free to do so. I don't want to see the people I like in pain."

"You must not like many people."

"I don't. But speaking of people I do like, is Michael single?"

I growled.

"Okay. What about Gabby?"

I extricated myself from her and rolled my eyes. "I'm pretty sure she doesn't date women. Or, you know, Satan."

Dee was unmoved. "I don't have to be a woman. Hell, I could be a phosphorescent unicorn, if that's what she's into. You want me to be a phosphorescent unicorn?"

"Not really."

She looked disappointed. "Well, the point remains. Accommodating personal preferences isn't a problem."

"Yes, but there's still the Satan thing, isn't there?"

Dee shrugged. "I'd like to think that a modern, progressive person like Gabby won't be subject to that kind of prejudice."

"Have you heard her thoughts on soup?"

Dee waved the matter away.

At this point, I desperately needed more alcohol. I stood and walked to the kitchen without another word. I opened the fridge and leaned into it.

"If you're looking for beer," Dee called in, "I finished the last of it this afternoon."

I whipped the fridge door closed and said, "You don't even like my beer."

"Yeah, but it was the only thing in there. Don't worry; I've got a friend coming over and he's bringing some with him."

You know when someone throws so much crazy at you all at once, you don't even know where to start? That was me. I stood in the kitchen door, paralyzed by an overload of indignation. I guess part of it was how much this situation reminded me of my childhood.

Dee was stretched out on the couch. She lifted her head and asked, "That's okay, right? Answer in the affirmative by staring slack-jawed and saying 'what.'"

"What?" I asked, eliciting a grin from Dee. Then my brain rewound far enough to get the point. "God damn it!"

She cackled in triumph.

"Has anyone ever told you you're a complete and total asshole?" I asked.

She grinned at me. "In fourteen thousand, five hundred and seventy-eight languages, on six different continents."

"Still working on Antarctica?"

"I'll get it one of these days." She looked toward the front door. "Ah, he's here."

My eyes followed hers. Something knocked on it. Actually, that doesn't quite do justice to the moment, so let me try to describe it again.

Ahem.

There came three claps against the door, each reverberating through the walls, rattling my teeth, turning my blood to ice, sending my heart leaping against the walls of my chest. The eldritch sound was permeated with a malignant, oily, depraved quality that I shudder to remember even now.

I knew not what unutterable malevolence lurked beyond the door, hidden from my sight by a mere inch of oak, but the booming crash of its appendage against that feeble portal spoke of horrors too perverse for the eyes of men. Whatever slithered on the other side, it was ancient and amoral, yet somehow familiar, as if a part of it hid forever within the stygian shadows of the human soul—its presence embraced by only the psychopathic, the degenerate, and the damned.

There we go.

While I was still recovering, the devil looked at me and said, "Aren't you going to answer it?"

"Fuck, no!" I cried. In fact, I was already thinking about fleeing out the back. I would have done it already, except I wasn't sure how *big* the visitor at my front door was. I worried that it might possess slimy tentacles that stretched all the way around the building.

Dee rolled her eyes. "He's not going to hurt you. Well, unless you piss him off by keeping him waiting."

I couldn't help but remember my childhood and the parade of guys who *probably* wouldn't snap and murder us, if we were careful not to piss them off. But while some of them certainly carried an aura of death about them, it wasn't, you know, a literal aura of death.

A deep rumbling shook the furniture and informed me that I faced the same dilemma now. I knew that refusing to let it in was the quickest way to make it mad. I crept to the door, growing more unsure with every step and imagining the perverted horror that lay on the other side. I thought of looking through the peephole but knew it would be a mistake. My only chance at surviving this with my mind and body intact was to act without thinking, without first seeing the ichorous thing waiting outside. I closed my eyes as I worked the deadbolt with shaking fingers. I drew back the security chain and turned the knob.

And there my courage failed. But even as I shied away, the door swung open of its own accord, creaking on the hinges. I whimpered as I felt clammy appendages wrap around my shoulders and a gelatinous mass press against me.

But the appendages felt strangely like arms, and the mass was lumpy in a way that suggested ribs. At the end of one of the appendages, a hard mass had the shape of a wine bottle. I opened my eyes and saw that the creature resembled—indeed, had the precise form of—a slob. But, you know, a completely human slob.

And he was hugging me.

"Jordan!" he said, in a raspy but chipper voice. "Girl, it's so great to finally meet you. Dee talks about you all the time." He released me from the hug, stuck a cigarette in his mouth, and held out his hand. "I'm Death."

I took his clammy hand and shook it. What the hell else was I supposed to do?

He patted me on the shoulder. I just stood there, gawking like an idiot, while he went past me and into the apartment. Dee came from the living room to meet him. He plucked the cigarette out of his mouth, shifted his bottle between hands—turns out it was tequila, not wine—and embraced her. They even kissed each other on the cheek.

It was weird.

"They didn't have any beer," he said, holding up the bottle. Only then did I notice the scorched label and the splash of blood on it. "I hope that's okay?"

"No, that's fantastic. Hey, Jordan, you have a blender, right?" I could only stare. "Okay, she's spaced out, but I think I saw a blender in one of the cupboards. We can make frozen margaritas!"

"Yes!" Death said. "I love frozen margaritas." He kissed the bottle right on the blood splatter and said, "Thank you, drunk drivers."

Dee looked at me and pointed at the kitchen. "You in?" When I still didn't answer, she made a sympathetic face and asked, "What is it, sweetie?"

My eyes darted to Death, then back to Dee. I stammered out, "I just...pictured him...slimmer."

While Death looked awkwardly at his feet, Dee shook her head and clucked her tongue. "Wow. You're, like, the rudest person ever, aren't you? You're just going to up and comment on other people's weight, huh? You're one to talk, Pudge."

"I'm a healthy weight for my height," I said.

She snorted. "Oh, yeah? I didn't realize you were eight feet tall." This brought a snicker from Death. Dee lowered her voice, but not so much that I couldn't hear her clearly, and asked him, "Hey, did you get a look at her ass in those pants? What does it remind you of?"

"I dunno," he said, "like a pot roast or something?"

I sighed and said, "I didn't mean your weight." I really didn't. Death wasn't even overweight, but he was flabby. He looked like a man who hadn't exercised since he was born. "I just mean, I always pictured you more...gaunt. You know, skeletal."

He took a drag from his cigarette and blew smoke at the ceiling. "You should meet me in the slums of Burundi." He turned to Dee and said, "I hate that place." Then he looked back at me. "Here in America, this is the face of death." He began to tick off on his fingers. "Heart disease, cancer, lung disease, diabetes…" He hesitated at the thumb, apparently trying to remember the next cause.

"And brain diseases," Dee said.

"Oh, yeah, I always forget those." Death held a straight face for about two seconds, then cracked up laughing. When he finished, he asked, "So, we having frozen margaritas or what?"

As Dee shuffled Death toward the kitchen, she looked at me inquisitively.

I sighed and said, "Yes, I'm in." Judge me if you will, but you cannot possibly comprehend how much I needed alcohol at that moment. I shuffled after them.

As I entered the kitchen, Dee put an arm around me and squeezed. "You have to excuse some of the things she says," she said as Death plugged in the blender. "She grew up right before they outlawed lead paint. But she's a fun person." She gave my shoulders another squeeze and looked at me. "Remember when you stabbed me and buried my body in the woods? Those were good times."

"I'm just here for the margaritas," I said, voice and posture both quite wooden.

Death paused as he took ice from the freezer, looked at me, and said, "Somebody's a grumpy bunny."

"You should have seen her earlier."

Death turned and started pouring ice cubes into the blender. "How much should we make?"

"Fill it to the top," I said, without a second's hesitation.

"See?" the devil said. "Isn't she fun?"

He filled it to the top, and let me tell you, Death makes a damn strong margarita. I just want you to know that, in case it ever comes up.

I finished most of mine before we even left the kitchen for the living room. As I sank into the couch, Death took my glass and returned to the kitchen to refill it. I made no complaint.

And then the phone rang. I froze where I was, sitting on the couch. I wouldn't say that the sound of the ring was as bad as Death's sonorous knock, but it was in the same ballpark. It rang again.

"I unplugged that," I said, as if stating that fact would make it stop ringing.

"I plugged it back in this afternoon," Dee said, from the other corner of the couch. "I needed a phone so I could order some premium channels. By the way, your cable bill's going to be a hundred and eighty dollars a month for the first year. Which means I saved you, like, a thousand dollars compared to the regular price."

I was a little too panicky to process that, so I ignored her as I got up to unplug the phone. But before I even made it to the kitchen, the third ring cut off.

"Yo, you're on with Death," he said as he answered.

I stopped short, rooted in place just outside the open kitchen door.

Death looked at me. "You want Jordan? Yeah, she's right…"

I swung my arms wildly and shook my head.

"…not here at all. I think she's at the, ummm…grocery store? Who am I? I'm just her… casual sex partner, I guess?" Honestly, my only complaint was that he didn't sound convincing enough. "Yeah, I'll tell her. No problem." He hung up and looked at me. "Simon called. He says he still loves you, no matter what you do."

I took two quick steps into the kitchen and pulled the plug.

"You have to talk to him one of these days," Dee called from the sofa.

"Yeah," I said, "but not today." Death was looking at me curiously, which is perhaps the most disquieting type of look a person can get from the personification of death. "I think I'm going to go to bed."

Now he just looked awkward. "Oh, well, uh…"

"Stay as long as you like," I said, heading down the hall.

As I turned into the bedroom, the last thing I heard was Death asking, "What the hell was that about?"

# 7

They were gone by the time I woke up. I made it all the way to work and straight through the morning without seeing a sign of Dee. I was beginning to hope I'd have a whole day of peace when, an hour before lunchtime, she popped her head over the back wall of my cubicle and said, "Oh, there you are. This place is like a maze."

She was glassy-eyed, a little wobbly, and glitter clung to her face. "Jordan, seriously," she said, hanging an arm over the cube wall, "next time Death is in town, you have to come out with us."

I leaned closer to my monitor, until the screen eclipsed Dee's head, and for the first time in many years, I focused my full attention on doing my job. Dee whined with displeasure.

Then she was behind me, draping her arms over my shoulders. I could smell alcohol on her breath. "Oh, Jordan. Jordan, Jordan, Jordan," she said, and sighed melodramatically. "Jordan, Jordan, Jordan, Jordan." She took a deep breath. "Jordan, Jordan, Jordan, Jordan, Jordan, Jordan… Jordan." She leaned her head against mine. Her face was oily, her hair sticky with dried sweat. "Is Jordan a Norwegian name? Because it starts to sound Norwegian when you say it incessantly over and over again, without pause."

I ignored her, though I could see her pouty face reflected in the monitor.

"Jordan, don't you like me?" she asked, her voice lilting up at the end.

"What makes you think I don't like you?" I asked at a whisper. "You're like the sister I never had a chance to move far, far away from."

Dee brightened up instantly, laughing and making a tiger-claw gesture with her hand. "Mrow!" she said. "I like this side of you! I should get hungover and say your name over and over more often." She danced back and forth, spinning in a half-circle around my chair and squealing, "Jordan, Jordan, Jordan!" She said it again and again, occasionally interspersing some sisterly nuggets, such as "If you're looking for your dolls, I buried them in the backyard!"

It was still three quarters of an hour until lunch—which is pretty much how I always measure time at work. I don't like to eat lunch early, because it throws off my internal clock—kind of like daylight savings—but I couldn't deal with this shit on low blood sugar.

Before heading to the break room, I checked the news alert I'd set up for the "Wellesley Stabber," as the papers were now calling me. Several news items had popped up since I'd last checked, but none contained anything new. Every story may as well have carried the headline, "Beautiful Victim in Wellesley Stabbing Case Remains Unidentified, Dead."

Then, as I made my way across the cube farm, I checked the second, backup news alert I'd set up on my phone. Because, as someone once told me, "you can never be too careful when the police are looking for you." Thanks for that advice, Mom. It's served me well.

The devil was still doing her little dance, pirouetting around me and saying my name as I walked. She only gave it up at the entrance to the break room, where she stopped in the doorway, slumped her shoulders, and said, "Ugh, I guess you ran out of cool."

"Yeah," I said. "It's not an unending supply, like you and smugness."

I stepped into the break room, and it was full of, like, half a dozen people—all of them looking past me, waiting for whoever I was talking with to enter the room. Oh, and one of those people was my boss.

I guess every disaffected person of my generation has to have a boss who takes themselves way too seriously. I think it's a rule or something. Mine was Ruth, a woman who came from a proud lineage of tedious bosses. I bet her ancestors were mid-level managers for the pharaohs, convinced that only they possessed the skills to tell other people to push on a giant limestone block.

I didn't recognize the rest of the crowd, which meant they were probably the government auditors we were expecting this week. *Awesome.* I kept walking, and one by one, they seemed to realize there was no one behind me, and politely looked away.

Obviously, I couldn't retrieve my lunch from the refrigerator now, or these people might get the right ideas about me. I made a snap decision to get a cup of coffee instead, but as I approached the coffeemaker, I realized it was in the middle of brewing.

"Jordan," Ruth said, and nodded as I took a cup from the rack.

"Ruth," I said, and nodded back.

In the quiet that followed, the trickle of coffee became the loudest sound in the room, save for one of the auditors occasionally clearing her throat, or Dee making a fleshy sound with her armpit. I have to say, I prefer her when she's merely abusive.

"Slowest coffeemaker ever," I said with a nervous laugh as I watched the coffee trickling into the pot. That's the kind of humor government auditors like, right?

"Well, Jordan," Ruth said, "we're not about to bill the taxpayer for some expensive, fancy kitchen appliance just because you don't have the patience to wait for coffee."

I smiled, nodded, and died just a little more inside.

Dee moved effortlessly through the crowd of auditors and looked Ruth up and down. "Is this what she's always like?" she asked. "How have you not snapped and brought a gun to work?"

"I've definitely considered that," I said, answering both of them at once.

"Good, you ought to have," Ruth said. "That ought to be the first thing on everyone's mind these days." She smiled expectantly, as if waiting for a pat on the head and a biscuit from the auditors.

"Oh, I've asked around, and it definitely is," I said.

"Mind you," one of the auditors said, holding up a pen and waggling it thoughtfully, "it could be argued that, at the average rate of pay of a government employee, productivity lost while waiting for coffee justifies the purchase of a more expensive machine, if it does indeed minimize dead loss and, of course, if you can find one that's manufactured domestically, as per the requirements set forth in the Buy American Act." She laughed. "Obviously, we can't let you have equipment of foreign manufacture."

I suddenly understood why our printers never worked.

The auditors went into a huddle and whispered amongst themselves. I think they finally resolved to commission a study on the matter, but between their conspiratorial volume and penchant for jargon, I could only understand half of what they said.

I did understand my boss's seething glare, however. It said that this turn of events was a total catastrophe, and it was all my fault. I'll leave it to you to decide whether her assessment was true—keeping in mind that if you agree with Ruth, then you're probably a jackass. Ha, what am I even saying? You're definitely a jackass.

The coffeemaker finished brewing with a slurping sound, and I dove in before anyone else could get to it. I poured my cup while the last few drops sizzled against the heating element, and handed the rest of the pot to Ruth.

I wasn't being mean. I just wanted to get the hell out of there as fast as possible. I grabbed a sugar packet, and as I was going for the creamer, Dee said, "Don't take that packet. The sugar has rat piss in it." I was all set to ignore her, but she must have seen the skepticism written on my face, for she went on. "The mill owners know about the rat problem, so they cover their stock with a layer of fresh sugar whenever the inspectors show up. Most of the turds get sifted out before packaging, but you can't sift out piss, can you? Take one from the bottom. Those are clean."

Just to be on the safe side, I stopped and put the sugar back. Despite the odd and harrowing look Ruth gave me, I dug around until I got to the very bottom of the box and plucked a packet from there. I looked at Dee as I brought it up, and she nodded her approval.

When we were a safe distance from the break room, I whispered, "Do you really know what does and doesn't have rat piss on it, or are you just messing with me?"

"I know the history of things," she said, "especially where unethical behavior is concerned. If I told you about the living conditions of the people who made your blouse, it would turn you white. The people who made your slacks, on the other hand, were surprisingly content—for, you know, sweatshop workers."

"Super," I said. I sat down, checked my news alerts again, and started researching how to get rid of the devil.

# 8

Sooner or later, I was going to end up in a church.

I chose the Cathedral of the Holy Cross because it came with the best references on exorcism-related message boards and it possessed a fragment of the True Cross. I took real comfort in knowing that if they needed a holy relic to exorcise the devil from me, they wouldn't have to send away for it. Plus, it was right on the Silver Line.

"You really think they can help you?" the devil asked, as I stepped into the narthex.

"Maybe," I said, my voice echoing off the stone.

"You know," Dee said, her voice not echoing, "these people talk about exorcising demons and curing leprosy, giving sight to the blind and hearing to the deaf, but they're not half as effective as their promotional material suggests. In fact, judging from the balance of evidence, you're better off asking a doctor to get rid of me."

"Yeah. I'm going to listen to the devil's opinion on religion."

There were only a few people inside the cathedral. One was kneeling near the front and praying on a rosary, while the rest were sitting in the pews and looking expectant, like maybe they got the address wrong and were waiting for a movie to start.

"Hey, I'm not against religion," Dee said. "Shit, man, everyone needs a hobby."

"Like undermining God and all his holy works?" I asked. My voice drew the attention of a man sitting near the back. He turned around and glared at me.

Dee snorted. "You know what holy work is? It's someone who takes himself way too fucking seriously, trying to make everyone else take him way too fucking seriously, too."

Huh. I wonder if Ruth is religious? Putting the question out of my mind,

I stopped at the back row of pews and tried to figure out where the hell they kept the priests in this place.

"What were you expecting?" Dee asked. "A bunch of holy men milling inside a little enclosure, like at a petting zoo? Or, oh, I know, maybe a discreet sign that reads, EXORCISMS THIS WAY, PLEASE FORM AN ORDERLY QUEUE?"

Well, it would have been helpful, wouldn't it? As it was, I just wandered down the aisle, heading for the altar and hoping for a sign. I'm not usually the type who expects a sign from God, but this was a special case, right? I knelt at the foot of the stairs at the front, cast my eyes beyond the altar, up to Jesus on the cross, and silently begged for guidance.

Behind me, the devil said, "Why are you talking to someone who doesn't exist?"

I tried to ignore her. I really did. But seriously, how the hell do you ignore something like that? My head shot around and I narrowed my eyes. "Do you think I'm stupid?" I whispered.

She considered it and said, "Well, a smart person wouldn't tee themselves up like that."

"I meant, are you honestly trying to tell me there's no God, when you're *the devil?*"

She gave me a look that, measured in sheer patronizing force, exceeded even Ruth's best. "Why would you assume there has to be a God just because there's a devil?" she asked. "What, you think mystical beings have to come as a set? You met Death last night. So, do you just assume there's also a personification of the other three Horsemen of the Apocalypse? Famine, War, and…who's the last one?" She frowned. "Damn, that's going to bug me until I remember."

"Pretty sure it's my mom." I turned back to the altar and tried my best to ignore her.

"That reminds me. Death and I got to talking, and we think you should call Simon, or at least pick up the phone when he calls."

I tried my best to ignore her.

"He's not angry, you know. He's just worried about you. Maybe you could, I don't know, talk to him about these issues you're having, instead of going to a stranger in a funny robe and expecting him to use magic on your problems."

Ignore harder.

"Come on, Jordan. He's your brother." And on the last word, her voice finally echoed through the nave. What a drama queen.

I succeeded in ignoring her, and she soon became suspiciously quiet. After a few minutes, all I heard was the occasional metallic click, accompanied by a little *sproing* sound.

I just had to know what she was up to, even if she was playing me. I turned to see her sitting in a pew with her feet up. Her eyes slid up to meet mine, and I saw her lips curl into a smile of triumph. What really drew my eye, however, was the crossbow in her lap.

No one else in the cathedral seemed to see it, though several gave me nasty looks when I turned around. Maybe you're not supposed to kneel on the steps or something. I dunno. If not, it's the church's fault for not putting up a rope.

I didn't give it much thought, because, you know, the crossbow. For one thing, it was loaded. For another, it happened to be pointed at my head. I stood and took two big steps out of the way, then approached her from the side. She had her hand on a little crank at the back end of it and was idly turning it back and forth.

"Where the hell did you get a crossbow?" I asked.

She looked up. "Fourteenth-century Genoa. Why, where do you get yours?"

"You can just make stuff appear?" I asked. "So, why didn't you do that instead of drinking all *my* beer?"

"That question answers itself." She held the crossbow out. "Want to try it?"

I'm not going to lie. I did. Because, seriously, how fucking cool is a crossbow? But I was almost definitely on the edge of refusing when Dee tossed the thing at me.

"Careful now. It has a hair trigger."

It was heavier than I expected, too. I caught it, but I was still fumbling, trying not to drop it.

"Pestilence!" Dee cried, snapping her fingers.

And the damn thing went off. I heard the twang of the arrow hitting somewhere behind the altar.

"That's the fourth horseman's name. Pestilence." Dee looked past the altar. "Hey, man, nice shot."

I couldn't quite tell where she was looking. I searched until my eyes reached about a third of the way up the crucifix. Then my mouth fell open.

"Oh, God," I said, my voice a low but pitiful wail, "I shot Jesus in the dick."

Dee walked up next to me and tilted her head. "Maybe no one will notice," she said. "The bolt's buried so deep in there, there's hardly half an inch sticking out." She tilted her head the other way. "I tell you, though, if they do notice, they'll have to ream it out with an electric drill. Or I guess they could just cut it flush and paint over the area. Of course, every time they look up there, their eyes will be drawn to their savior's junk, and they'll remember it has a crossbow bolt buried in it."

I pushed the weapon back into Dee's hands and ran for the exit.

# 9

I ran and kept running, across the road and straight down the nearest cross street. I don't know what the criminal penalty for desecrating a cathedral is, but I didn't want to find out.

I was ready to give up my quest for exorcism entirely, to assume that not only Christianity but faith in general was closed to me because I'd shot Jesus in the dick. At that moment, I don't think I would have dared walk into a Hindu temple, for fear word had already gotten around among deities. But the more I ran, and the more I thought about it, the more it seemed that I could not possibly have bullseyed Christ's bullseye of my own accord.

What got me was the sheer improbability of it. Really, what were the odds? I was increasingly convinced that Dee had orchestrated the entire thing, and that she'd done it to throw me off the right path.

Speak of the devil, she ran past me, wearing white track shorts and a sports bra. She turned around and jogged backward. "Whatcha thinkin'?" she asked.

I gave her the finger.

"Fascinating," she said. "Could you expand on that?"

I gave her both fingers.

"See, this is why I like hanging out with you: the intellectual discourse."

"Was any of that even real?"

"Jordan, it was as real as it was hilarious."

"But you made the arrow hit where it did, didn't you?"

"It wasn't an arrow. It was a bolt." We jogged on in silence for a few seconds. "But yes. Congratulations, Jordan. You saw through my elaborate web of lies."

"Don't think this will stop me," I said.

Dee grinned. "Hey, there are plenty of churches left in town. What are the chances you'll have a chain of mortifying incidents in every single one, each one more mortifying than the last? Hardly worth considering."

♦

There *are* a lot of churches in Boston—Dee was right about that—but my research had revealed that only a few were open to the idea of exorcism. My next best prospect was St. Jacob's, all the way over in the West End. Getting there was a pain in the ass, of course, because Boston. Nothing in Boston connects to anything else the way you'd expect. It's like navigating a cat's cradle.

It took two bus connections and a hike of several blocks, but I eventually made it. This time, I learned from my earlier mistake and stayed well clear of any valuable or sacred objects. Instead, as soon as I entered St. Jacob's, I looked for the old lady praying on the rosary. I knew I'd find one, because every time I've been in a Catholic church outside of scheduled mass, there's always been exactly one old lady praying on a rosary. I think they come with the building.

I sat down behind this one, and when she got to the end of her set of Hail Marys, I tapped her shoulder and asked whether any of the resident priests had experience with exorcism. I half-expected her to slide away from me, but she actually recited a name and phone number from memory. I was so impressed, I almost gave her a tip.

Only half an hour later, I was sitting in the parish office, looking across an oak table at Father Cunningham, a kindly, older man dressed in a black cassock and white collar. Later on, I'd do more research and learn he was one of only a handful of priests in the country officially licensed by the Vatican to do exorcisms. Because, yeah, that's a real thing.

"Okay," he said, "what seems to be the problem?"

I'd been rehearsing this in my head, and decided that the best plan was to dive right in. I took a deep breath and said, "The devil talks to me."

"Okay. Does he tell you to do things?"

"No," I said. "I think she's just here to punish me. If I'm being honest, I probably deserve it, but she should have to wait until I'm dead, right?"

"Okay," he said, with the exact tone and intonation as before. "And is the devil talking to you now?"

"No," I said. "She's lying with her back on your desk, with her legs around your neck." I figured it was best not to mention the motions she acted out. "Don't worry. She's wearing pants." She was not wearing pants.

"Okay," he said, unfazed.

"Wow," Dee said. She rolled off the desk and landed on her feet. "This guy's a lot harder to shock than I expected. Probably because he masturbated furiously every night in seminary school and never confessed it, because he blamed it on demons." She idly picked at her nails. "Better than diddling kids, though, right?"

"Okay," Father Cunningham said again, "the first step in the process is to make certain it's not a mental condition."

I told him about the waffles.

"Okay," he said, still in the exact same tone. It seemed to be a verbal tic.

"God, I'm sorry about your fucking waffles," Dee said, from her new seat, hovering and grinding just above the priest's lap. "I'll buy you more waffles. Will you just get over it, already?"

"I believe you," he went on, "but that diagnosis will have to be confirmed by a psychological professional. You understand?"

I nodded. I knew this was going to be a pain in the ass going in. I've seen *The Exorcist*.

"Then we have to prove that you're under the influence of the Evil One."

"Hey, that's me!" Dee said, quite cheerful.

Father Cunningham went on, oblivious to her. "Evidence of his influence might be something like, say, exhibiting supernatural strength."

Wow, that would be cool, wouldn't it? There were a few books on his desk, so I picked one up, double-checked that it wasn't the bible, and tried to tear it in half.

It didn't work.

"Okay," the priest said. God, why did he keep saying that? It was starting to unnerve me. "That's okay. It isn't a requirement to prove possession."

"Oh, good," Dee said, "they grade on a curve."

"You might shout profane things, uncontrollably."

"You mean since the devil started talking to me?" I considered. "Yeah, I would say I've been doing that a lot more."

"Okay."

Dee, who was now sitting on the edge of the desk, just snickered. "Jordan, you should definitely trust this guy. I have a good feeling about him."

"Okay, and you may commit acts of sacrilege. Have you committed any acts of sacrilege?"

I looked at the desk to avoid making eye contact as I said, "You know the crucifix at Holy Cross? I shot it in the...uh...in the penis with a thirteenth century Genoan crossbow."

"Fourteenth-century," Dee corrected. "And it's 'Genoese.'"

"I meant fourteenth-century Genoese," I said.

"Okay," he said, and hung in silence for many uncomfortable seconds before continuing. "I will have to...confirm that, but I'm afraid it still doesn't quite reach the required level of proof for a possession. Hmm, what else?"

"I love how disappointed he looks," Dee said. "Like he's afraid he might fall behind in the exorcism standings."

"Ah," Father Cunningham said. "Do you know anything you couldn't possibly know, absent the possession?"

After a moment's thought, I said, "Rats pissed in the sugar I was about to put in my coffee this morning."

Dee sighed. "I knew that was going to come back to bite me in the ass. You try to do something nice for someone, and they just use it against you." She shook her head.

"Okay, good," the priest said. Yeah, by this point, the "okay" thing was getting weird. "But I can't just take your word for it, you understand? It has to be something I can confirm."

Dee just grinned wide at me, as if daring me to say what I was thinking.

I swallowed. "Umm," I said, "it's true that the devil will mix truth with lies, to try to corrupt us, right?" I was almost positive I remembered that from *The Exorcist*.

Father Cunningham nodded.

I took a deep breath and ripped the bandage off quickly, saying in a fast patter, "Okay, I'm not saying this is true. Maybe it's a lie, but she says that, when you were in seminary school, you masturbated every night and never confessed it."

He went bug-eyed with shock.

I was braced for another "okay," but he just stared at me for a while. Like, a really, deeply uncomfortably long time—so long that I began to worry he'd had a stroke. I was on the verge of calling for help, when his lips twitched and he mouthed a completely silent "Okay."

He mouthed it several times more before I heard the faintest breath in it, and the string of silent "okays" grew into a string of muttered "okays."

Dee exploded into giddy laughter and said, "Holy shit, you broke the priest! Hey, you don't like your job, right? Wanna come work for me? In my organization, a talented young go-getter with skills like yours could go straight to the bottom."

While Father Cunningham was still rebooting, my phone vibrated, shaking loose a sharp bit of casing that jabbed through the pocket of my slacks and into my thigh. I pulled it out just long enough to send the call to voicemail. I didn't even look at who it was.

"That was David," the devil said. "You keep stringing that man along and you're going to lose him. He ain't like Simon. He won't give you a hundred more chances. Speaking as someone who knows about these things, it's a miracle you got this one. Turn up your nose at it and you might as well delete his number, 'cause if you keep him waiting any longer? That boy's gonna take a cue from you and not pick up the next time you call."

It was another attempt to throw me off the path.

It had to be, right?

Then again, between the trip to Tampa and the whole devil thing, I had been brushing David off since our first date. It was surprising, now that I thought about it, that he hadn't gotten the wrong idea and given up entirely.

Dee leaned across the desk and spoke right into my face. "Jordan? Do you think you're ever going to get another chance at someone like him?"

It can't be good when the devil is trying to get you laid, right? That just has to be bad.

As I contemplated this, the priest finally recovered himself and said, "Okay. I believe you. Okay. Okay. Ordinarily, we'd need the consent of the bishop to do an exorcism, okay, but sometimes he doesn't have the clarity of vision needed to see these things for what they are, okay, okay, so I can talk to a friend of mine at the Vatican, okay, and—"

"Excuse me," I said. "I need to make a phone call."

"Okay, if it isn't long distance."

I was momentarily baffled, then realized he was offering the use of the office telephone, which must have been a very polite gesture in whatever decade he thought it was. "Thank you, I have my own," I said, waggling my phone at him. A small piece fell off of it and skittered under his desk, but he was still too dazed from the masturbation thing to notice.

He nodded with one last "Okay" as I stepped into the hall.

I closed the door in Dee's face, which only prompted her to walk straight through it, leaving a barely noticeable dusting of ash around her outline. I felt her breath against my ear as she looked over my shoulder at David's entry on my contact list. "I think you have to swipe from left to right to make a call," she said.

"I know how to use my own phone, thank you."

"Really?" she asked, and walked in front of me. "Because you're just standing there, staring at it. Is this some new smartphone interface I haven't heard of, or are you having one of those hesitant, dramatic moments that people only drag out this long when they know someone else is watching them?"

"The second one," I said, still looking down at my phone.

"Would it help if I played thoughtful, reflective music on a cello?"

"No."

"What about a fiddle? I'm a great fiddle player."

"So I've heard."

I swiped left to right and put the phone to my ear, part of me hoping he wouldn't pick up, the rest trying to formulate something I could say if he did. The ringing cut off and I heard a smooth and sonorous voice say, "Jordan, hello."

"Heeey, Agent Dave," I said, and immediately winced. Yeah, that was the best I could come up with. Fuck you. I was under a lot of stress.

He laughed softly. "If I am a secret agent, I'm not a very good one. Everyone seems to know."

"Well, maybe that's your cover. You're such an obvious secret agent, no one would suspect you of being a secret agent." God, why was my mouth still going? I really wished I could make it stop. Even the devil was shaking her head. "They call it a double bluff. But you already know that, of course."

Against all odds, he laughed. "Or maybe I just want you to think that I know that."

"This conspiracy runs deeper than I thought," I said. The devil gave me a thumbs-up.

"So," David said, "I have a couple tickets to *The Walking Dead: The Musical*, down at the Orpheum. Curtain's at seven-thirty. Interested?"

"Tonight?" I asked, like a complete moron.

"Yeah. With the Lithuanians after me, I can't afford to make plans too far in advance."

I hesitated. The devil looked at me and said, "You know, you could just tell him what happened, explain *why* you've been brushing him off, and say you need some time. He'll understand. Or, I guess, you could make up another implausible excuse that'll make him think you're an asshole. Whatevs."

"Jordan? Still there?"

"Yeah, I, umm, kind of have a thing tonight." I looked back at the priest's door.

David sighed. I guess I'd used that one a few too many times.

"But I can cancel. I'm not too far away. I'll meet you there, okay?"

"Oh, good." I could hear the smile in his voice. "I'm having some issues at work, and I just need to do something pointless with someone awesome, or I'm going to lose it."

I grinned. "Pointless I can manage."

I made my excuses and headed out. The devil followed in silence, until we were nearly there. I avoided talking to her all the way, though I could hear her footsteps immediately behind me. When we were nearly at the Orpheum, she said, "So, why don't you just tell him what happened in Tampa? Why don't you tell your friends, for that matter? Do you think they'd blame you for things that are beyond your control?"

"I don't want them feeling sorry for me."

She laughed, humorlessly. "Yeah, because that would just be a fucking tragedy, wouldn't it?"

I spun around to face her.

She was gone.

I was probing the little circle of ash she'd left with my toe, when David's voice came from behind me. "Don't want who feeling sorry for you?"

I spun back and smiled. "Just talking to myself."

"Seemed like a heated conversation," he said.

"Sometimes it's hard to find common ground."

"With yourself?"

"Yeah."

And that seemed, for the moment at least, to convince him that I wasn't dangerous. It didn't stop the situation from being incredibly awkward, of course, but I think I covered for it quite nicely, by eye-banging him.

David is all the things you want in a man, and all the things you're too embarrassed to admit you want on top of that. He has a body like Daniel Craig's, a voice like Roger Moore's, a face like Pierce Brosnan's, and he wears the sort of endearing, self-assured smile that Sean Connery perfected and all the other Bonds merely imitated. He's also incredibly smart—he started his own biotech company—and he has a great personality, but I guess those don't really come through in an eye-bang.

It was a goddamn tragedy when we found our seats and the theater went dark, because I had to stop objectifying him. I wanted to make up for it by nibbling his ear, but I wasn't sure it was a good idea, even though the musical numbers were a B minus at best. Then again, I thought I saw him glancing over at my own ear during Morgan's love ballad.

We held hands on the way out, though, so that was something, right?

As we walked under a marquee advertising *Stargate on Ice*, he asked "Want to grab a bite? I know a great little place in the North End."

I agreed, if only because I worried he'd take it as a rejection if I didn't. Outside, the wind had picked up, blowing in from the bay. I was dressed for fall, not for a mile's walk through icy wind. He noticed and suggested we take the Orange Line.

At that moment, I knew we had something.

I knew we had something, because you don't take a second date onto the Orange Line in the middle of the night, unless you've already achieved a level of comfort and ease that most married couples will never reach. The Blue Line, sure. The Red Line, maybe. But the gloomy Orange Line, with its tacky, wood-paneled interior and guess-the-stain upholstered seats? No. The Orange Line is one of the most unglamorous places in Boston—a city filled to brimming with unglamor—and I couldn't have been more thrilled that David suggested it.

"Why are you grinning like that?" he asked.

"No reason."

He gave me an odd look, but when I glanced over again, he was grinning too. It was one of those magic moments that in future years you tell your kids about, not just once but over and over, until they're sick of the story. It was the moment when I first thought, *This is the man that, barring unforeseen incompatibilities, I'm going to have a high probability of spending the rest of my life with.* Because, you know, I'm a romantic but still a realist.

And then I remembered Dee.

# 10

I knew she was out there, plotting, and I watched for her the whole way.

"You know, I was only joking about the Lithuanians being out to get me," David said, noticing my wariness. "It's actually the North Koreans."

"You should have said. I would have brought my acid-shooting pen."

We arrived at the restaurant, ordered, and then there was a bunch of boring date stuff that you probably don't give a crap about. I understand. There's nothing more tedious than people talking about how great their kids are or how well their dates went.

You know what, though? Fuck it. I'm going to tell you anyway.

We were effortless together. The only strain on our conversation came from the fact that we wanted to rip each other's clothes off.

It was so nice, I didn't even mind when the conversation turned to work bullshit. "We lost a big NIH grant," he said, "so now I have three months to convince the investors we can bring our drug to market with half the money we were expecting to have. I think we can do it, but my team is so demoralized, they're hardly making any progress, and we're falling behind by the day."

I put my hand over his. "Damn. That sucks."

"So, what do you think I should do?"

I was too stunned to respond, at first. I thought he just needed to vent, so I'd resisted the natural impulse to spew ignorant advice at him. "You want to know what I think?" I asked, still not believing it. "About biotech issues?"

He shot me that Connery smile and shook his head. "You have a way with people, whether you realize it or not. You inspire loyalty."

"Huh." It still seems weird, but I guess he was right, wasn't he? Gabby and Michael supported me in ways that were not just beyond what I deserved but beyond what was plausible. I don't know if David was the first person to notice this, but he was the first person to make me aware of it. It wasn't exactly an Orange Line moment, but it was nice.

"So?" he asked.

I considered the problem as I munched some garlic bread. "If I had to guess," I said, "I'd say there's one person at the heart of your morale problem—probably the person who believed the most in what you're doing and worked the hardest. But now their belief has been shaken, and they're coasting because they think the whole thing is doomed."

"No, not Debby," he said, too quickly.

"It's Debby," I said. "And she's infecting the others. See, I bet they've always looked to her to set the patterns of their behavior."

"Fuck," he said. His face confirmed that he thought I was right. "But how did you know?"

I shrugged. "Debby is me. Except Debby is coasting until your company fails, whereas I'm coasting until society fails."

"You think big. I like that. Ever consider a job in biotech?"

"Hell, no."

Between the garlic bread and the main course, a fiddle player emerged from a back room and began serenading the tables. Yeah, a fiddle player. Could Dee be more obvious? I made an excuse to leave the table and went straight for the supposed musician.

"You think this is funny?" I asked, nosing in next to him while he played for a couple in a booth. "You know, it's not like real Italian restaurants even have violin players. That's just shit from the movies."

He didn't miss a note of his song, though his lips formed a scowl and his eyes darted over to me. The couple at the table just stared, one frozen with a forkful of lasagna halfway to his mouth and the other in the middle of taking a sip of red wine.

When I noticed them looking at me, I flashed a little smile and said, "Excuse us." I grabbed the violinist by the back of his collar and dragged him away, his song ending in an abrupt staccato as the bow stuttered down the strings.

I got him into a quiet corner, gave him a hard look, and asked, "What the hell do you think you're playing at?"

"Nocturne in E-major?" he said, in a squeaky voice.

I was half a second from slamming him against the wall when I heard Dee's voice from behind me. "Is there a problem here, Jimmy?"

"This lady doesn't seem to like the music, Mr. D'Angelo."

I turned to face Mr. D'Angelo, who was just Dee dressed in a tuxedo. "Let me have a word with her," she said. "You get back to work."

As Jimmy scampered off and resumed playing—his performance rather worse than before—I narrowed my eyes at her. "Mr. D'Angelo?"

"He saw what I needed him to see," she said. "Just like you."

"So, are you throwing up illusions around yourself, or inhabiting the actual Mr. D'Angelo, or what?" I asked. "Did that body I buried belong to someone?"

"Don't change the subject. Maybe you've realized by now, but that poor violinist is not the devil. In fact, the most evil thing he does is masturbate to a Japanese kids' show."

I was torn between regret for bothering the guy and regret for not calling the police on him. "Ew," I said.

"Say what you will, at least he's good at hiding his crazy. Unlike a certain person I won't mention, except to say that it's you."

"Are you trying to ruin my date?"

She sniffed indignantly. "If I was, I wouldn't have to inhabit a cliché. I'd just sit back and watch you do what you're best at: turning peace into mayhem." Her expression became thoughtful. "Hey, have you ever thought of running for president? Because I could make you president. Usually, I'd want your soul in payment, but in your case, I'm willing to call it a freebie."

I didn't say anything. I just peered at her, half suspicious and half accusing.

She rolled her eyes and shooed me away. "Go on. Get back to your little friend. And be secure in the knowledge that I will not mess with you in any way whatsoever for the rest of the night." She said it so earnestly, I really believed her. "I'll merely be watching you, like I always do. Every minute of every day, watching everything you do."

"That's almost as bad as that guy masturbating to a Japanese kids' show."

She shrugged. "The two situations are similar in another way, too."

My mouth opened but no sound came out.

"In that you're all as stupid as children to me," Dee said. "Why, what did you think I meant?"

I just shook my head and went back to the table. I checked over my shoulder as I sat down and saw that Dee was gone, replaced by an ashy spot on the tile.

"What was all that about?" David asked.

*Shit.*

I had to come up with an explanation, and fast. "Oh, I was just telling the violinist that, if he comes over here and plays for us, I'd smash that violin over his head." I set my napkin in my lap and picked up my fork. "I hate that shit, don't you?"

Confusion dominated his face. At first. It was slowly replaced by a soft, contemplative smile. I recognized it: he was having an Orange Line Moment.

I smiled back.

# 11

I didn't get home until after eleven. I really wanted to invite David over, but the place was a mess. I went straight to bed but took my laptop with me and spent half the night on research. I must have fallen asleep while scrolling through Dante's *Inferno*, because I woke up at 9:15 am, spooning the computer—I think because of the warmth, not because I'm a latent technosexual.

While contemplating this deeply personal question, I noticed the time and screamed, "Motherfucker!"

I went straight for the alarm clock, checking it in a panic. I don't know why, but that's the first thing I do when I oversleep. Some part of me must earnestly believe that, by determining the reason for the alarm clock's failure, the mistake will somehow be undone. I found that there was nothing wrong with it. The alarm had simply been deactivated.

Dee's voice came from behind me. "Oh, I turned it off."

I hardly even jumped, by now accustomed to her unexpected appearances. I only turned to glare at her.

"What?" she asked. "You looked like you needed the sleep. You were up so late, reading that travelogue."

I would have hurled curses and threats, but time was of the essence, so I proceeded directly to Jordan Liang Oversleep Contingency Plan Number Three. I don't want to brag, but Plan Three may be the world's most abbreviated process for preparing for work while still maintaining the appearance of hygiene. It involves dressing in my least complicated work clothes, which have been pre-positioned in a handy spot in anticipation of just such emergencies. A bra is not included in the dressing process, unless you can get it on in under five seconds, but it can be thrown into a handbag for later use. No breakfast is prepared, but fruit may be taken for consumption en route. Makeup is absolutely out of the question, but a rudimentary cleanliness is maintained by moistening several paper towels with tap water and including them in the aforementioned handbag for later use. Dental hygiene may at first appear tricky, but if one considers the trivial cost of replacement toothbrushes, a solution presents itself: as the final step in the preparation process, toothpaste is applied to a toothbrush on the way out the door. In this manner, the teeth may be brushed during the walk to the bus stop and the toothbrush discarded when finished.

I was out the door in under three minutes, and it only took that long because Dee distracted me. And then I waited fifteen minutes for a bus. That's probably the biggest flaw in the Jordan Liang Oversleep Contingency Plan Number Three, but at least you aren't left wondering if you missed a slightly earlier bus.

"Can I just say that I admire your savoir faire?" Dee said, while I waited for the bus.

"Uck you," I replied around my toothbrush. I finished and spit the brush into the gutter, where it landed next to two earlier toothbrushes which had arrived there in the same manner. It's not that I like to litter, mind you; it's just that there isn't a trash can close by. Anyway, the street cleaners come through often enough that it's rare for more than ten toothbrushes to pile up.

When the bus pulled up to the curb, I had one hand stuffed down my shirt and was cleaning my armpit with a damp paper towel.

"Hey, Jordan," said the unflappable bus driver.

I caught the paper towel under my arm as I boarded, so I'd have both hands free to find and tap my fare card. It was nearly ten by the time I made it into work, but it would have been much worse if I wasn't prepared. I snuck in, my head low to keep out of sight behind the cube walls. Dee crept ahead of me, doing shoulder rolls between cubicles and giving hand signals like some kind of Green Beret. I ignored her and walked faster.

I made it to my cube without being spotted, but as I turned into it, I saw the dreaded sticky note on my monitor. It read *See Me – Ruth* in magic marker.

Dee plucked the note off the screen, made a show of studying it, and said, "Wow, this is really angry handwriting. I bet if you told her you murdered the devil with a boning knife, she'd be more polite."

"No, she's already said that what I do outside of work hours doesn't concern her. It was part of a speech about how I'm not supposed to like my job. Or that if I like my job, it means I must not be working hard enough at it, or something like that. I don't remember. At the time, I was concentrating on lighting her on fire with my mind."

Dee eyeballed me and asked, "Why are you staring at me with that strangely determined expression?"

"No reason."

I set my things down and made the long trek to Ruth's office. As I entered, she looked up from whatever the hell it is mid-level managers do all day and flashed me a phony smile. I mean, all of Ruth's smiles are phony. I don't think I've seen her smile sincerely in all the years I've worked there, but she usually puts some effort into the deception. This time, it was like she *wanted* me to know how phony she was being.

She held up her forefinger, pointing it at the ceiling before sweeping it up and back down to point at the chair on the other side of her desk. It's how she tells you to sit down when she's pissed off. I think she saw it in a movie and thought it looked intimidating, but when she does it, it just looks like she's not sure where the chair is.

"Jordan," she said and sighed. "Jordan, Jordan, Jordan."

As I sat, Dee went around to stand next to her. She wagged her finger at me and echoed Ruth, saying, "Jordan, Jordan, Jordan."

I smiled sheepishly. "Sorry I was late. My alarm didn't go off."

"Jordan, I don't think the problem here is with the alarm."

"Well," I said, "insofar as it didn't go off, I'm not sure I would—"

At this point, Ruth put her finger to her lips and silenced me. She leaned forward and spoke in a very concerned tone. "Jordan, I won't need you to talk for most of this meeting."

I crossed my arms over my chest and just stared at her, at which point her face caught on fire. Or so it appeared. I realized, as the skin burned away and the hair went up, that Ruth was either sufficiently focused to ignore being set on fire, or this was a harmless illusion generated by Dee. I glanced at Dee, whose smirk seemed to confirm the latter.

I went from utter shock to holding in laughter. Ruth shook her flaming skull and sighed again. "You know, this is your problem, Jordan. You don't take things seriously."

I nodded, trying to look as stern as possible.

"You were late today," said the chattering, fire-wreathed teeth of Ruth's skull. "But you're late a lot, aren't you? Don't think I don't notice." Ruth's fiery eye sockets turned toward her monitor. "And the websites you've been visiting…"

"Whoops," Dee said, as the flames extinguished. "Looks like someone installed web monitors."

Ruth's face rebuilt itself from the bone out. I held my hands out and said, "I can explain that…"

"I don't need you to talk yet," she said, matter-of-fact. Her eyeballs unmelted and looked over her screen. "Let's see what you've been reading during work hours. Exorcism. Satanic ritual. The devil. Demons. The *Huffington Post.*"

I leapt to defend myself. "Now, wait a minute, I don't read the *Huffington Post!*"

"Sorry, that was me," Dee said. When she saw my puzzled look, she shrugged and added, "What? They have a lively comments section."

Ruth put on her I'm-not-mad-I'm-just-disappointed-but-yeah-also-mad face and said, "I'm sorry, Jordan, but I'm going to have to give you two written warnings. One for the websites and one for your tardiness."

Okay, now, let me just say that the technical merits of those warnings cannot be denied. I was late. A lot. And I did visit those websites during work hours, except for the last one. But holy fuck, are you fucking kidding me with this fucking shit? Sure, so I don't put a hundred percent into my job. I put maybe twenty-five percent into it, but I'm still more productive than anyone else in the goddamn department. But were any of those useless assholes getting two motherfucking warnings for it?

Sorry. Sorry. I didn't mean to get worked up. It's all in the past. It doesn't matter now. There's no need to discuss it further, so I'm just going to let it go.

But what the fuck, right? What a fucking bitch! Where the hell does she get off, giving me two warnings in one day? Three and you're fired, and they'd be losing their best goddamn employee, if not—obviously—their hardest-working one.

It's okay. I'm breathing. I'm breathing. It's okay. I'm not angry. It just frustrates me, is all. I'm going to stop now.

*But fucking seriously*, what the fucking fuck is fucking wrong with that fucking bitch? I think she just hates me. I think that's the real problem right there. She doesn't like me and she was picking on me. She's just a fucking bully. That's all she is, really. A fucking bully.

Okay, I'll stop. I'm calm. Seriously, I'm calm. It's okay. We're cool. Everything is cool.

I think for real, this time.

Yeah.

*So.*

I left Ruth's office having said absolutely none of those things to her. I didn't say a word, actually, which at least seemed to make her happy. I walked back to my desk and sank into the seat. "This is your fault," I said to Dee. I couldn't see her but I knew she must be lingering somewhere behind me.

"Oh?" she said, from over my left shoulder. "It's my fault you hate your job?"

I turned the chair toward her. "No, but it's your fault I'm on the edge of losing it."

She looked up from examining her nails and laughed. "Which is another way of saying that I'm helping you get a new one."

"More of your help, huh? Well I don't want your help. I don't need your help."

She went back to examining her nails. "You obviously do, considering how long you've been at this job. It's coming up on your ten-year anniversary, isn't it?"

Holy shit, it was, but I hadn't realized it until that very moment. I sat there, too stunned to talk, counting off years in my head.

"Your problem, Jordan, is you refuse to deal with things until someone kicks you in the head."

"I do not refuse to—" I started to say, until she silenced me with a certain arch of her eyebrows, which threatened to provide evidence if I persisted in this denial. So, I just settled for "I fucking hate you."

"You know, speaking as the Lord of Lies, I find it funny how people hate me most when I'm telling the truth." She flashed a sly grin. "Don't you find that funny?"

I turned back to my desk. "I have work to do."

Even though I couldn't see her, I could *hear* that oily smile in her tone as she said, "Sweetheart, the Damietta ain't just a river in Egypt."

I went to work on my reports, ignoring her. I finished in record time and was all ready to spend the extra hour I saved looking for a psychologist who could give me a letter certifying that Dee wasn't the result of a documented psychiatric disorder. But when I tried to print my work reports, I could hear the crinkling, grinding sound of a paper jam from halfway across the office. I spun my chair around and found Dee right where I left her. "Did you break the printer?" I asked.

She held her hands up and shook her head.

Throughout the office, a dozen heads popped up above cubicle walls. Half of them asked some variation on the question "Is the printer broken again?"

When I arrived in the printer nook, the damn thing was still going, trying to ram more and more paper into the jam. I lurched to hit the Stop button. The printer tried to cram one more sheet into the jam before it stopped, as if to assert its dominance. Only then did it flash *Paper Jam* across its unhelpful little LCD screen. I gave Dee a good, suspicious eyeballing and was getting ready to call IT when I noticed the sign posted above the printer nook, reminding us to attempt to fix printer problems ourselves.

See, the way our budget is structured, it makes more fiscal sense for me to spend hours of my time trying to fix the printer than it does to have the IT goblins come up and fix it in five minutes. As a consequence, the entire IT department sits idle most of the time, but none of the department heads care, because idle IT hours don't come out of their budgets, whereas IT hours spent repairing printers do. This, by the way, was someone's idea of making government operate more like a business.

Lucky for those of us who don't want to take night classes in printer repair, we can just go downstairs to print our shit out.

Except that, on this occasion, an admin from downstairs came over and asked, "Is the printer up here broken, too?"

"Fuck," we said, together.

I had to make a good-faith effort to repair it before calling IT—or at least make an effort that appeared to be in good faith—so I opened the printer's side panel to assess the situation. It was a nightmare of twenty-pound bond paper in there, with torn and crumpled sheets stuck five thick between rollers meant to accommodate only one. I got to work yanking the top sheet out of the jam, but it just wouldn't budge. I gritted my teeth and yanked harder, because that's the kind of mood I was in.

My last yank tore the sheet in half. It made an even bigger mess of the printer's guts and sent me tumbling back against the cube wall. I cracked my head against it so hard, I nearly sent the entire wall toppling over into the adjacent cubicle.

And, naturally, that's when Ruth walked by. I don't know what instinct allows managers to appear at the exact moment you're at your worst, but Ruth has honed it more finely than anyone I know. "Everything okay down there?" she asked. She said it cheerfully, too, like she hadn't been scolding me less than an hour before, like that shit never even happened, like we were the best goddamn chums in the whole world.

"Yeah, we're good," I said, avoiding eye contact and rubbing the back of my head.

"If it's too much for you, just call IT," she said, and breezed away, as if she hadn't berated us all about calling IT as recently as a week earlier.

So, at that moment, I knew I would absolutely not be calling IT. Not just because I smelled a trap, but because I was feeling extremely contrary toward Ruth. I rocked forward, took a firm grip on the paper, and...

"You'd have more luck pulling the middle sheets first," Dee said, as she hopped up and sat on top of the printer.

I eyed her suspiciously, my grip loosening but not moving.

She shrugged. "Or do whatever you want. It's none of my business."

"And yet your nose is always in it. Hey, if you want to help me, why don't you just fix it?"

"That's much too vulgar a display of power."

I arched an eyebrow at her. "Isn't that from *The Exorcist?*"

She grinned. "One of my favorites, yeah. But it's true. I have to be very selective about who I reveal myself to. I can't just go around doing spooky, supernatural shit out in the open, where ordinary citizens can see it."

"Can't or won't?"

She seemed to honestly consider the question. "That's...complicated. The line between *can't* and *won't* is blurrier for me than it is for ape-monsters like you. Let's put it this way: I could fix it. I could even choose to fix it against my better judgement, but I can't *make myself* choose to fix it against my better judgement. Does that make sense?"

Is it weird that it did? I guess it isn't, considering that I'd taken expert-level classes in convoluted nonsense as a child, taught by one of the best professors of drug-addled nonsense in the country, my dear mother.

I nodded.

"Which is all beside the point, because I don't want to fix it, anyway."

I offered her a rude gesture and turned back to the printer. "So, was Ruth's face really on fire, or what?"

Dee snorted. "No, but if you set up a plausible explanation, it could be. Like, I dunno, maybe put the batteries for her laser pointer in backwards, or something. We could start a national scare."

"Tempting, but that's a hard pass," I said, as I tried to dislodge the top sheet. When that didn't work, I finally resorted to pulling on the middle sheet. I felt it beginning to give and pulled harder. With some effort, I was able to work it out, then two more the same way. With them gone, getting the last two was easy.

"See?" the devil said. "I can be helpful. If you want, I could show you how to stop those jams from happening again. We could turn this disaster into an opportunity to make you an office hero." She waggled her eyebrows and looked down at me. "After all, isn't the Chinese character for 'crisis' a left falling stroke, a turning stroke, a horizontal stroke, another left falling stroke, and two more turning strokes?"

I blinked at her. "I have no idea. You know how to fix printers?"

She hopped down and laughed. "Absolutely! Who do you think made them so difficult in the first place?"

I had to wait for a coworker to pass, but once he did, I said, "I should have known."

"So, will you do what I say, or what?"

I sighed. "Fine."

She smiled proudly. "Okay, so there are a few problems here that add up to these frequent jams. You've got the wrong paper type listed in the printer settings, the alignment guides aren't adjusted right, the mechanisms in there have never been cleaned or oiled, and the rollers were manufactured by a guy who cares about his job even less than you do. So, here's what you do..."

She guided me through every step. Half an hour later, I had the guts of the printer disassembled and lying on the carpet. When I looked at them spread out across the alcove, I was certain I'd made a terrible mistake. When I started to draw a crowd of onlookers, I was even more certain. But I kept following Dee's instructions, because at that point, I had nothing left to lose.

Slowly, I put all those little pieces back into the printer in the places Dee pointed to. Lo and behold, when I reassembled the last part, closed the bay, and hit the power button, the printer sprang to life and spat out the rest of my print job, along with all the jobs that had queued up in the meantime. And it did it faster than I'd ever seen it run. A couple of the people watching actually applauded. The commotion attracted Ruth, who complimented me in front of everyone. I really was an office hero. Hell, I was a living legend—the only mortal in history to fight the printer and win.

"We make a pretty good team, huh?" Dee said, as the crowd dispersed. "We should form a crimefighting duo. I'd be the brains and the muscle, and you'd be…uh…the other half of the duo."

My day was going so great that Dee's comment didn't sting me. I didn't even mind when, a little before noon, she followed me to the cafeteria and ate half my lunch, snatching bites when no one was looking. I didn't mind when she followed me out afterward.

I began to grow concerned, however, when I arrived back on my floor to see a thin line of smoke rising from the printer alcove. I grew somewhat more concerned when I noticed the tops of two heads poking over the wall there. I recognized the first as Ruth's, and I thought the other belonged to one of the IT goblins.

I shot a nasty look at Dee, then rushed the rest of the way to my cube. I peeked over the wall. "I wish I knew what they were saying." The moment I said it, I could hear them, crystal clear, all the way across the office. I glanced at Dee, who smiled.

"So, what caused it?" Ruth asked.

"It's hard to tell with all the soot and charring." I heard metal clinking against metal as the IT guy spoke. "Ah, hell. See this? Someone took it out and put it back upside down. The weird thing is, anyone who knew how to take it out in the first place would never make that mistake. If I didn't know better, I'd say it was deliberate sabotage."

Ruth's head rose higher. As her eyes came over the wall, they were already pointed right at me. I ducked below my cube wall and huddled against the desk. "Did she see me?" I asked Dee, who was still looking.

Dee nodded. "I think so. She's coming over here."

I sat in my chair and focused like a laser beam on my work. When I heard Ruth's footsteps behind me, I didn't turn. I waited, pretending to work harder than anyone in that office has ever pretended to work before.

And then Ruth said simply, "There will be an investigation, and appropriate action will be taken."

And as I turned, with a blank look plastered carefully over my face, she was already walking away.

# 12

After work, I headed straight for St. Jacob's and that whackadoodle exorcist priest. None of my research or phone calls had found a psychologist who might be sympathetic to a pre-exorcism evaluation, so I was hoping he'd have a few in his Rolodex. That's one of the problems with the American medical system, isn't it? You can never find the specialist you need.

In the meantime, I needed some psychological support of my own. I called Gabby as soon as I got off the subway, and recounted my day while I walked through the West End. I left Dee out of the story, of course, which left a few unanswered questions.

"Why were you reading the *Huffington Post?*" Gabby asked, when I'd finished the story.

"They, uh, have a lively comments section?"

"And what possessed you to think you could fix the printer?"

"Nothing *possessed* me," I said, laughing nervously. "Why would you think something *possessed* me? That's ridiculous."

I noticed Dee walking shoulder to shoulder with me, though I hadn't seen her approach or appear. She shook her head.

Gabby asked, "Jordan, what's really going on? You've been acting strange lately, and I say this as someone who put a ten-thousand-dollar retainer on a soup lawyer this morning." I could almost hear mental gears turning on the other end of the phone. "And since when do you go on business trips? What social worker goes on business trips to Tampa?"

"It was a conference," I said. "On social work."

"Well, you should stop going to conferences. They make you mental. I bet you don't remember this, but in the bar the other night, you thought you were talking to the devil."

"I am not mental!" I said, loud enough to turn several heads up and down the sidewalk.

"Jordan, you took the printer apart. Why would you take the printer apart?"

I went from loud and defensive to quiet and meek. "Someone told me I could fix it. I was lied to."

Dee smiled proudly.

"By whom?" Gabby asked. "Some rogue motivational speaker? What person tells someone they can fix a printer, and why would you ever believe them?"

"I guess I've just been in a weird place lately," I said, and switched to Bluetooth so I could look through recent news updates about the body I buried in the woods.

"You should see a psychologist," she said.

"I am!" I said. "I'm going to see someone right now so they can help me find a good one."

"Why can't you just Google it?"

"Already tried."

"You don't need a psychologist," Dee said. "Because *I'm* here to help you with any emotional problems you might be having, Jordan. You can even lie on a couch, if you want. Clothing optional."

"If you want my advice, just go to one and see how it works out," Gabby said. "You can change later. You have great insurance."

"I'm just not sure that's a good idea right now."

"Well, you need to see *someone* about whatever's going on with you lately. We're all worried."

I paused on the steps of St. Jacob's and looked at the big Doric columns flanking the door. "I tell you what. I'll book an appointment with whoever this guy recommends."

Gabby made a suspicious *hmm* sound. "Who are you going to for advice, again?"

I swallowed. "A priest."

I expected a sudden exclamation, but Gabby only sighed and became quiet. After a few seconds, she said in a soft voice, "Jordan, you're an atheist."

"Yeah, well, about that…"

"Why would you take advice from someone who tells people not to work on Sunday but has a job where that's the only day he works?"

Beside me, Dee laughed. "Have I mentioned how much I love Gabby?"

"It's just," I began. "I think he can help me, is all. He's a special sort of priest."

I couldn't see it, but somehow I knew that Gabby's eyes were narrowing. "Have you gotten involved with a cult?"

I took some time to process that and then said, "No."

Dee snorted. "I'm sure the long pause before answering has convinced her of your sincerity."

"Jordan," Gabby said, "they prey on people with your background—people who grew up in an unstable environment and yearn for the steady guidance they missed as children. But it's all a lie. Whatever they're telling you, it's a lie. Don't get involved and don't give them any money, okay? Promise me."

"I'm not going to give them any money, obviously," I said.

"And you're not going to get involved with them?"

"Well…"

"Promise me, Jordan!"

"It's not a cult!"

"Jordan, it sounds exactly like a cult. Don't do anything until we get a chance to talk face to face, okay? Can you promise me that?"

"Okay," I said. I climbed the stairs and stood before the big church doors. "I won't do anything until we talk. But I have to go now. I'm going into a subway station. I'm about to lose reception. Gotta go. Bye."

I ended the call and took a breath. I'd called Gabby to get support and all I got was…well, technically it was more support than I expected. The point is, I felt even shittier than before. My phone beeped with an incoming text message, and I looked down to see:

**Michael:**     *please dont join a cult*

**Michael:**     *or if you do at least watch jonestown frst*

**Michael:**     *i think its on youtube*

"Your friends really care about you," Dee said, over my shoulder.

"Shut the fuck up." I looked back at Dee, who stepped briskly aside to reveal a woman behind her, dressed in a habit. "Oh sorry, Sister."

The nun shook her head and went past me. I stood on the steps, shaking hard, weighing the importance of my promise to Gabby. As I pondered the pros and cons, my phone rattled a piece loose, and a text from David popped onto the screen, asking if I was doing anything tonight.

Well, what was one more day, really? The shrink appointment would probably be weeks out. I could talk to Gabby the next day, fulfill my promise, and then go back to Father Cunningham in the evening, right?

I stood staring at the door for a while, then went to the contact list in my phone and swept left to right across the top name.

"Hey, David," I said. "What did you have in mind?"

# 13

David answered his apartment door with a dish towel in hand, a pot under his arm, and an oven mitt in his teeth. "If I were the Russians, you'd be dead now," I said. Goddamn it, why did I keep going back to the secret agent thing? At the Orange Line stage of our relationship, I should've been able to come up with better conversation-starters.

He shrugged, spit the oven mitt into his hand, and said, "If you were a Russian agent, I'd just use the awkward charm of the moment to seduce you."

By sheer willpower, I refrained from blurting out, "I'm a Russian agent!" Because that might have been a smidge too forward. Instead, I smiled and said, "As long as you have a contingency plan. Need any help in the kitchen?"

"Nah, it's all under control," he said. "I'm just about to put the paella on. Have a seat." He disappeared into the kitchen. "There's wine in the cabinet."

I poured a glass and settled onto the couch. A big, fluffy, brown-and-cream Himalayan cat hopped up with me, gave my wine glass a cursory sniff, then chirped with impatience. "Hi there, Gus!" I said, scratching under his chin. "How's the best cat in the world?"

Now, at this point, you may be thinking that your cat, or some other cat you know, or a cat you've seen on the internet, is actually the best cat in the world. You're wrong. Gus is the best cat. Sorry your stupid cat sucks.

I heard a pan go onto the stove, then David came out from the kitchen. He stood, staring in disbelief as Gus hopped onto my lap and curled into an adorable snuggle-ball, his face pressed into my belly. "Admit it," he said. "You only came over to visit my cat."

"Eh," I said, scratching Gus behind his ears, "I'd say it's about sixty-forty."

"Who's the sixty and who's the forty?" he asked. He sat next to me and reached over to fluff Gus's coat.

"If you have to ask..."

"I'm surprised he'll even let you touch him. He hates people. He's the most misanthropic cat I've ever had."

"Exactly. He's *my* kind of cat."

David smirked. "How can a person be a social worker and a misanthrope at the same time?"

"By doing social work."

He leaned a little closer. "It can't be that bad, can it?"

"Some days, it isn't bad. Those kinds of days are getting farther apart, though. Most days, it seems like I hardly make any headway. But that's just the world."

He leaned even closer. "You know, heroes don't accept the world the way it is. They change it."

"That's beautiful. Is that Foucault?"

He shook his head slightly. *"Buffy the Vampire Slayer."*

And that's the moment I realized I was in love.

I'm not sure when the kiss started. I don't remember the exact moment, and I'm not entirely clear on when a deep, long kiss becomes a make-out session, or whether there are special conditions beyond simple duration. Which is really neither here nor there, since I don't know how long the kiss lasted, anyway.

I do know when it ended, however. It was when the smoke alarm went off. Now, I don't know how long it takes paella to burst into flames, but the cooking time was supposed to be twenty minutes, so we must have been preoccupied for at least that long. That's a very long kiss, or possibly an average make-out session, depending on what the rules for these things are.

Smoke was still pouring from under the pan cover when we rushed to the kitchen. I had to stop David from lifting the cover to check under it, which is everyone's first instinct. But I've started enough kitchen fires to know better, so we left the lid on to let it burn itself out.

While we were waiting for the embers to cool, David pulled the battery from the smoke alarm while I tried to coax Gus out from behind the entertainment center. I never did manage, and I still worry the poor cat will be terrified of people kissing for the rest of his life.

When I judged it safe to check on the paella, David and I leaned over the blackened crust of our dinner. I shrugged. "Good paella's supposed to be a little burned, right?"

He smirked. "Yeah. On the bottom, not the top."

"So, we'll just turn it upside down. Then the top will be the bottom and everything will be fine."

He donned the oven mitts of shame and picked it up. "Nope. I'm calling it. This paella has succumbed to its wounds."

I followed him to the trash, saying, "But you can't throw it away. We have to perform an autopsy and track down its killer."

As it went into the compost bin, he said "Yes, detective. What do you want on the pizza I'm ordering?"

I balled my fist and said, "Justice."

"Okay, but if they're out of justice, would tomato and basil be okay?"

One pizza delivery later, we were leaning out of David's living room window to avoid the lingering paella smoke. A chunk of tomato slipped from my pizza slice and fell five stories to the sidewalk below. David leaned next to me. Though the window wasn't quite wide enough for two people, and the air was freezing outside, neither of us seemed to mind.

Finally, something in my life was going right.

# 14

Dee didn't reappear until the next morning, while I was fixing my brown-bag lunch.

"You know, your sandwiches would be less soggy if you kept the bread separate until lunchtime," she said, looking over my shoulder as I was sliding a BLT into a plastic bag. "And I like more lettuce on them."

I didn't look up. "I'm not making it for you."

"Why not? I'm going to end up eating it anyway."

I stopped in the middle of zipping it up and turned to her. "So, I should start making *my* sandwiches to *your* liking?"

She shrugged. "Well, there isn't much point making them to your liking, is there?"

For a brief moment, I felt beaten. Then I grinned at her, holding eye contact while I tossed the sandwich right into the trash.

"See, that's just spiteful," she said, leaning over the bin and looking down into it.

"I thought you, of all people, would appreciate good spite." And with that, I set off for work.

"Don't you know there are starving kids in some shithole country somewhere?" she asked, as she followed along.

But I didn't care. I mean, I cared about the starving kids in wherever, but I didn't care about Dee's running commentary. It was a brand-new day, I had another date with David that evening, and I felt fucking fantastic.

I got into work a little early and went straight to Ruth's office. Her receptionist wasn't in yet, so I stuck my head inside the open door and tapped on the frame. Ruth looked up, then checked her watch. She looked shocked by what she saw.

"I just wanted to apologize about the printer," I said. She scowled, but I plowed on before she could say anything. "I really thought I could fix it, and I wanted to show you that I take this job seriously. I guess I got carried away. Maybe we can take the cost of replacing it out of my pay. I wouldn't object to that."

Dee peered at me and waved a hand in front of my face. "What the hell is going on? Are you on drugs?"

Ruth's scowl didn't want to fade, but it did in the end. She even smiled a little. "I don't think that'll be necessary," she said. "You meant well."

"Yeah," said Dee, "just like those missionaries that kidnap aboriginal children."

I ignored her. "I've been going through some personal problems lately," I said, "but that's no excuse. I won't let it interfere with my job anymore."

And now Ruth genuinely smiled, or at least came as close to a genuine smile as her emotion-emulating robotics software would allow. She said, "You're a hard worker when you want to be, Jordan. I do care about your welfare, so if you have any personal problems I can help out with, I want you to come straight to my office and talk to my secretary."

Dee put a hand on her hip. "This is the person you're sucking up to," she said. "This person. This person here. You're sucking up to her. What the fuck is wrong with you? Did you have a stroke in the night?"

"Thank you," I said. It was insincere, but not blatantly insincere, and I'm pretty sure Ruth can't tell the difference, anyway.

I went to my desk and set out a picture of David. Technically, this is against office policy, as we're not allowed to have personal effects in our work areas. But I got around that by setting a picture of David as my Frankenphone's wallpaper and leaning it up against the cube wall where I could see it. I left it plugged in, so if anyone challenged me, I could tell them I was only charging the battery.

Dee was quietly fuming. She stepped into the next cubicle over, which was unoccupied this close to nine o'clock. I heard the phone come off the receiver. Shortly after, my cell vibrated to an incoming call, one of the pieces of the case came out, and it fell over.

Dee hung up and stepped back, flashing a little smile.

I returned it with a grin and said, "See, that's just spiteful." And then I went right to work.

I got a week's worth of work done before lunchtime, while Dee sat on my desk and stewed. She'd occasionally ask me "why the fuck" I even wanted to keep this "fucking job," but I let it slide off me like water off an unusually productive duck's back. Hell, if staying employed here pissed Dee off, it was worth it. Being the devil's favorite hobbyhorse had finally allowed me to put the term "soul-crushing job" into its proper perspective.

I worked a few minutes past twelve before heading for the cafeteria and buying a sandwich. To forestall Dee's lunch-stealing proclivities, I made the ultimate sacrifice: I sat down with my coworkers, where an invisible person eating my lunch would be too vulgar a display of power.

Dee paced back and forth on the other side of the table, like a caged animal. "Are you shitting me with this shit?" she said. "Don't fucking grin. You don't like these people. You don't want to talk to them. Do you even know their names?"

I don't, actually. I think the guy directly across from me was Tom, or Tim, or something, but the others I had no idea about. I'd worked with some of these people for nearly ten years, and I didn't even know who they were. And the longer I chatted with them, the more I remembered why. They were incredibly boring people. But hey, as long as it pissed Dee off, I was content to pretend interest in their stupid little lives.

She almost got me when I bit into my sandwich, and she said, "You know, there's horse meat in the salami."

I nearly choked, but was able to pass it off as food going down the wrong pipe.

"The supplier sneaks it into the ground beef, and no one's caught on yet."

I looked her right in the eyes as I took another bite, chewed, and swallowed. I like horses, don't get me wrong, but this one was already dead, and quite frankly delicious.

"Hey, you know what I've always wanted to try?" I asked the table, with a smug glance at Dee. "Horse sashimi."

This was met with a chorus of distaste from my coworkers and a roll of the eyes from Dee. Only Tim-Tom seemed supportive. He said, "I've thought about trying it, but it's really expensive."

I shrugged. "Yeah, well, how often does one of those fishing boats catch a horse?"

This was met by nothing but blank stares. God, I really hoped Dee would get bored with me soon, because I wasn't sure how many days I could eat lunch with these people before I had to murder them.

While my mind was on murdering people, I realized I hadn't looked at my news alerts since the previous evening. I'd been so preoccupied with David, then so preoccupied with devil research, then so preoccupied with work, that I'd forgotten all about it.

I checked my phone, and my heart dropped through my stomach, came out somewhere around my liver, and kept falling until it bounced off one of my kidneys and rolled to a stop against my iliac crest. The top story on my news feed was "Source in Wellesley PD Leaks Video of Alleged Jane Doe Killer." Accompanying it was a grainy picture of an intersection in the woods, showing a person pulling a lumpy, rolled-up carpet from the hatchback of a green subcompact.

I stood up so fast, my flimsy cafeteria chair flipped over and bounced away. "Holy mother of fuck!" I cried.

You know how, in the movies, someone makes a sudden exclamation and the entire room goes silent? And then, a second and a half later, someone in the background coughs?

That's pretty much what happened.

Dozens of faces were staring at me, demanding an explanation. I stammered out, "I...just realized I forgot my brother's birthday." Life began to return to the room, and conversations resumed. "I have to go."

I walked back to my desk, to the accompaniment of Dee's giddy laughter. I sat down, hit the power button on my computer, and waited an agonizing minute for it to wake up. The moment I got to the desktop, I lunged for the browser and went to a local news site.

I was in the second article from the top. I stared at my own picture. It wasn't very flattering, taken in bad light and pixelated as hell, but I knew it was me, even if the cops didn't. How the hell had they gotten it, though?

A little research revealed that the town of Wellesley installed a bunch of cameras at their intersections a few years back, to monitor traffic flow and improve the timing of their red lights. And where does the video from all those cameras go? Directly to the Wellesley police department.

Awesome.

"You knew about this?" I asked Dee.

She spread her hands. "Yeah, but I didn't think it would be an issue. Who knew they'd find the body so quick? Honestly, I think this is on you for not burying it deep enough. Didn't one of your mom's boyfriends go to prison for murder? How did you not learn to be cautious, from his example?"

I watched the video several times. It was too grainy, and the light too low, to distinguish one person from another. In fact, the article kept referring to the perpetrator as "he." You could barely even tell what kind of car it was, and the license plate was nothing but a blur. But don't they have ways of enhancing that stuff?

I was beginning to wonder how suspicious it would be if I left work right then and got on a train to Mexico. Unfortunately, after a few minutes of checking, I found that you can't actually take a train from Boston to Mexico.

"Fleeing a murder investigation is a lot harder when you don't own a car, ain't it?" Dee asked.

"Yeah," I said, sighing.

"Why don't you get in touch with your mom's friends in that motorcycle gang?" she asked. "I bet they have lots of experience in sneaking people into Mexico. Hell, I bet they'd even set you up with a job and shit, for old time's sake."

That...was actually a pretty good point. Despite being violent, drug-trafficking bikers, they had always been really nice to me, possibly because my mom was as much their pain in the ass as she was mine, so we were kind of like brothers-in-arms.

"Of course," Dee said, "you'd probably have to pick one and be his woman. Or not pick one and be his woman."

"Nope," I said, the word coming as a reflex. "We're not doing that."

"Well, then, we could get you a car, if you think you need one. Mind you, you'd have to murder some more people for it."

I went back to ignoring her as I contemplated escape.

# 15

All the way home, Dee was trying to scare me. When I got off the Red Line at Harvard Station, she suddenly screamed, "Cheese it! It's the fuzz!"

I set off sprinting in an instant.

"The fuzz," in this case, turned out to be a transit cop just making his rounds, which I didn't realize until I got to the bus terminal and looked back. And yes, asshole: while fleeing from the law, my first instinct was to run to my usual bus stop. I don't know what I was planning to do after that. I'm just lucky that people making a mad dash for their connecting bus is a common sight on the T.

I didn't feel safe until I was home and had the door locked behind me. Not that a locked door would do any good against a SWAT team, but I wasn't exactly thinking with perfect clarity. I'd closed the door in Dee's face, but as soon as I turned around, there she was, coming out of the kitchen with a pudding cup in one hand and a spoon in the other.

"Thank you so much for that warning at Harvard Station," I said.

She put a spoonful of pudding into her mouth and spoke around it. "Are you being sarcastic? I can't tell through that hipster miasma."

"I am not a hipster!" I screamed.

She rested the spoon against her lower lip as she studied me carefully. "I still don't get that," she said, pointing the spoon at me. "Are you saying that hipsterism has gone too mainstream?"

"I'm just not a hipster!" I screamed, louder than before. "I'm not a too-hipster hipster, or a not-enough-hipster hipster, or a just-right-hipster hipster! I'm just not a hipster at all!"

The devil seemed to contemplate this, then said, "If that's true, it's only for lack of talent." She ate another spoonful of pudding. "Mmm, this pudding is heaven, by the way. You should have one. The middle layer's caramel."

And yeah, I went straight to the kitchen to get myself one. Make all the fat jokes you want, bitch, but let's see how you eat when the law's closing in. Besides which, I'm very suggestible when stressed.

I opened the fridge to find them all gone. Dee looked over and said, "Oh, right. This was the last one."

"There were six this morning!" The other thing about that morning was I wasn't going to let Dee push my buttons anymore. Maybe my pudding cups ended up in the same place as that plan.

"Sorry," she said. "If you want, I'll let you smell my breath when I'm finished."

"If the police do close in on me, I'm going to stab you again. I want you to know that."

She waved it off. "Oh, stop worrying about the police. They won't suspect you. And even if they do, just stick to your story and you'll be fine. Remember: you went to the movies in Burlington. You took the back roads. There was a red light on the way. You stopped at that red light on the way there and also on the way back. That's all you know."

My phone beeped. For a second, I was worried it was a text message from the police. I have no idea what they'd be texting me with. Maybe *You have the right to remain in silent mode.* But it was just David, running early for our date and promising some juicy news about work.

Well, shit.

I forgot he was coming over, or I'd have cancelled. I'd wanted to clean the apartment, change out of my work clothes, take a shower, and put on some nice music. As it was, I'd be lucky if I had time to clean the stinky terror sweat from under my arms.

Thankfully, hurry-up protocols had been drilled into me by years of oversleeping. I wet a hand towel on the way to the bedroom and wiped under my arms in the middle of changing my shirt. I stopped off at the bathroom to brush my hair and proceeded smartly to the living room.

I fell onto the couch and pulled my shoes off, then pulled one foot up to my nose to give it a test whiff. The smell was bad but not knock-you-over bad. I shuffled my feet across the carpet to scrape the worst of it off.

Don't judge me.

Dee was judging me. She stared at me, her lips tight and eyes narrowed.

"Sorry we can't all be as effortlessly cool as you are," I said, as I ran my fingers between my toes and wiped the foot sweat off on the underside of a couch cushion.

"Oh, cool is easy. It's just confidence minus sincerity." She looked down from her contemplations, and her nose scrunched up. "And not ever doing whatever the hell you're doing right now, obviously."

Before putting the couch cushion back, I tossed the worst of the living room clutter—mostly library books about the devil and exorcisms—

underneath it.

That's rule one, by the way, when it comes to making your apartment presentable in under a minute: don't clean. Conceal instead. It's faster, and it has a definite stopping point. Hurried cleaning tends to get uneven, because it's hard to judge when you're safe to stop.

I got my shoes back on and went to the kitchen, where I slid an outstretched arm over the countertop to gather all the dishes and utensils strewn there, and pushed it all over the edge, into the open mouth of the dishwasher. It took a couple shoves to get the door closed, and there was a crunching sound when the door finally latched shut, but dishes are cheap, while David's impression of me was priceless.

That's rule two for tidying in a hurry: things can be replaced.

I pushed past Dee, who was loitering in the entryway to the kitchen. She followed me with her eyes, saying, "One thing I'll say for you, Jordan: you've got 'not having your shit together' down to a science. You could teach classes in it, if and when you lose your current job."

In the hallway, I gathered all the cardboard boxes I'd collected from the past several years of online shopping and had kept in case I needed them for returns. Or possibly it was laziness. You know what? Fuck you.

I tried to get the boxes into the hall closet, but they wouldn't fit without being flattened, and I had no time to do that, so I opened a window and tossed them all into the alley behind my apartment. I made a mental note to go out there and move them to the recycling bin the next morning.

Rule three: it's not littering if you clean it up before the authorities notice.

I was just finishing up by washing the toe-stink from my hands when the doorbell rang. Perfect timing. As I breezed past her, Dee said, "You may want to wait a second."

I ignored her.

"Really, Jordan, take a moment to compose yourself before you open that door."

I continued to ignore her. As I opened the door, I put one hand on my hip in what I hoped would be a cute little pose.

I'm not sure the police officer on the other side appreciated it. I just stood there, staring at him for a few seconds, my eyes running from his badge, to his gun, to his neatly pressed blue pants, to his boots—shiny in places and scuffed in others. It's strange, the things you notice in a crisis.

"Don't panic," Dee said behind me, in a soft and reassuring voice. "Just stick to your story and you'll be fine."

Of course, my story. I flashed the officer what I now realize must have been a manic smile and said, "I went to the movies in Burlington!"

I heard a sigh behind me, and Dee said, "Smooth."

I was surprised when the police officer merely looked at me funny rather than handcuffing, Tasering, and/or shooting me. He said nothing, and took a step to the left to reveal a short, slender woman dressed in civilian clothes and carrying a clipboard.

"Jordan Liang?" she asked. She didn't offer her hand. In fact, she never came closer to me than the cop was to her. "Hi. I'm Rachel. Health and Human Services sent me over."

My brain shuffled through several possibilities, very quickly. If she was from HHS, she was probably a social worker. Were the police using social workers to assess suspects in murder investigations? Probably not. So, maybe it was about work. Maybe HHS wanted to hire me away from my current job. But then, why the cop? And why not an e-mail? I looked at him. He seemed more bored than suspicious, as if he was only there for her protection. But what kind of social worker needs a police escort?

And then I finally realized.

"Are you trying to section-twelve me?" I asked, looking between them.

She held the clipboard against her chest, but in trying to hide it, she might as well have revealed the whole thing. The form on it had crossed my desk often enough in the previous ten years. I could have recited it back to her, word for word. The first few lines flashed into my memory, unbidden. They read,

Commonwealth of Massachusetts
Department of Mental Health
Application for an authorization of temporary involuntary hospitalization

"Fuck me," I muttered.

Behind me, Dee quickly said, "I'm game if she says no."

"Now, now, it's not so bad," Rachel the social worker said. "I'm only here because there are people worried about you. It's just an assessment. It's not uncommon for people to be concerned about a loved one's faculties, especially when they join a cult."

"Wow," Dee said, "way to blurt out confidential information."

In Rachel's defense, the cop was surely under a confidentiality agreement, and she had no way to know that Dee was eavesdropping on the conversation. On the other hand, a simple glance over her shoulder would have revealed the achingly handsome man with an armful of flowers standing within earshot in the hall behind her. Rachel (hereafter referred to as "that dirty bitch") was lucky she'd brought a cop along, is all I'm saying. She would have been in real trouble if she hadn't.

"David," I said, maintaining a truly superhuman calm as I looked past that dirty bitch to address my at-this-point-almost-certainly-ex-boyfriend, "could you wait in the hall for a bit? It should only take these people a few minutes to finish ruining my life."

"Uh, okay," David said, his hand drooping until the flowers hung upside-down at his side.

That dirty bitch finally bothered to look behind her, saw David, and promptly turned bright red. So, she at least had the decency to be abashed, for all the good that did.

I led her to the living room, the cop never more than three steps from her. He closed the door, right in David's face.

"Is he really necessary?" I asked, indicating the police officer.

"He's here for your protection," that dirty bitch said.

"Ah. So, you're afraid you might attack me?"

"May I have a seat?" she asked, moving to sit on the couch. The couch stuffed with books about the devil.

"Not there!" I lunged in, meaning only to direct her somewhere else, but the cop instantly had his hand on his gun. I froze where I was and held my hands up. "On second thought, please sit wherever you'd like."

She sat and looked uncomfortable. Still holding the clipboard secretively to her chest, as if that mattered now, she reached under her cushion, fished around, and pulled a book from underneath. It was bound all in black and the front cover read, *The Satanic Rituals: A Companion to the Satanic Bible.*

"At least it wasn't one of the embarrassing ones," Dee said, lounging on the other end of the couch.

I chose to remain standing, in case sitting down was considered a threatening move and therefore grounds to shoot me. "There's no law against worshipping the devil," I said.

Strangely enough, it was Dee who looked most shocked. "Worshipping?" A smile blossomed on her lips. "Oh, Jordan. You've made me so happy."

My comment, of course, was purely strategic. Religious beliefs are not considered delusional thinking under psychiatric guidelines. They couldn't commit me for even the most abnormal behavior, as long as it didn't hurt anyone else and I could credibly blame it on my unwavering allegiance to Satan.

She pulled out another book. It was, *A Manual on the Exorcism of Demons: A Step-By-Step Guide to Escaping Satan's Ranks.*

Ah, shit, I was so boned.

"So, actually, you're trying to rid yourself of demons?" that dirty bitch asked.

"I didn't say that," I said. "I'm just doing…" I grasped for a way out. "…research on the opposition."

"The opposition being?"

"God and all his holy works," I said, without hesitation.

Dee beamed brighter and brighter. "Jordan, you know when people say there's a special place for you in Hell? In your case, you should take that literally. What kind of amenities do you want? Extremely heated floors? Hot and cold running Styx water? Jacuzzi tub of boiling blood? Say the word, buddy, and they're yours."

"Mmm-hmm," the social worker said, making a mark on her little form. "And when did you decide that God is your enemy?"

♦

The whole thing took nearly an hour. I wasn't expecting that, but I think finding those devil books put Rachel on the warpath. What she wasn't ready for was my intricate knowledge of how these things went. I knew the rules, I knew the paperwork, and I was able to counter her, move for move.

I was so sure I had her that, toward the end, I was barely paying attention to the interview. I was already planning how I could best get rid of Dee, using all the time that would be freed up by David leaving me. In hindsight, maybe I should have worried about one thing at a time.

I only realized I was in trouble when I noticed her signing the form. "You are not under arrest at this time," she said, "but I will now transport you to a psychiatric care facility, where you will be evaluated by a physician. If you attempt to resist, you may be restrained for your own protection."

The cop put his hand on his Taser, like he was just itching to use it. Maybe it was the new model.

"I won't resist," I said, "but I want it noted that I believe this is a violation of my constitutionally protected religious beliefs."

The dirty bitch looked up from her clipboard. "I'm not transporting you because of your religious beliefs," she said. "I'm transporting you because I'm afraid you're going to kill yourself."

I really should have paid more attention. Let that be a lesson: when someone really wants to commit you, they don't have to stick with the first reason that pops into their head. "Fuck me," I said.

Dee shook her head, sadly. "Jordan, when are you going to stop propositioning this floozy and see me for who I am? When will you finally notice that, behind my dorky exterior, it turns out I was beautiful the whole time?"

The social worker led the way and I had no choice but to go along. In the hall, slumped down and sitting on the floor with his back to the wall, David was still waiting. I was hoping he'd gotten bored and gone home. As he looked up, I shrugged my shoulders and said, "I think tonight is kinda canceled."

The poor guy didn't know how to react. What are you supposed to do, anyway, when your date gets committed to a mental institution? David just stood up with his mouth slightly open, looking hopeless. He reminded me of a lost puppy—a lost, incredibly sexy little puppy.

"Oh, by the way," Dee said, "you have your shirt on backwards and inside out. I meant to tell you earlier, but in all the excitement, I forgot."

I lowered my eyes and sighed as they led me away. David still hadn't said a word.

# 16

Dee sat beside me in the hospital waiting room. "Look at it this way," she said, after a long silence, "If the police track you down now, you'll already be locked up in a mental ward, so it'll be that much easier to plead insanity."

I checked to see if anyone was listening, because the waiting area of a mental ward probably isn't the best place to be caught talking to invisible people. "As soon as I get out of here, I'm heading straight back to that exorcist priest."

Dee recoiled. "Oh, no," she said, her voice quivering with feigned terror, "that's my one weakness: a skeevy old priest. Bitch, do you even remember who I am? I'm the Princess of Darkness, Queen of Hell, Mother of Lies, Her Satanic Majesty..." She paused, at a loss for more feminized devil names.

"Mephistophe-lass," I suggested. Yeah, I know, I really shouldn't have encouraged her, but it just popped into my head and I was too proud not to say it.

She grinned. "See, Jordan? This is why I love you. You get me. And it doesn't have to be all pranks and mental institutes and running from the law, either. Friendship's a two-way street, babe. There are all kinds of things I can do for you—and to you, for that matter. You only have to ask."

I rolled my eyes and looked away.

"Oh, Jordan. Don't be like that. Some people have a cute pout-face, but you just can't pull it off. Not with jowls like yours."

For the record, I was not pouting. I continued to not pout.

It took mere seconds for Dee to get bored and resume her chattering. "Hey, you seem good at this stuff. What do you suppose our celebrity couple name would be? Dee and Jordan. Deedan?"

"JorDee," I said, without thinking. Goddamn it.

"Yes!" she said in a giddy squeal. "Like on *Star Trek*!" She put her arms around my shoulders, gave me a squeeze, and lingered in that unwelcome position.

"Why are you doing this?" I asked.

"Well, you see, it's the only part of you I can get my arms around." She pantomimed straining to wrap her arms around my waist, which she could have easily done. And I don't have jowls, either.

"You know what I mean. Stop playing games."

"I've told you over and over: I'm here to help you."

"Bullshit," I said. "There are people all over the world who need help. Why don't you help any of them?"

She released me and shrugged. "Well, for one thing, I don't like them. I like you."

I turned to her, and believed her for the first time. She really did like me. At least, she was amused by me and wanted to squeeze as much amusement as possible out of me, like a cat playing with a baby bird. "How do I get you to unlike me?"

The question brought her even more glee. "Oh, Jordan. I'm not sure that's possible. You're just too much fun."

I groaned as I looked away. "Couldn't you just appreciate how fun I am invisibly and inaudibly? From a tremendous distance?"

"In most cases, I would. But on special occasions, when someone I really, really like does something really, really stupid, I've been known to make a house call. Out of concern."

I looked at my feet. "I don't know what you're talking about."

She disentangled herself from around my shoulders but left one hand to linger on my back. "I have every confidence that you can fool these morons," she said, motioning to the reception desk, "but if there's one single absolute truth in the universe, it's that you can't fool me."

I didn't answer, because a stocky man had entered the room. Which was just as well, really, because I didn't have a fucking answer. "Jordan?" the man asked. "I'm Dr. Parks. Would you mind coming with me?"

Would you mind? Why is it that authority figures only ask politely when you don't have a choice? I swallowed down my resentment, gave him my friendliest smile, and said, "Sure."

He led me to his office, where he offered me the chair in front of his desk. "We're just going to do a little assessment on you, to determine whether you belong here," he said as he sat behind it. "Is that okay?"

I nodded, despite the pure, unrefined bullshit coming from his mouth. You see, if a social worker wants to section-twelve someone, a certified psychologist has to sign off on the order. This is a commonsense fail-safe, since being a social worker doesn't make you a psychiatric expert. And yet, I've never *once* seen the psychologist fail to sign off on a section twelve order, and that isn't because of any particular competency on the part of social workers. It's more like a professional courtesy. It would be embarrassing, after all, if you were to section-twelve somebody and then have the psychologist overturn your assessment. Your coworkers might make fun of you. You might get a bad performance report. It could have a negative effect on your self-esteem.

If you're tempted to point out that the patient is in a much more embarrassing situation, that their entire life and career might be destroyed by the fickle whim of some idiot social worker that a psychiatrist is just too damn polite to contradict, then you don't understand how the world works.

"Absolutely, it's okay," I said with a smile.

He opened a manila folder, scanned the top document, smiled warmly, and said, "Tell me about your mother."

I arched an eyebrow. "Are you shitting me?"

◆

So, my assessment didn't go so well, obviously, but I still had an ace up my sleeve. When they brought me to the check-in desk, I said, "I'd like to be voluntarily committed."

The nurse on duty looked up and laughed. Then, over the course of the next few seconds, his amused expression faded. "Oh, you're serious."

"I've been having thoughts of self-harm," I said, "and I would like to voluntarily commit myself to this institution."

He had the involuntary commitment paperwork already printed out, filled in and waiting only for a couple of signatures. He looked down at it, then up at me, then over to the nurse who'd escorted me to the desk. She shrugged.

"You've already been assessed," he began, but ran out of steam after that.

"But I haven't been involuntarily committed. Not yet. Nor will I be, because I'm checking myself in voluntarily."

"You can't do that."

"I absolutely can."

"Hold on a second," he said, and picked up his phone. "Dr. Parks? Could you come out here?"

The doctor arrived shortly, and the three of them went into a huddle behind the check-in desk. They muttered something among themselves, then all looked up at me simultaneously. I smiled back.

The huddle grew in size, at first because people were called from nearby offices to consult. After a few minutes, though, nurses and social workers who happened to be walking past were drawn in by the attraction of a crowd. As word of the situation got around, people arrived from other wards, with rulebooks in hand and lists of state laws open on their phones.

I remained patient, and my patience was rewarded when the admitting nurse came out of the huddle, shoulders slumped, and stood across the desk from me. He looked back at the larger group, who collectively shrugged at him. He sighed, turned to me, and said, "Okay. Sure. We'll let you do that."

*Let me? Yeah, try to salvage what little dignity you have left, asshole.*

The fact is, there wasn't a damn thing they could do about it. The law says you can voluntarily commit yourself at any time, and you can't be involuntarily committed once you've requested voluntary commitment. It's one of those little, accidental quirks of the legal code that would have been fixed decades ago if it didn't benefit people with good lawyers.

After I read through and signed the voluntary commitment paperwork, the nurse said, "Now, if you'll just be patient, I'll find someone to escort you to—"

"Sorry," I interrupted. "May I have a blank sheet of paper?"

The admitting nurse looked as blank as the sheet he handed me, but a few of the people in the huddle were catching on. Dr. Parks shook his head, but I think I saw admiration hidden deep in his eyes. I wrote a short note, signed and dated it, and slid it back across the desk.

"I am informing you in writing," I said, "that I, who am currently a patient at this facility, admitted voluntarily, wish to be released as soon as possible. Please countersign it and note the date."

"Oh, come on!" the admitting nurse cried. "You said you were having suicidal thoughts!"

I nodded. "Yes, but I feel that my time here has been a tremendous help, and I no longer wish to harm myself."

"You've only been a patient for two minutes!"

I shot him a brilliant smile. "A testament to the skill and efficiency of your staff."

The nurse seemed to be having a breakdown, and was nearing tears when Dr. Park calmly put a hand on his shoulder. "We'll schedule a hearing for release within seventy-two hours." He took the pen out of the nurse's shaking hand, countersigned my request, and wrote down the date and time. I heard clapping, and thought it must have been Dee, but it turned out it was one of the staff, standing in awe of my social-work-fu. Dr. Parks silenced them with a glance, then looked hard at me. "That hearing will be exceptionally comprehensive, of course."

*Fuck.*

Those hearings are often shit shows already, and Dr. Parks was promising to dredge up every turd he could find. That's a lot of turds, sad to say. And if I wasn't released after this hearing, it would be three months before I could request another. My brilliant maneuver had just blown up in my face.

They were extra nasty as they checked me in, of course. They took my shoelaces and left me to shuffle around in loose sneakers. They took most of my money, supposedly to protect me from theft, and left me with just a few dollars for the vending machines. They took Frankenphone too, but the joke was on them. That just meant I wouldn't have to deal with the constant barrage of texts and voicemails from Simon.

My escort nurse wrapped an ID bracelet around my wrist, double-checked to make sure it was just a little too tight for comfort, and led me a few doors down the hall. "Usually, we'd get you settled into your room first," she said, as she opened the door for me, "but I think you've kept him waiting long enough already."

I arched an eyebrow. "Kept who waiting?"

"Your visitor." She just stood there, so I played along and shuffled my limp sneakers into the room. It was a small activities room, the kind of place where I'd soon be making chalk drawings and macaroni art to express my emotions.

But right now, the only other occupant was a big, awkward-looking dork leaning by the window, looking out at the yard.

"Hey, brother," I said.

# 17

"Hey," Simon said.

"Hey," I replied.

A moment of uneasy silence passed before he burst into a torrential wave of words. "I didn't know they were gonna lock you up like this. I just called the police because I was worried about you and they said if you were hanging up on me then there was no reason to do a, do a, a whatchacallit…"

"Wellness check."

"A wellness check. And they told me to call social services, so I did, and they transferred me to mental health, and they were asking me questions and stuff, and I just told them about you 'cause I was confused and 'cause I didn't realize they were gonna commit you, and I told them not to, 'cause I'd come up myself, but they said they got a call from someone else too, and they were gonna send someone out today, so I got the first flight up, and I would've made it on time but there was a delay and I missed my connection, and I was on the phone to the airline, and I was begging and pleading, and—" His voice rose steadily in pitch as he spoke, until it was a squeak.

That's when I grabbed him and wrapped him up in my arms, pushing his head against my shoulder as I said, "Shh, shh, shh. It's all okay. I have it all under control."

"I'm sorry," he said, his nose full of snot.

"Don't you worry about it," I said, as soothing as I could. I petted his hair, a gesture that was very familiar, even though the last time I did it, there'd been more hair to pet.

"If I knew they were going to do this to you…"

"You would have done it anyway. You'd just be a lot less contrite about it."

"That's not true," he said, and sniffed.

"Yes, it is. I know you, and you're only ever sorry for things you didn't mean to do."

He sniffed again. "That sounds more like you."

I relaxed my arms around him, enough to lean back and look him in the eye. "Don't pout," I said. "You can't pull it off."

He rolled his eyes and turned away, shrugging my arms off as he did. "See?" I said. "This is what I'm talking about."

He went back to staring out the window, and a lull settled over us.

I looked out the window myself, if only because it seemed like the thing to do. As my eyes swept up past the bocce ball courts, I suddenly remembered something about this facility. "You know," I said, "this is the only mental hospital in the state—or maybe anywhere—that has its own nine-hole miniature golf course."

He looked at me and arched an incredulous eyebrow. "Is this one of your stupid little jokes?"

I put a hand on his shoulder and said, "I would never joke about mini-golf. Not to you."

♦

It took a little doing, but I managed to check out putters and obtain permission to use the course before it got too dark. Simon went first, then I set my ball down and lined up my shot.

At the top of my backswing, Simon said, "So, about Mom…"

The distraction made me chip the ball right off the damn course. It bounced off the sidewalk, into the grass, and rolled against the fence at the very edge of the compound. I looked hard at Simon. "You did that intentionally."

He shook his head. "No!" He looked away. "Maybe." He looked back and saw I wasn't mad. "Yes."

I narrowed my eyes and said, "Well, ordinarily I'd bludgeon you to death with this golf club, but I think that's against the rules here."

"Yeah," he said, "I hear they're real strict about that kind of thing."

I retrieved my ball, set it back in place, and took my shot—in silence, this time. The ball came to rest right next to Simon's, along the back edge of the green, three feet from the hole. In the gloom of the evening, it was hard to tell the color-coded balls apart.

When he walked over to take his next shot, he paused next to them and scratched the bald spot atop his head. "Which is mine?"

I shrugged. "Hard to tell them apart, but I think it's that one." I pointed with my putter.

He took his stroke and sank the ball perfectly.

I stepped up to the hole and pulled not a green but a red ball out of it. "Oops, looks like this is mine. That's a one-stroke penalty for you, for disturbing an opponent's ball."

He peered at me. "You knew that."

"No, maybe, yes," I said.

"Do those anti-bludgeoning rules apply to visitors?"

I smirked. "Probably."

On the second hole, as he was assessing the green, Simon said without looking at me, "I'm not mad about it, you know. No one is. It doesn't matter. We just want to know why."

"Know why about what?" I asked, as he took his shot.

"Why you weren't there."

I guess I should back up a bit. You see, I haven't been entirely honest with you. Remember when I said I was in Tampa for a conference? Well, you already knew that was a lie, because you're not stupid. Or, then again, maybe you didn't know it was a lie, because actually you are pretty stupid.

But the fact of the matter—which isn't to say the truth of the matter—is that I was in Tampa for the funeral. I got into town early on Friday so I could go out and get drunk with Simon. I don't know if that's an appropriate thing to do the night before a funeral. You tell me what the protocol is when your drugged-out lump of a mother finally kicks.

I met him at a bar we knew in Ybor City. We remembered the good times and, after the thirty seconds it took to get through all of those, the bad times. Like "Remember the time Mom was practicing with her .45 and nearly shot us by accident?" Or "Remember when she took us to work at the strip club?" Or "Remember that time she got drunk and crashed her motorcycle?" And, of course, "Remember that *other* time she got drunk and crashed her motorcycle?"

Then, because my brother is the sweetest and most clueless person on the planet, there was the inevitable "Remember that time you slit your wrists? That really sucked." You kinda have to hear it in his voice, I guess, to appreciate the sweetness hiding amid the cluelessness. You also have to appreciate that I'd been waiting for someone to say that for twenty years.

Right after the attempt, I didn't want to talk about it. I was embarrassed, if not mortified. Ha! Get it?

Not so much into suicide puns, are you? Okay. Fair enough.

The point is, as soon as the pills and the therapy helped put my broken pieces back together—and I ain't talking about the scars, obviously—I *wished* someone would talk about it. I wanted to explain myself. I wanted to work out the feelings. I wanted to get rid of the disconcerting sense of embarrassment, which was the last thing I expected to feel after a suicide attempt, but there we are.

But no one would talk about it, except Simon. He was the only one who didn't pretend it never happened, who didn't go on like everything was normal, like I didn't have forty-six stitches in my wrists.

So, you see, it's not as strange as it seems that we were talking about the bad times in a bar in Ybor City, the night before our mom's funeral. He called me a "stupid moron" and I punched him. It was really very therapeutic for both of us.

But the thing about the bad times, the fundamental thing about them, is that I eventually escaped them, and Simon never did. I got into college and he barely passed his GED. When I left, while I was watching Florida slide past from the window of a northbound bus, I was thinking one thing, over and over again: *She'll be dead soon, and my brother will be free of her, and then I'll get him out of here.*

But it took fifteen years. I never thought it would drag out that long—long enough for him to get a bald spot. And now I don't know if he'll ever get out. I don't know if you ever can get out when you've spent your whole life trying to save someone who doesn't want to be saved, and you've failed. Where do you go after that? What do you do with yourself?

Also, where do you go after you've spent four hours doing shots in Ybor, trying to convince your little brother that the death of his mom is actually a good thing? That, at least, is a question I have a definitive answer to: the floor of the ladies' room, in a rapidly cooling puddle of your own vomit.

After that, things get a little hazy. My next clear memory involves my motel room, a screaming headache, a bottle of orange juice from the continental breakfast bar, and a bottle of vodka from God knows where. I don't know if screwdrivers are an appropriate drink for the morning of your mother's funeral, but yadda yadda whaterthefuck, like I even give a shit what you think.

The funeral started at one, and it was eleven-thirty by this time, so I set aside an hour for me and my vodka to get to know each other—because, when something's important, you make the time.

Sitting at a wobbly plastic table in the little lobby of the motel, I considered the possibility of getting absolutely fucking sloshed, then showing up halfway into Simon's eulogy to push him aside and deliver the drunk version of mine. I think I would have started off with "*Webster's Dictionary* defines 'funeral' as," and then winged it from there. I'd remember, of course, to raise a toast to the pimps and drug dealers of the Tampa / St. Pete area, without whom this blessed occasion would not be possible. It seemed appropriate, even poignant, but in the end, I decided against it.

As the hour drew near, I slouched off to my room and dressed in my dour best. I finished with time to spare, but the last thing I wanted was to show up early for a funeral. That seems wrong, somehow, like you're trying to prove how much you love being there. So, I turned on the television, sat on the corner of the bed where the blast from the air conditioner caught me full in the face, and stared out the window until it was time to go.

But even then, I didn't go. I sat motionless while the TV droned in the background. I stared out the window, looking across an alley at the back end of a shoe store, as the minutes on the clock ticked past. My phone rang at fifteen past. I glanced at the phone and saw the call was from Simon, but I didn't answer it. It rang again at twenty past, and kept on ringing with only momentary interruptions for the next quarter of an hour. And then it stopped for the rest of the afternoon, as if it was pouting.

I sat and stared out that window for a good while longer. I wasn't always motionless, exactly, but every time I moved, I felt that I was somehow cheating, that I'd unforgivably compromised…something. I don't know what. I tried to imagine what the people at the funeral had thought of my absence, what my uncles, aunts, cousins, and friends—if there were any friends—were saying about me at that moment. Not from any feeling of guilt, mind you, but from idle curiosity.

I went to sleep that night without changing out of my mourning clothes. I just slumped over onto the pillow and, eventually, dozed off. I woke before it was light, stuffed the dark clothes into my suitcase, and changed into the same clothes I'd arrived in. And then, without even knowing why, I went out and walked around the motel. And when I'd finished the circuit, I veered across the parking lot and wandered through the sort of streets you really shouldn't be walking alone in the wee hours of a Tampa morning.

It wasn't until I returned to the motel, well after dawn, that I realized I'd left without bringing my keycard and couldn't get back into my room. It wouldn't have been such a problem if I hadn't also neglected to bring any form of identification. The guy at the front desk was no help. He'd never seen me before, so he wasn't about to cut me a new card. The lady who'd checked me in and knew my face wasn't scheduled to show up until the next shift, so he told me to wait by the pool until then.

That's exactly where I went to wait, not because I like pools but because I'm very suggestible when stressed. But when I got out there, I couldn't get past the gate. *Because you need your fucking keycard to get into the pool, dipshit motel front desk guy.* I rattled the gate a few times on the theory that it might respond to intimidation.

I was on the point of giving up on the pool and instead extending my tour of dangerous neighborhoods, when a slender hand came through the bars from the other side of the gate. It settled on mine, and I looked across at a woman's smiling face.

"You look like you could use a friend," she said, and opened the gate from the other side.

"Oh," I said. "Thank you, uh…"

"Call me Dee."

♦

"I hadn't even seen her in fifteen years," I said, as I lined up my putt in the dim light from the facility windows. "I never wanted to see her again. And now she's dead, which makes that a lot easier."

"I wish you wouldn't talk like that," Simon said. "She was your mother, too."

"Only in the most technical sense." I putted, and my ball bounced off the back barrier and ended up farther from the hole than it started. "Goddamn it."

Simon had already sunk his last shot, so he could just stand there and look smug. When I missed my next shot, too, his smugness faded. "Have you cried?" he asked.

I didn't understand the question at first. I had to roll it around my brain for a few seconds to realize what he was getting at. "Over Mom?"

"No, over the fucking trade deficit," he said, rolling his eyes. "Obviously, over Mom."

"No," I said, putting my eyes back on the ball. "Not over that."

He made a knowing little *hmm* sound.

I looked up. "What the hell was that?"

He shrugged. "Nothing."

I narrowed my eyes and gave the ball a little tap that put it right into the hole. As I reached in to get it, I asked, "So, who won?"

Simon furrowed his brow. "I dunno. I forgot to keep score."

"Oh. So did I." I laughed. "Well, we better get this equipment back. I bet they're going to be super pissed we kept it out as long as we did."

They were more pissed, as it turned out, that we'd gone over visiting hours, and they weren't interested in learning that it was their own damn fault for taking away my phone and leaving me oblivious to the time. While I was checking in the equipment, I checked out my keys and gave them to Simon, so he'd have a place to stay.

As he hugged me, he said, "Promise me you'll cry."

I only rolled my eyes. "Yeah, I'm not going to promise that."

"You'll feel better," he said.

"I feel fine already."

He rolled his eyes back at me. "You're talking to the guy whose calls you haven't been answering for an entire week, and I've been calling you constantly."

Oh, right. "Well, maybe I'll try stubbing my toe and see what happens from there."

He hugged me again and didn't say anything else.

# 18

Everything you know about mental institutions is wrong.

No one thinks he's Napoleon, and no one's screaming gibberish in the halls. The closest you get to that is the occasional muffled sob on the other side of a closed door. The majority of the patients are in for depression. They're mostly poor, mostly women, and mostly voluntary admissions.

And most of them get to keep their fucking shoelaces, as I observed with envy while scooting and shuffling down the hall behind the ward nurse. "You weren't scheduled for mini-golf today," she said, in her best tut-tut voice, "so we'll have to take that out of your rec time for tomorrow."

That's the one thing you know about mental institutions that's actually right: the staff like to infantilize the patients. Being in a mental institution is a lot like being in elementary school except that, instead of detention, the teachers stick needles in your ass when you misbehave.

When I got to my room, I was happy to find only one bed. You don't always get your own room in these places, and roommates are a crapshoot. Just because a person knows they're not at the Battle of Austerlitz doesn't mean they're fun to be around, right? So now, at least, I'd get time to myself, free of bosses and coworkers and annoying neighbors.

"Hey, roomie!" Dee called, as soon as I closed the door.

I turned around, already preparing myself for an extended argument, but I was struck dumb by what I saw—or rather, by what I didn't see.

"What?" she asked, perfectly innocently.

I took a deep breath and counted to ten, then took another deep breath and counted to twenty. I still wasn't calm, but I could have taken deep breaths until I hyperventilated and I still wouldn't be calm, so I just dove right in and asked the obvious question. "Why the hell are you naked except for a pair of fluffy slippers?"

Dee looked down at her toes, then back up at me. "Because I have sensitive feet," she said.

"You know what I meant," I said, but I knew by her coy smile that she wasn't going to answer until I put it plainly. "Why is the rest of you naked?"

She smiled and said, "I heard one of the nurses say they practice nude therapy here."

I started counting, and made it to three before I couldn't hold it in any longer. "Mood," I growled. "They practice *mood* therapy."

"I dunno," she said, bouncing across the room and flopping down on my bed, "I'm pretty sure I heard *nude*." She stretched out on top of the blanket and frowned. "Not a very big bed for two people, is it? Well, that's okay. I'm a snuggler."

"You know," I said, "I've been thinking about it, and I bet they can't send someone to jail again for killing the same person twice. Double jeopardy, right? And if I killed you, like, twenty or thirty times, it might be too confusing to prosecute."

Beelzeboobs sat up and grinned. "Oh, Jordan, you're so sexy when you're threatening murder. Hey, that reminds me: is Simon single?"

She must have noticed the look on my face transitioning from infinite irritation to infinite repugnance, because she didn't look like she was having fun anymore. "You will stay the hell away from my brother," I said. It wasn't the first time I'd said it, either. I was very protective of him back in Tampa—someone had to be—and I must have said those exact words at least once a fortnight. Now I said them to Dee with as much certainty and as much unspoken promise of violence as I ever had before. At that moment, I was no more afraid of the devil than I was of any other dirty skank who made the mistake of putting their eyes on my brother.

Which might be unfair to dirty skanks; I don't know. But if you're allowed to have just one marginalized group that you don't want dating your brother, that's a pretty safe choice. No offense to you personally, of course.

Dee still looked like she wasn't very happy, but thankfully, her unhappiness wasn't translating into me being consumed by flames or anything like that. "Sorry" was all she said, and I think she actually meant it.

I left the room without a word, taking off my shoes at the door. Fuming and walking barefoot through the corridors, I went in search of the vending machines. I found them inside the darkened common room, where a girl from a goddamn Dickens novel was standing in the fluorescent glow of the snack machine. *Waif* didn't begin to describe her. She was a little wisp of a thing in her late teens or early twenties, dressed in shabby clothes, all hunched up like she expected someone to hit her. She peered longingly through the glass. It kind of put things in perspective, and my anger cooled.

She held a dime in her hand and spit on it as I approached. She noticed me and froze. After a few seconds, her eyes whipped from me to the machine as if she'd been caught doing something naughty. She fixed her gaze on a pack of peanut butter crackers while she rubbed the dingy coin between her fingers.

I knew better than to ask about it. It would only agitate her. She was already looking more anxious, her other hand clutching tight around, I assume, a pile of spare change that added up to a dime less than the price of peanut butter crackers.

I stood well outside her personal space and knelt to get a good look at the bottom row of the snack machine, where the hygiene items were. "Well, there goes my record," I said. When she looked down at me, I glanced up and smiled. "I've flossed every night for the past ten years. Haven't missed it once. But I forgot to bring my floss from home, and they don't have any in the machine. Now at my next appointment, I have to tell my dentist that I only flossed *almost* every night since I last saw her. I think she's going to be pretty disappointed."

At first, I didn't think the waif would respond. She just stood there, looking more and more anxious. And then, in a tiny little voice, she squeaked out, "Don't you think it's weird that so much of your self-worth is tied up in the opinion of someone you only see once a year?"

I snorted. "It is weird, but I have more of my self-worth tied up in people I see less than that."

The corners of her lips curled down as she looked spastically from me to the machine and back again. Her face screwed up, then suddenly unwound as she blurted out, "That's fucked up, man." With a jerk of her head, she looked back to the machine and put her dime in the slot with trembling hands. It rolled straight through and came out the change return. It was still bouncing around in there when she stuck her fingers in and snatched it out, as if she was afraid I'd steal it from her. She spit on it again and resumed trying to rub the corrosion off.

"Mind if I go in front of you?" I asked.

"Sure," was all she said.

I put two dollars into the machine and bought a toothbrush priced at a buck fifty. I reached into the bin, took the toothbrush, and left my change in the return, as if I'd forgotten it. I waved as I turned, saying, "See you around." I was halfway across the common room when I heard her hand go into the return bin and pull my quarters out.

As I left, I saw Dee—mercifully clothed—leaning against the wall outside. "And there came to that place a dumpy lady dressed in mom jeans," she said, "who gave unto the poor waifish girl two small coins. And verily I say unto thee, that this dumpy lady in mom jeans gave more than all the rich merchants gave together, with all their gifts of silver and gold."

"That's nice," I said as I breezed past her. It was still pretty early, well before lights-out, but I wouldn't have been in the mood to socialize even if there was someone around I wanted to socialize with. So, I went to the washroom, brushed my teeth, took a shower, and noticed that the towels weren't kept within arm's reach of the shower stalls—in that order.

As I was contemplating a dash for the linen rack, Dee handed a fresh towel over the top of the stall door. "There," she said in a grudging tone. "And I'm going to let you have the bed to yourself tonight. Make sure you mention that when you're telling this story and you spin it so I come off as the bad guy."

As if.

# 19

I got as good a night's rest as can be expected when institutionalization is the least horrible thing that's happened to you in the past month. It was one of those nights where you get up feeling like you haven't slept at all, except you figure you must have gotten some sleep, because your memories of staring at the ceiling have an unexplained break between five and six in the morning.

By six thirty, I was ready to give up. Rest had been a worthwhile experiment, but it was time to cut my losses and face the day with resolve and bloodshot eyes. Coffee was the first order of business, obviously, so I set off to find the cafeteria. Breakfast wasn't for another hour and a half, but there was a drip coffeemaker with a sign instructing patients not to operate it on their own. The more pertinent fact, however, was there wasn't anyone around to stop me.

As I was pouring the grounds in, Dee appeared at the edge of my vision, scribbling on a clipboard. "That's another sin for the list," she said.

I rolled my eyes as I set the machine brewing. "I didn't know contravening hospital policies was considered a cardinal sin."

"Venial," she said. "And of course it is. Somebody went to the trouble of writing it down."

I snorted. "So, anything someone writes down is a sin? Is that all it takes?"

She looked at me as if I was an idiot. "When has it ever taken more?"

I was running on practically no sleep and in no state to argue transcendental theology, so I just gave her the finger. She shook her head and made another note on her clipboard.

I put my cup under the spout as the first of the coffee filtered through. I spilled a bit in the process and it sizzled against the hot plate below. Dee made another note. "You sure are racking up the sins, and it's not even breakfast."

"I like to get a running start on the day," I said. I took my first sip of the morning, and suddenly everything seemed just a little bit better. It was pretty good coffee for pre-ground, and I was beginning to feel that my time there wouldn't be so bad. Shit, I think I could live at the bottom of a mineshaft if they had an espresso bar down there.

Dee looked up from her clipboard. "Do you think we're best off with a tunnel or a laundry basket?"

I didn't even want to know. "I think we're best off on opposite sides of the continent. Can you arrange that? Preferably with you on the arctic side, inhabiting the bellies of several different polar bears."

She *tsk*ed at me.

"Come on, you'd be doing them a big favor. They're a threatened species."

"No, silly," she said. "I mean, are we better escaping this place by tunneling out or by hiding in a laundry basket and trying to smuggle ourselves?"

I tried to concentrate on the nice warm feeling the coffee made in my stomach. "You're the one who got me into this place," I said. "Now you're trying to get me out?"

She shrugged. "I figure I owe you one."

I snorted. "I'd rather you owed the polar bears."

She examined the silverware rack on the counter. "I suppose we could use a spoon to dig," she said. "I don't know about these spoons, though. Most of them have been up somebody's ass."

I spit a mouthful of coffee in a fine mist.

Dee reached up to casually wipe her face dry. "It's true," she said. "The hospital got them cheap from a secondhand dealer who picked them up at a garage sale. You'd be amazed at how many garage-sale utensils have been up somebody's ass." She gingerly picked a spoon up, holding it between her thumb and forefinger. "Really says something about the kind of people who hold garage sales." She dropped the spoon back into the rack and wiped her fingers on her pants.

I almost didn't want to know, but I asked anyway. "Where's the coffee been?"

"Oh, just the usual places. Planted in clear-cut rainforest by the exploited poor, grown in soil filled with the bones of murdered indigenous people, harvested by forced labor, processed by child workers, purchased by a drug cartel as a way to launder money for their heroin business, then exported to a company in the US that doesn't care about any of that as long as its quarterly profits look good."

I blinked twice. "No, I mean, has anything bad happened to it?"

"You mean, has it been up somebody's ass or something?"

I nodded, then eyed the cup suspiciously.

"No, no, nothing *bad* has happened to it. Although some people say the best coffee in the world is brewed from beans found in the excrement of the Sumatran palm civet."

"Oh, I've always wanted to try that." Don't judge.

"I've had it myself, and I don't really care for it," Dee said. "It's not that I'm fundamentally opposed to drinking from another creature's ass, mind you. I'm just uncomfortable doing it without a safe word."

I sighed. "You know, I would have thought a conversation about spoons in asses couldn't possibly take a weirder turn. Then you came into my life."

She beamed a smile at me. "If you're saying what I think you're saying, then how do you feel about 'batrachomyomachy' as our safe word?"

I didn't sigh. I think I'd run out of them. I just drained the rest of my coffee and said, "Maybe later. I need to make a phone call."

I headed down the hall to the lobby, where a dozen women were lined up, waiting for their turn on the hospital's one payphone. I strolled right past them, up to the desk, and said, "I'd like to check out my cellphone."

The nurse manning the desk didn't say anything. She didn't even make eye contact. She only reached for my arm, which I held out obligingly, so she could read my patient number off the hospital wristband. She went off into a back room, while a little storm of whispering rose in the telephone line behind me. By ones and twos, patients left that line to form a second line at my back.

The woman directly behind me leaned forward and said, in an embarrassed and strangely apologetic tone, "I didn't know we could do that."

I turned to look back and saw a line of faces all looking at me with a mild but distinct sense of awe. I glanced over the desk to make sure the duty nurse couldn't hear, then said, "You mean, she let you all line up for the payphone without telling you?"

The second woman back shook her head and said, "They don't give a shit about us. They're worse than my fucking social worker."

Oh, hell. Was she one of mine? I studied her face, my mind flashing through the thousands of cases I'd handled over the years. She wasn't one of mine, was she?

I didn't think so, though to this day, I'm still not a hundred percent sure. Among the cases that I handled in my first few years of social work, I can remember all of their faces with crystal clarity. If I met one of them on the street today, I'd know them in a heartbeat, and be able to ask after their relatives by name. But in the past few years, all the faces have sort of blurred together into a single, featureless blob. In any event, she didn't seem to recognize me.

"Well," I said, "you have to understand that these people can get burned out. They're just like anyone else."

The nurse returned with Frankenphone, saw the line formed behind me, and shook her head. "Ugh. See what you did?"

And, then again, some of them are just natural assholes.

"And don't forget to sign up for mini-golf," I said as I stepped away. "They have mini-golf here." A ripple of murmured surprise spread through both lines. When I reached a quiet corner of the lobby and turned around, the nurse was scowling at me.

You know those movies where a doctor gets sick and discovers that he can't cope in the very medical system he's heretofore been an architect of?

This was nothing like that. As a social worker suddenly thrust into one of the programs I used to put people in, I was the queen of everything. I was functioning better than I ever had before, sticking it to the man while being adored by the indie crowd. I was truly in my element. In the days to come, whenever my mind wandered, I would fantasize about staying here forever. I could invent a continuous stream of symptoms and mental disorders that would keep me committed indefinitely. Admired by patients and feared by staff, I'd become a sort of folk hero—the Robin Hood of the psych ward.

A girl can dream, can't she?

But for the moment, I set my dreams aside and dialed work. Hopefully, Ruth wouldn't be in at this hour and I could just leave a voicemail message. I heard a click and then she answered with a forceful "Ruth. Go." What a fucking twit.

"Hey, Ruth," I said. "It's Jordan. I don't think I'll be in this morning."

"Oh?" she asked, ready to pounce on whatever excuse I offered.

"Yeah, I have a really nasty stomach virus. Puking. Diarrhea. The works. I can't even hold down water. I think I got it from a sandwich in the cafeteria. Might want to look into our vendor."

Some might have claimed a cold or flu in this situation, but that's a rookie mistake. You can't convincingly fake chest congestion, so don't even try. For that matter, some bosses will expect you to fight through it and come in anyway. A stomach virus, on the other hand, has disgusting symptoms, no effect on the victim's voice, is easier to fake if you do end up coming in, and is incredibly contagious. That last point is particularly important, because it brings to bear your best resource for any kind of social manipulation: fear.

"I'll try to make it in this afternoon," I continued.

"No, no, no," she said. "You stay home. That's the only way to get better." See what I mean? In just a few short seconds, she'd abandoned her skepticism and was now trying to talk me into staying home. That's the magic of fear.

"Oh, no, it's okay. I have so much to do, and both ends of me have to be empty by now."

"Jordan," she said, "I admire your resolve, but I have to insist. You stay home. Take the weekend to recover. Take Monday off, too, just to be sure."

"Well," I said, drawing the word out.

"No, Jordan. It's decided. Stay warm and try to drink some fluids. Take tiny sips. That'll help you keep it down." There was no legitimate sympathy in her voice, but she was managing a fair approximation out of sheer self-concern.

"Okay, okay," I said. "I'll see you on Tuesday."

"Or Wednesday, if that's what you need," she quickly added. "Rest up, Jordan."

With that task checked off the list, I returned the phone and left the duty nurse to her phone and mini-golf requests, and the patients to make their own sick calls. My next stop of the day was the hospital library, where only one of the two public computers was occupied at this early hour. As I sat down and opened the web browser, the sweet, elderly lady at the other computer glared at her screen and said, "Fucknuggets. They've blocked HuffPo. Why would they do that?"

"Somebody in the comments must be upsetting patients."

"Fucknuggets," she repeated.

"That's just the pinnacle of wit for you, isn't it? An old lady saying fucknuggets."

The old woman shrugged. "I'm a creature of simple pleasures, my little fucknugget."

"You're going to keep saying *fucknuggets* until you get a laugh out of me, aren't you?"

She rolled her eyes. "Nonsense. That's pure fucknuggets."

I found a sigh I'd hidden away for emergencies. I put on my best approximation of a smile and said, "Ha ha. Ha ha ha. Ha. What a funny thing that is."

She returned a smile that appeared much more genuine. "See, Jordan? This is why we're so great together. We're on the same wavelength. We have a connection. We really get each other." She leaned over to look at my monitor. "Whatcha reading?"

"Articles about banishing the devil."

Out of the corner of my eye, I saw her arms cross over her chest. "Talk about upsetting. And yet it's HuffPo they block."

I did my best to ignore her while I read, and frequently checked over my shoulder to make sure no patients or staff had wandered in to observe my reading choices. I got a solid hour of research in before people started waking up for breakfast, and I decided not to push my luck. The last thing I did before heading back to the cafeteria was to check on the progress of the Jane Doe Killer investigation.

Even a week later, the killing of a mysterious, attractive woman was still the top story on all the local news sites. The headlines made my heart sink. Earlier in the week, when I first saw that freeze-frame image of me unloading the body from the back of a rental car, I thought I'd landed at the bottom of a pit of hopelessness and despair. Now I knew the pit had subbasements.

The headline at Boston.com was "CASE CLOSED" and the subheading read, "Wellesley Police Chief: 'We Have a Confession.'" The mugshot photo and the caption below it told the rest of the story. Some poor woman who'd been squatting in the woods of Wellesley was arrested, based on a passing resemblance to the blur of pixels in the intersection camera footage, then bullied into signing a confession. The supposed perpetrator looked like she'd had a hard-enough life before she became a suspect in a murder case. By the picture alone, I could tell she wasn't exactly sober and lucid when they arrested her.

I jumped when I felt breath on my cheek, but it was only Dee looking over my shoulder, her elderly-lady ruse discarded. She whistled. "False murder confession, huh? Well, it looks like somebody has a decision to make."

A small fraction of my terror turned itself to anger. "You did this?" I hissed.

"Nope," Dee said, "but only because I didn't think of it. You've been feeling a little too smug about your own virtue lately. Maybe this is just Karma putting you to the test. I'll have to ask, next time I see her."

# 20

I barely remember breakfast, but I know I didn't use a spoon. I also recall returning my tray and hearing a cafeteria staffer say, "Wow, you sure cleaned your plate," as if she were complimenting a well-behaved child.

Dee, who was standing at my side, swallowed a piece of bacon and said, "Tell her the scrambled eggs were overdone." As I left the cafeteria, she called after me, "Hey, come on. How will they improve if they aren't given feedback?"

I had group therapy at ten. I'd never been in group therapy before, never even seen it except in movies. The nicest thing I can say about the group leader, Gary, is he didn't infantilize us, but that's only because he didn't do much of anything. Mostly, he just sat there and nodded while the others talked. Even when the group strayed from therapeutic topics and wandered into outright gossip about celebrities, he didn't say a thing. He only nodded in the same familiar way. I thought at first that he had a plan, that he'd turn the latest tabloid news into a lesson on depression, but he just sat and stared and bobbed his head up and down like one of those drinking-bird toys. And I bet this guy went home at night thinking he'd made a difference.

I began to wonder what qualified someone to have a job like this. What was the degree program like? I figured the first day was probably the toughest, with the instructor shoving students down into chairs and telling them to start nodding in unison. "Half of you will not pass this course and become group therapists," I imagined him shouting, like a drill instructor at Navy SEAL training. "And one of you will quit today, because this day does not end until I get one quitter. Nod if you understand, you pussy-ass sons of bitches!"

I'd been quietly speculating about this for half an hour before Gary looked at me and said, in a questioning tone, "Jordan?"

Shit. He'd finally stopped nodding and asked me something. But what was it?

Dee appeared at my side and said, "He wants to know the three things you'd most want to bring on a desert island."

I gave her a silent look of thanks and said, "I'd like to bring a radio, lots of beer, and the complete works of Jane Austen."

Everyone in the group stared at me, including Gary. His expression was the most perplexed and judgmental of all, which I figure isn't something they teach you in Group Therapist Academy.

"Or, I dunno," I stammered, "maybe Toni Morrison?"

"Jordan, it's only down the hall," Gary said. At this point, Dee doubled over and suffered a giggle fit. An annoyed voice came over the PA, driving the point home as it summoned me, by name, to the front lobby. I must have missed it the first time.

"Right," I said. "I'll just go and see what they want, then."

Silence ruled the room. The floors were carpet, but my footsteps seemed to echo as I walked toward the door. The handle squeaked as I turned it and pushed fruitlessly on the door.

"You have to pull," the group leader said.

"Yup, got it," I said. "Thanks."

As I closed the door behind me, I heard one of the patients ask, "What's wrong with her?"

"I heard she used to be a social worker," another said, "but a couple years ago, she lit a printer on fire and they gave her electroshock at Mass General. She's been like that ever since."

And all I could imagine, as the door clicked shut, was Gary nodding along in vacant agreement.

Fuck Gary.

The lobby desk was still manned by the same asshole who begrudged getting off her butt to check out my cellphone. I sure hope it was worth three years of her life in a nursing program so she could come here and be a glorified receptionist.

"You have a guest," she said. "Remember that morning visiting hours end at eleven."

"Thanks," I said, and gracefully refrained from adding, "Hey, did you know a tape recorder could do most of your job?"

My visitor was Simon, of course. He hugged me in his awkward way.

"I'm glad you came," I said.

He shrugged. "Yeah, well, none of the other mini-golf courses are open this early."

The nurse looked up from her computer, poorly concealed glee shining in her face. "The golf equipment is all checked out. Don't complain—that's your own fault."

Simon returned the appropriate expression, which was complete and total bafflement.

As I led him away down the hall, I whispered, "The staff here are all crazy."

"You don't suppose they're secretly patients who've overthrown their keepers, do you?"

"No, no," I said. "The patients would give themselves away by pretending they gave a shit."

He nodded and, when no one was around, leaned toward me as he walked and said, "I brought you some cigarettes." He patted his jacket pocket, then tapped the side of his nose.

"I quit smoking years ago, Simon."

"I know, but you can use them as currency."

"I'm not in prison!"

We'd nearly walked a circuit around the entire ward before I got him to understand that I didn't have to beat somebody up on my first day to prove I was dangerous.

"Although," I said, "they do make you work on a chain gang, cleaning up trash along the side of the highway."

He thought about this. "And does one person on every chain gang play the harmonica?"

"Yeah. That's state law."

"Nice to know that some things are still sacred." He was silent for a while, then asked. "Have you cried?"

"Not yet."

"You should."

"We'll see."

We drifted into other topics, covering all the light minutiae that you talk about when you're trying to talk about anything but the subject at hand. By the time we made three or four laps around the ward, we'd exhausted the weather in Boston, the weather in Florida, and the weather in Chiapas, Mexico, which was being hit by a hurricane. And all the time, the only thing I really wanted to say was "If you had to pick a life to ruin, would it be some drugged-out tramp who got bullied into a murder confession, or would it be someone who's actually tried to make the world better, and might still succeed if she got half a chance?"

But I never did. I'm too much of a coward, I guess. When eleven o'clock rolled around, the ReceptioNurse came looking for us. I hugged Simon goodbye and said, "Things may get worse before they get better."

I don't know what kind of response I expected. Resistance, maybe. Scorn for the idea that things could get any worse, when Mom just died and I'd been committed to a mental hospital. But he already knew something was wrong, must have heard it in my voice or worked it out somehow. He only squeezed me tighter and said, "I know it'll be okay."

◆

The next time they called me out to the lobby, I was in art therapy. Art therapy, if you're not familiar with it, is when a licensed art therapist has to psychoanalyze a chalk drawing instead of the patient. I think it works on the principle that, no matter how depressed you are, you come out of it knowing that things could always be worse, because you could have been an art therapist.

My drawing was a globe with the children of the world holding hands across the equator. I turned it face down when I was unexpectedly summoned from the room, in the hopes that Dee couldn't mess with it while I was gone. She's the type who'd redraw one of the children of the world naked, just to see if the therapist noticed. I knew this because she'd been suggesting I do it since the beginning of the session.

"Aww," she whined, "turn it back around and I promise I'll only redo one of them."

I did my best to ignore her and made my way to the lobby. There, waiting on the far side of the reception desk, were Gabby and Michael. Michael had a box of chocolates.

"Afternoon visiting hours end at four," the nurse said. I could almost hear the slight change in pitch that would accompany the word *four* when they finally replaced her with a machine.

Gabby and Michael ran over to hug me, but I couldn't bring myself to hug back. These two were the reason I got locked up, and now they showed up with hugs and chocolates and they expected warmth in return? And yes, asshole, Simon did the same thing, but Simon only wanted someone to make sure I was all right. His biggest sin was ignorance. Gabby and Michael knew exactly what would happen, and they did it anyway.

Suffice it to say I didn't want to deal with them. I had enough to worry about, to have to act nice and pretend they hadn't just fucked me over, the day before.

"These people are upsetting to me," I said to the nurse.

And I have to give her credit, because that nurse came through for me. For all her grumpy indifference, the moment she thought my mental health was threatened, she leapt out of her chair like a mother bear protecting her cub. While Gabby and Michael looked increasingly bewildered, she grabbed them each by an arm and said, "You two are going to have to leave."

"But" was all Michael could manage to say before she yanked him away from me.

"Sir, I need you to leave *right now*, or I will call security. This way, please."

They were nearly out the door when I was struck by a sudden pang of regret. "Wait!" I said.

Nurse, Gabby, and Michael all turned their heads back to me.

"You can leave the chocolates," I said.

Still held firm in the nurse's iron grip, Michael dropped them on the floor before being escorted away. When they were set free in the parking lot, I ventured over, picked up the box, and opened it.

When the nurse returned, she gave me a conciliatory smile and said, "If you need some time on the mini-golf course, you just let me know."

"Thank you," I said, and offered her a chocolate. She took a macchiato praline and patted me on the shoulder.

So, yeah, I turned my back on my two closest friends, who might have provided invaluable guidance and support at this trying time, but I'd already found a worthy replacement in What's-Her-Name at the front desk. Things were looking up.

"You're the stupidest fucking person I've ever met," Dee said, the moment I returned to art therapy.

"Chocolate?" I asked, as if speaking to the entire room, and holding the box lid up to give Dee cover from the eyes of the other patients.

Still giving me the stink-eye, Dee grabbed a dark chocolate truffle and stuffed it into her mouth. "Oh my God, that's heaven," she said. "But you're still the stupidest fucking person I've ever met."

I left the box on a table near the door and, while several patients and the therapist hovered around it to take a piece, I returned to my seat. Having learned not to underestimate Dee, I flipped my paper over and checked it carefully for any alterations.

There, uh, were some alterations. Where there was once a pleasant, floating planet Earth, there was now a pentagram in a circle. Where there had been children holding hands, there were naked people, covered in blood and dancing. And looming over it all was a goat-headed, black-winged figure that I recognized from my research as Baphomet, the Sabbatic Goat. As in most modern representations of Baphomet, this one had bare, pendulous breasts and an erect penis with snakes wrapped around it.

It took me quite some time to form a coherent thought.

When I finally managed it, I was filled with an odd sort of admiration. It was, after all, a very good drawing. It would have looked wonderful on the side of some creep's van.

"You like it?" Dee asked from somewhere behind me. "I'm thinking of putting it on the side of a van."

I couldn't look away from it. It was like a train wreck. "Why?" was all I could manage to say.

"Negative reinforcement. I was only going to mess with your little drawing a little, but then you went and did something monumentally stupid, so I did this instead. It's the same principle as training a dog to not shit in the house."

"Oh," I said. Or maybe I only thought it. I could have gotten angry, I suppose. Angry at myself, if not at her. I didn't, though. I guess it was because I was still processing what I'd done a minute earlier. I mean, I've made a lot of dumb mistakes in my life, but turning out Gabby and Michael was surely the worst of them.

"Wow," said the licensed art therapist, when he came around to look at my work. "This is, uh, really...something." He was supposed to be evaluating it, looking for themes that might identify psychological issues, and encouraging me to use art to work through inner turmoil that I couldn't express in words. Instead, he stood staring, occasionally scratching his scraggly beard. "It sure is something."

"What does it mean?" asked another voice.

I looked over my shoulder to find the entire art therapy group huddled behind me, studying the chalk drawing.

"Harmony," I said without missing a beat. I'd had some time to plan for that question, and figured something direct and baffling was my best strategy. Art is subjective, which is another way of saying you can bullshit your way through it pretty easy. Who's to say, really, that the best representation of harmony isn't a breasted goat-man with snakes on his dick?

As one, the entire group took a small step backward. There followed a lot of polite nods and a chorus of noncommittal, subvocal sounds. "Oh, ah, mmhmm." That sort of thing.

The therapist stood scratching his beard.

♦

It's not all art therapy and mini-golf down at the old mental institution. You get some time to yourself to read, watch television, or reflect on the woman who's falsely accused of a murder you sort of committed. Dee was proving an impediment to that last one, though, confusing the issue with bizarre logic, invented facts, and personal insults. It was a lot like that time I started a Twitter account.

It wasn't until the lights were off and I was lying in bed that I had the peace and quiet to think through my situation. And the more I considered it, the simpler the matter became.

Look at it from a utilitarian standpoint. Who could society most afford to lose? Obviously, it was her. Even on my most useless days, I still contributed more than some homeless woman could contribute on her best. And yeah, that wasn't her fault, but we're not talking virtue. We're talking utility, right?

Even if we were talking virtue, everything that happened to that poor woman was Dee's fault. Granted, the poor tweaker lady wasn't responsible for the body they found in the woods, but neither was I. It was a thing that happened to me, not something I did. So, on the culpability front, it was at worst a toss-up, leaving the score steady at one to zero in favor of leaving that lady to her undeserved fate.

But really, it was more than just a toss-up, right? Because I'd already suffered for what happened. I'd been stressed out of my mind for the previous week, recoiling from every cop and wondering each morning if this was my last day of freedom. And I was still saddled with Dee, maybe for the rest of my life. That was the greatest punishment of all, worse by far than spending twenty-five to life in the slammer. To add prison on top of that was simply unreasonable. I ask, if you had no choice but to mete out a fixed quantity of unfair punishment to two innocent people, wouldn't you try to divide it equally? Wouldn't it be even more of a travesty to put the entire burden on one of them—i.e., me?

And how did I know this drugged-up hooligan was even innocent? She did confess to a murder, after all. Why would a person do that if they didn't have something to feel guilty about? Obviously, she didn't commit this *particular* murder, but maybe she'd confused it with a different murder. Maybe she'd killed someone, taken their money, and in the heroin haze that resulted from that sudden windfall of cash, she accidentally confessed to the wrong crime.

If you really think about it, jail was probably the best place for her. It would give her time to get over her various addictions and come to terms with all the crimes she'd committed—so many she couldn't even keep them straight. Out in the world, she'd probably die of an overdose or get stabbed to death by her pimp. In jail, she was safe. She'd come out older, sure, but drug-free and ready to make a difference. Maybe someday I would find her and tell her, with tears in my eyes, that I knew she was innocent and I did nothing. And I'd be expecting her to be angry, to attack me, but instead she'd hug me and thank me for saving her life.

QED, I should under no circumstances endanger my own freedom on her account. Cold, hard logic bore me out on that point, by a score of four points to zero. As much as I wanted to be selfless, as much as I might wish to throw myself in the fire to protect a tweaker heroin junkie crackhead multiple murderess prostitute drifter, I had to keep a cool head and remain rational. I had to remember all the good I could yet do in my time, and when in doubt remember to ask myself, "What's left of my own life, if I do this?"

I must have said it out loud, because a voice in the darkness replied, "You know, a lot of people continue to have very fulfilling lives in prison."

"Good point," I said.

"So, if you're worried you won't be able to do your favorite things, just think of all the people you'll have the chance to feel superior to. In many ways, your life will barely change."

Oh. She meant me.

I rolled away from her, and Dee took it as an invitation to climb into bed. She was, at least, wearing pajamas. As if to compensate for that consideration, she hooked one leg over me and draped an arm across my chest.

"You agreed not to do this," I said, with scant hope that it would stop her.

"I am the Lord of Lies, Jordan. I have certain standards to uphold. Besides which, I agreed not to do it yesterday. I made no promise about tonight. Rule one of dealing with the devil: gotta read the fine print. Everyone knows that."

"Are you going to help that woman? The one who signed the false confession?"

After a moment's thought, Dee said, "Nah."

"Why not?"

"Because I'm the devil. Unlike you, I don't have to come up with an elaborate rationalization for doing the wrong thing."

"It's not a rationalization," I said without thinking.

That just started her laughing. "Oh, Jordan. You're so predictable. Now, don't tell me. Just let me guess. You figure even an incompetent public defender has a shot at getting that woman's confession thrown out, on the grounds that she was drugged out of her mind at the time. Whereas, if you confess, between the physical evidence and the rental car records, it'll be open and shut. So, by a simple probabilistic assessment, it makes sense for you to do nothing. Am I warm?"

Shit, I didn't even think of that. So, let's adjust the logic score to make it five to zero, shall we?

I scooted away and turned to face her in the darkness. "That's not it at all," I lied. "I'm leaving this for you to fix, because you can fix it without even going out of your way. Besides which, this is all your fault anyway."

"How do you figure?"

"How could I not? It's not my fault I stabbed you. You arranged it, just like that time I shot Jesus in the dick."

She responded to my cogent argument by falling into a fit of giggling. When it finally subsided, she gasped for breath and said, "Okay, you've convinced me. You've won me over to your side."

"So, you'll put this right?"

"No, no," she said, "I mean that since we have such great times together, it just wouldn't be fair *to me* if you had to go to prison. So, you're definitely justified in pinning all the blame on that poor, innocent woman."

I rolled over again and scooted farther away, right up against the wall. "Well, I'm glad we agree."

# 21

I had another night of rotten sleep, half because that poor tweaker woman haunted my dreams, half because Dee kept hogging the covers. I woke up at 2 am to find her rolling in her sleep like a fucking dervish, reeling the sheets in until she was cocooned in them and I was left clutching a tiny scrap of fabric. I clung on until it too was ripped from my hands. If I hadn't been so tired, I might have called it a metaphor, but as it was, I just kicked her until she fell off the bed. It would have been a win, too, if she hadn't dragged all the sheets down with her.

The moment I fell back asleep, I woke to the sound of pigs being slaughtered, and rolled over to find her back in my bed, snoring. And so it went until six, when I gave up. I left Dee asleep in my room, but when I got to the cafeteria, she was sitting there with her feet up on a table.

She answered my aggravated grunt by looking up from her newspaper and saying, "Morning, sunshine."

I went for the coffee machine with such speed that I forgot to shuffle, lost a shoe, and decided to leave it behind instead of bending over to pick it up. Sometimes you have to sacrifice a sailor for the good of the ship, you know. I knew it was worth it as soon as I got a whiff of the heavenly aroma of brewing coffee.

But when I poured a cup, my first sip tasted like steamed ass. I opened the lid on the machine and pawed through the grounds, expecting to find rat turds or worse. When I found only hot, moist, delicious-smelling coffee grounds, I looked at Dee. "What the hell happened to the coffee?"

Without looking up from her newspaper, she said, "It's probably curdled."

"Coffee doesn't curdle," I said. I peered down into my cup, which had already made a liar of me. Globs of oily goo bobbed up to the surface as I watched. I skimmed one onto my fingertip. It smelled rancid and looked like smoker's phlegm. "Why do you do these things?" I asked.

She tilted her newspaper down and leaned over to examine my finger. "You can't blame me for this one. You did that."

I knew she was setting me up for something, so I didn't say a word. I just put my hand on my hip and stared at her.

"Don't think you're special or anything," she said, returning to her newspaper. "All witches can do it."

I sighed as I poured myself another cup. "Nice try, but I'm an atheist. Or, you know, whatever. But not a witch."

She set down her paper. "Au contraire. You mean you're not *Wiccan*. You are a witch, which—ha!—involves four prerequisites." She started ticking off points on her fingers. "You have to anoint yourself with the blood of the Beast, which you did when you stabbed me. Then you have to pledge your loyalty to Satan, which you did when you were breaking the printer at work."

I rolled my eyes. "I surely didn't."

"You absolutely did. And stop calling yourself Shirley." She doubled over in laughter at her own wit. When she finally recovered herself, she explained, "Let me refresh your memory. I said, 'So, will you do what I say, or what?' and you made one of those pissy little sighs of yours and said, 'Fine.'"

I was going to sigh again but thought better of it.

She ticked off another finger and said, "Then you have to repudiate God and all his holy works. You did that when you were talking to the social worker in your apartment."

Yeah. I thought I remembered something about repudiating God and all his holy works.

"Finally, you have to sleep with the devil, which we did last night. Et voilà, you're a witch."

I made one of those pissy little sighs of mine. "I surely... I mean, I didn't sleep with you. We slept in the same bed. That's not what 'sleeping together' means."

"Let's not split hairs," she said, returning to her newspaper. "Anyway, I don't see what you're so mad about. You have magical powers. Who doesn't dream of having magical powers?"

"You mean the power to ruin my favorite beverage? Yeah, I'm thrilled." I poured another cup and it curdled immediately. I tried to skim off the bits that floated to the top.

"Oh, it's not just curdling," she said. "You can also wither crops and afflict livestock."

I got rid of the last coffee curdles and took a sip of what was left. It was weak and nasty but just barely drinkable. "Why would I want to wither crops and afflict livestock?"

Dee shrugged and turned the newspaper page. "I dunno. If there's nothing on TV?"

I just glared until she looked at me.

"Oh, don't be such a baby," she said. "You can control it. You just have to remain calm and focused." She spent a moment studying me. "So, yeah, you're pretty screwed, aren't you?"

"Only as long as you're around."

She *tsk*ed. "I would never leave you, Jordan. Not now that we've consummated our unholy union."

"As soon as I get out of here, I'm going to find a psychologist who'll certify that you're not a hallucination, if I have to hold him at gunpoint, or reveal my disgusting supernatural power to him, or both, and then I'm going back to the exorcist. They can burn me at the stake if they want to. Anything to get rid of you. You crossed a line when you took away my coffee."

She turned another page and said, "Oh, look. The Galleria is having a sale on futile crusades."

I flicked a curd at her and walked out.

◆

I had to walk back in for breakfast, since missing a meal could be used as evidence against me at my release hearing. No, seriously. They take the three-squares-a-day rule real serious in psychiatric hospitals. I admit that this makes sense for patients with an eating disorder. You don't want anorexics passing out in the halls after dinner—that's when the janitor buffs the floors, so you'd have anorexic-shaped patches of grubby tile. But for everyone else, monitoring our food intake just feels like piling humiliation on top of embarrassment.

Dee showed up as soon as I sat down. After checking that no one was watching, she ate my bacon and pancakes, leaving me with nothing but soggy hash browns and a cup of freshly spoiled coffee. I went for a second cup, but for some strange reason, I couldn't remain calm enough to keep it from curdling.

As soon as I'd resigned myself to breakfasting solely on undercooked potato shreds, the PA called me to the front desk, so I left my shreds and my coffee curds untouched.

"You're scheduled for an individual therapy session," the weekend lobby nurse told me.

"It's Saturday." They don't do individual sessions on Saturdays.

She shrugged. "Dr. Parks said he was willing to take time out of his weekend since your hearing is tomorrow. He's waiting for you in his office."

Ah, so it was a witch hunt. No, wait. That's a poor choice of words. It was an attempt to scrape up enough evidence in seventy-two hours to have me involuntarily committed. If I'm being generous, I can admit that he might have been worried about my safety outside the facility. But let's be serious here: I pissed him off and now it was personal.

"And," she added, "there's a problem with your insurance that we need to take care of." She already had the forms out, and was handing me a pen.

"We must have our priorities," I muttered as I began to read them.

"Making you well is our top priority." She said it so earnestly that I thought she actually believed it. She must have been new.

I eyed her. "You're cutting into my therapy session so you can make sure you get paid. I think you might be confused about what the word *priority* means."

"Sign here, please," she said, cheerful and unfazed. I expected that. Cynical misanthropes aren't made in a day. In time, though, this blooming flower of optimism would surely wilt into a bitter little bud, its once-cheerful petals rotting on the ground beneath it.

I signed the documents and caught her rolling her eyes as I turned toward Dr. Parks's office. So it begins.

The first thing Dr. Parks said to me when I entered his office was "Hello, Jordan. I heard there was a problem with your insurance?"

"I think we got that sorted out," I said, sitting down in the chair in front of his desk.

"Good, good." I think that's what he said, anyway. My attention was fixed on the paper coffee cup in his hand. Not just coffee but a four-shot latte, by the looks of it. He set it down within arm's reach of me. So close. So very close.

"Sorry you had to come in on your day off," I said, my mouth wet from salivating.

"Making you well is my priority," he said, but without the energy or enthusiasm of the lobby nurse. He said the words as if reading them from a poster. And the circle of life moves us all. "In fact, I'd like you to come in for therapy sessions with me after you check out. Individual and group. Every day at first, and then we can see about reducing it to a few days per week. Of course, we only hold those sessions during regular work hours."

If that sounds like an impossible schedule to juggle and still hold down a job, it's because it is. He was deliberately steering me into a catch-22. If I refused his recommendation, *especially* if I refused it on the grounds that it was impossible to accept, he'd use it at the hearing to show I could only get the help I needed while involuntarily committed.

If he didn't lay it on so thick, I might have even fallen for it. "Well," I said, "it's going to be hard with my job, but if you think that's what I need, I'll just have to find a way to make it happen. Getting well is my priority, too." Too much, you think?

"Good, good," he said. The extra "good" made me smile, even as he tried and failed to form a smile in return. "For today, though, I'd like to continue the discussion we had yesterday, about your mother."

"I'd like that very much," I said, slowly sneaking my hand across the desk, until the tip of my finger was just brushing the base of his coffee cup.

"There's no right way or wrong way to grieve for a lost loved one, but there are ways that are much less…therapeutic than others."

Which is another way of saying that there are right ways and wrong ways, asshole. I snuck my hand a little farther out, until two fingertips and my thumb touched the coffee cup. "I admit that mine haven't been the most therapeutic so far."

"What do you suppose you could have done better?" He reached for his coffee cup, and I drew my hand back.

What could I have done better to handle the death of my mother? Well, I could have lied and told everyone I was adopted. "I should have opened a dialogue with Simon." There was no use running from the list of things that Dr. Parks thought I did wrong. Just disagreeing with him could be evidence in favor of committing me.

As much as it stung to act like Dr. Parks held the secrets of eradicating human misery, if only people would listen to his wisdom, I had to sit there and take it. It helped, of course, when he drank from his coffee and immediately spat it out. The mouthful of goo didn't splash but sat in a lump atop his mahogany desk, quivering.

"Are you sick?" I asked, tilting my head to the side and trying not to laugh.

He pulled the lid off his coffee and stared down into the coagulated horror within. As his accusing eyes rose to me, I leaned forward to look in. The contents of his cup looked like a spittoon. It was much worse than my coffee had been, probably because of the steamed milk. The stringy curds moved as I watched, and for a moment, I feared that I'd brought them to life—that I'd created a ravenous amoeboid monstrosity that would grow and consume living flesh until Steve McQueen finally managed to stop it. Then I realized that it was just settling into the cup, releasing fetid gas bubbles as it plopped in on itself.

Cooooooooooooool.

"You should go on Yelp and leave a bad review of that coffee shop," I said. Then I felt like an ass, because some innocent coffee shop might lose business.

He was still looking at me and, I think, trying to figure out how I'd done this. He might have seen my fingers on the base of the cup, but what did that mean? It's not like his patient could have supernatural powers, right? *Muhahah!*

He turned his attention to the glob on his desk, which by now had flattened and spread until it touched a piece of paper. From the point of contact, a halo of oily moisture was spreading in a semicircle. He lifted the paper, touching it only at the far side, and used it to scrape the glob up and drop it in the waste bin. Then he used his foot to push the bin a little farther from his chair.

So, at least there was a silver lining to this curdling thing. If I couldn't have coffee, neither would anyone who fucked with me.

"So, about my mom," I said.

"Right," he said. "Yesterday, you said this wasn't the first time your mother accidentally OD'd."

"Okay, let me stop you there," I said. "For one thing, she didn't accidentally OD."

I could see that he was about to contradict me, but then he stopped to think. And then he contradicted me anyway. *Asshole.* "You said they found thirty oxycodones in her stomach. You said everyone in your family was treating it as an OD."

I guess you really shouldn't laugh at the circumstances of your own mother's death, and especially not in front of a man who's determined to keep you locked up in a psyche ward, but I just couldn't help myself. "Yeah, and I thought it was obvious that everyone in my family is either lying or deluded. No one downs thirty oxys and expects to wake up in the morning. For one thing, you'd be out of oxys. That's why you never hear about someone who goes grocery shopping, checks on their 401(k), then takes thirty oxys. No, you hear about people who give away their stuff, put the cat out so it won't eat their face, and *then* they take thirty oxys."

"And when's the last time you went grocery shopping?"

"Sunday night." *Asshole.*

♦

As I was shuffling down the hall, pondering just how hard Dr. Parks was planning to fuck me over, Dee appeared at my side. "That's how it starts, you know," she said. "You curdle a latte here, you afflict a cow there, and pretty soon, you're eating babies under the gibbous moon."

I shrugged. "I never liked babies, anyway."

"Hey, have you given any thought to that woman who's in jail because of you?"

"She isn't in jail because of me." I said it so firmly I almost believed it.

"Really?" Dee asked, smirking as she walked. "Because, the way I figure it, you could get her out in an hour if you wanted to. It's by your inaction alone that she remains in jail. Even the cops who squeezed the confession out of her couldn't release her if they wanted to. Not now. Someone else put her in that cell, but you're the one who keeps her there."

I glanced up and down the hallway, then pushed her hard, up against the wall. Her only reaction was to bat her eyelashes at me.

"You have no right to stand there, accusing me of being at fault, accusing me of being responsible for that poor tramp being in jail, accusing me of being in the wrong, when you could get her out as easy as I could, and it wouldn't even cost you your freedom."

She looked back in silence, her eyes growing wider, and for a moment I thought I actually had her. Then a grin crept onto her lips and she said, "So, let me see if I have this straight. You're arguing your innocence on the grounds that your continued inaction makes you slightly less evil than the devil?"

"I…well…no, I mean…"

As I stammered, she began to slow-clap. "I love it," she said. "That's the kind of disruptive thinking I like to see in my servants."

"I am not your servant!" I said, and only afterward realized my voice would carry into the rooms along the hall.

"Fair enough," Dee replied. "A servant would only do what I tell them to, whereas you take initiative. You're doing my will in new and innovative ways. That makes you what? A sycophant?"

I only glared at her.

"No, you're right. You're more of a disciple."

# 22

It was Sunday—day three in the mental ward—and David still hadn't called or messaged, which seemed to confirm what I already knew. It was over.

"You done with that phone?" the weekend lobby nurse asked.

I scrolled through the message log one more time, hoping something was hiding in the cracks on the screen, but there was nothing. Not a word. At that point, I think I would have felt better if he messaged to break up with me, leaving no hope of reconciliation, because at least I could stop worrying about it. I earnestly wished for a text that read:

> **Agent Dave:** *We're through!*

> **Agent Dave:** *Because you're an insane cultist who didn't bother going to her own mother's funeral and I'm utterly humiliated just knowing you.*

> **Agent Dave:** *And Gus is getting a restraining order. He's very disappointed.*

> **Agent Dave:** *Sorry.* ='(

That would be something to work with, at least—a jumping-off point. Even if there was nothing I could do to change his mind, at least I'd know what he thought.

"I'm finished," I said, handing the phone back.

As I walked around the corner, Dee was there, leaning against the wall and already looking right at me. "I wouldn't worry," she said. "I'm pretty sure he knew you were crazy when you started dating, so this doesn't actually change anything."

"Thanks," I said, walking past her.

She caught up and said, "I'd be less worried about whether he's willing

116

to date a maniac and more worried about whether he's willing to date a maniac serial killer."

I sighed. "I am not a serial killer."

"Yeah, but everyone's going to think you are. That body in the woods was just the one they found."

"I didn't even mean to murder the first one!" Again, I neglected to check whether anyone was in earshot, and noticed too late that someone was listening from their room.

I grinned sheepishly through the open door, and the older woman inside nodded her head and said in a hoarse voice, "I believe you, honey."

"Thanks," I said, and hustled onward.

I could hear Dee's footsteps following behind me. "Hey, there's a chapel here. Shouldn't you be at Sunday services?" she asked.

"If I thought it would help, I would. But you're just trying to trick me into shooting Jesus in the dick again. Or worse."

"Jordan, let's be honest: if I could think of something worse, I'd have already tricked you into doing it."

As true as that was, I turned the corner toward my room, not the chapel.

"Come on, Jordan!" Dee said. "You're planning to visit an exorcist, but you won't even go to mass? Exorcism is a members-only service, you know. That means taking communion on a regular basis. You're going to have to eat his uncooked flesh and drink his unpasteurized blood. Although personally, I recommend joining the Church of the 160 Degree Internal Temperature for at Least Three Minutes."

"They do exorcisms on non-Catholics. That's one of the first things I checked."

Dee brushed the matter away with a flick of her hand. "Sure, they say that, but I bet they'll sneak a baptism in there, in between tying you down and beating you with reeds. Then they'll be all, 'Surprise! You're Catholic now. Please enjoy this starter kit containing a complimentary bible and, like, seven kids.'"

"They don't do that." We were coming up on my room, so I walked faster.

"I wouldn't put it past them. These are not healthy people, Jordan. It's not even their fault, really. They're only messed up because, two thousand years ago, their Father said he was going out for a pack of salvation and he hasn't been back since."

"Well, then, we have something in common, don't we?"

She walked in front of me and stood in the doorway to my room, blocking my way. Her eyes on the ground, she said, "I've been meaning to talk to you about your father, Jordan."

I sighed, shook my head, rolled my eyes—the whole nine yards. "Don't even try."

"Jordan, your father never really left you."

I pushed past her, still shaking my head. "Not buying it."

"Jordan, I'm your father."

"You aren't," I said, as I lay down on the bed and stared at the ceiling.

"It all makes sense now, doesn't it?"

"Nope."

She sat down on the corner of the bed. "You didn't even let me finish. You know, you could have pretended to believe me, just for a second."

"Sorry." I look over at her. "I just wasn't into it."

"This is why people don't like you," she said, sulking. "Well, this and a bunch of other things."

I just grinned back at her.

She twisted to face me, sneering. "There's another one. Has anyone ever told you that you're no fun to be around when you're this chipper? Why are you this chipper, anyway? What the hell do you have to be chipper about?"

I smiled, silent for a few seconds. "If I'm chipper," I finally said, "it's because you're right."

She arched an eyebrow and shot me a perplexed expression. "About what?"

"David did know I was crazy when he started dating me."

♦

Sundays are kind of slow down at the old mental ward. There are few doctors and therapists working on site, though there's always one there or on call to do emergency prescriptions. An emergency prescription could save a patient's life, after all, though I've never heard of it happening. Usually it's a stopgap measure for the understaffed weekend nurses, who make up in sedatives what they lack in manpower.

The point is, there wasn't much to distract me from the looming prospect of my release hearing. Weekend hearings for anything are kind of a crapshoot. Best-case scenario, you're dealing with semi-retired judges who no longer give a shit. Worst case, a regular judge gets called from home, and they come in already pissed off at the poor bitch who interrupted their key party, or whatever it is judges do on a Sunday.

I could almost imagine the phone call: "Yeah, this is Dr. Dickless down at the Belmont Hospital for the Criminally Maligned. We got a real sicko here, and we'll have to let her go if we don't get a hearing in the next few hours. Yeah, sorry about the rush. We were going to let her go without a hearing, but then suddenly this morning, she went from drinking four cups of coffee at breakfast to zero, which is a common sign of self-harm."

Worse, they hadn't let me see the evidence against me. Patients are supposed to get a copy of it before their hearings so they can adequately prepare, but *before* is one of those funny words that can mean just about anything you want it to—especially when we're talking about a shamed and infantilized minority. Which is all to say the bastards wouldn't let me see my files.

As I lay staring at the ceiling and imagining all the ways my hearing could go wrong, I could see, out of the corner of my eye, Dee crouched by the side of the bed. I tried to ignore her, but she had a unique talent for being incredibly annoying, even when remaining perfectly motionless at the edge of my peripheral vision.

"What?" I finally asked.

She was quiet for a second, then asked, "Whatcha thinkin'?"

"Just wondering if I have the ability to curdle someone's blood so it clots and they die of apparently natural causes, and how I should probably test that on you. Repeatedly. Every time you show up."

Dee laughed. "Don't be ridiculous. You don't have anything like that kind of talent."

I sighed, forlorn.

"Well, what do you expect?" Dee asked. "We only slept in the same bed."

"If it meant I could kill you over and over again without anyone being blamed, I might consider rectifying that and actually sleep with you."

"I dunno," she said, thinking about it. "Being repeatedly murdered is one of my turnoffs."

"Alas."

After I spent an uneventful few minutes staring at the ceiling, Dee asked, "So...whatcha thinkin' now?"

"I'm worried I'll be stuck in this place for the next three months." If I lost this hearing, that's how long it would be before I could present new evidence in favor of my release.

"I'm sure you'll do fine," Dee said. "You should call David now and get a date for tonight. Take him out dancing. It's a proven fact that excuses for bizarre behavior go over better while dancing."

"Well, that's a problem, because I don't dance."

"Don't or can't?"

"Don't and can't. Don't because I can't and can't because I don't."

"Oh, Lordy," she said. "I guess I should have seen the signs. You can't really dance to hipster music, can you?"

I rolled away from her and pressed my palms into my temples to fight the nascent headache.

I felt her poking me in the back with her index finger. "Come on," she said. "Get up. We're teaching you to slow-dance."

I looked back and narrowed my eyes, trying to figure out her angle.

She held her hands up and said, "No tricks. I'm suspending my scheduled abuse during the current lameness emergency."

I narrowed my eyes further.

"Come on, Lamey McLamerson. Up and at 'em. Slow-dancing is barely more than swaying back and forth. It's so easy, you'll feel like an idiot for not learning before now."

The funny thing was, if someone I trusted wanted to teach me to slow-dance, I probably would have refused. Out of embarrassment, if nothing else. But I didn't give a shit what Dee thought of me, so I eventually gave in.

And, for once, it wasn't a trick. The devil actually taught me to slow-dance. Go figure.

"Now let me teach you to lead," she said, when I had it down. "You'll need that in prison."

"Okay, we're finished," I said, moving my arms well clear of her and backing away.

"Suit yourself," Dee said. "Oh, and let me know when you graduate middle school. I'll give you ballroom lessons."

I was working on a pithy response when someone knocked on the door. My first instinct was to conceal all evidence that I'd been dancing, as if I imagined myself the teenage heroine from an eighties movie, hiding her dancing hobby from oppressive parents. When I came to my senses, I opened the door.

"Hi, there," I said to the orderly who'd knocked. "Just give me a second."

He nodded and milled about while I ran a brush through my hair, gathered up some notes, and checked my makeup. "Let's hurry it up," he said, clapping his hands twice for emphasis. "You don't want to be late."

Or, rather, *you* don't want to spend any more time with me than you have to, *asshole*. I shot him a perky smile and said, "Almost ready."

On the way out, he gave me the folder containing my copy of the evidence. I paged through it on the short, shuffling walk to the hearing room, and grew chill with sweat. I had already braced myself, ready to stay calm and not let them put me into an agitated state they could use against me at the hearing, but this was just too much.

This evidence was a masterwork of framing. Framing in the sense of "frame-job," or "to frame," or "did you hear about that poor framed-up bitch they put away for life in a mental ward because she sassed a psychologist?"

No reference to Satanism or the devil appeared anywhere in the evidence, except as a vague allusion to "feelings of guilt, worthlessness, and pessimistic thought culminating in an abrupt and capricious shift in the patient's core worldview." Meaning that if I so much as mentioned the devil—you remember the devil, right? The reason they sent a social worker out to commit me in the first place—if I so much as mentioned the devil, it would make me look like a complete loon in front of the judge, and I would be instantly, incredibly fucked.

Worse, according to the documents, Gabby and Michael had both called social services out of worry for me, and had both answered yes when the social worker asked if they were worried I'd harm myself. I'm sure they were hesitant yeses, but that doesn't exactly show through in a transcript, does it?

The coup de grace was the transcript of Simon's call. I hadn't had a single documented thought of self-harm in two decades, but the thing about suicide attempts is they kind of stick with you when it comes to psychiatric evaluations. Simon spilled it all to the cops when he called for a wellness check, then he repeated it to a clinical social worker. And he didn't just mention it; he repeated everything I said at the bar in Ybor, as best he could remember. On the transcript, it looked like suicidal ideation and arguably a concrete plan. That last is, honestly, kind of my own fault. I probably shouldn't have analyzed my failed technique quite so much. Hey, can I help it that I know more about arterial anatomy now and can pinpoint exactly how I got it wrong?

The point is, it looked *real* bad, and I hadn't even made it through the file before we reached the hearing room. The hearing room was the same room I'd had group therapy in the day before, which is pretty typical. They like to hold these things inside the facility, for the convenience of the patient and the psychiatric witnesses, and for the inconvenience of whatever witnesses the patient themselves might want to call. I'd called Simon in, though I was kind of worried he'd break down on the stand, to the point they might hold an immediate, second hearing to commit him. Simon is... Well, you know. He's sort of fragile.

Inside, the judge was sitting at an art table with papers and a gavel in front of him. To his right, Simon sat fidgeting, covered in sweat in a chair he'd pushed back against the wall.

*Shit.* I'd already lost, and I'd only just stepped into the room.

And next to Simon? Michael and Gabby, looking abashed but confident. I hadn't called them, nor had I called the professionally dressed lawyer who stood up from the left-hand table when I approached. "I'll be your counsel today, if that's all right with you." He handed me a business card from a primo downtown law firm. He had a copy of the same folder of evidence I had, except his was bulging with sticky notes and extra printouts. He and a gang of paralegals must have spent the whole weekend in focused research.

I searched the room for Dee and found her leaning against the back wall, smirking at me. In response to my unspoken question, she only shook her head and pointed to Gabby. My eyes whipped over, and Gabby's lips formed a silent grin as she mouthed the words *"Soup lawyer."*

# 23

Soup Lawyer went at it like the fucking Tasmanian Devil, making motion after motion to toss out the evidence Dr. Parks had so carefully assembled. The thick sheaf of my damnation was cut up and discarded page by page, without a pause, until Dr. Parks and his counsel looked shell-shocked as they paged through their documents, trying to figure out what they had left.

The hospital's council made an objection to every motion, but every objection was cut off at the knees by a flurry of Soup Lawyer's citations and precedents. Towards the end, the judge started giving the hospital's lawyer a nasty look when she objected, as if to say "Why are you wasting everyone's time by even existing?"

When the motions were through, and the judge asked, "Are counsels ready to proceed?," the hospital counsel's "Yes, your honor" was a broken little squeak.

And that was pretty much it. Soup Lawyer's motions left so little evidence—not much more than Dr. Parks's interviews with me—that they had nothing to hang an argument on. It was a matter of half an hour for the judge to find in my favor, and then I was escorted back to my room to gather my things.

I was still trying to process this when I walked outside to find Gabby, Michael, and Simon waiting to hug me. A lot.

"Was that really your soup lawyer?" I asked.

Gabby smiled. "Yep. He let me use my retainer on this when I told him what happened."

I resisted the urge to cry. "But your soup crusade…"

"Jordan, I'd give up two soup crusades for you. Maybe three."

♦

The alarm clock went off, and as I reached over to hit the snooze button, Dee whispered in my ear, "Happy Monday, sugar." If there's anything that could make Mondays worse, it's waking up to the tender whispers of the devil. But at least I woke in my own bed and not a mental ward.

I stared at the clock and pointedly away from Dee, trying to decide whether to go into work. I could take the day off. Ruth said I could, so she'd have no basis for complaint if I took her up on it, right? It would also make it easier to get to my group counseling session on time. It was set for 5:15 pm exactly, as if it meant to mock work hours from just outside them.

But with Dee as the dominant source of misery in my life, taking the day off hardly seemed worth it. I felt her breath on my neck as she leaned over the bed to join me in staring at the clock. "The secret," she said, quite softly, "is that it changes once a minute."

I rose and was about to ask her to leave the room so I could dress, but quickly realized how counterproductive that would be, so I ducked into the closet and picked an outfit in the dark. I was worried she'd appear in there with me, but she just skulked around the room and picked through my stuff.

When I emerged, she was kneeling over my dirty-clothes pile, rifling through it. "There are like twenty jelly beans in here," she said, looking at me in wonderment. "Are you trying to hide them away, like a squirrel?"

"It's more like two," I said as I left the room, "and they're not mine. They were probably just in my pockets."

I checked on Simon, still sleeping soundly on my couch, and went into the kitchen. Dee was already there waiting for me, leaning against the dishwasher. She looked me over and said, "That raises more questions than it answers." Then she popped one of the jellybeans into her mouth.

"That's been on a crack addict's carpet," I said, keeping my voice low.

When Dee heard, she promptly spit the half-chewed jellybean onto my kitchen floor, completing its life cycle. "Wow. Stealing jellybeans from a crack addict. That's low, Jordan."

Actually, the beans were from a bag that I brought for her kids. The kids dropped a couple on the carpet, so I grabbed them to keep anyone from eating them. "I thought you knew the history of things," I said. "How come you didn't know where those jellybeans have been?"

"Oh, I did," she said, grinning. "I just love spit-takes." She popped the second bean into her mouth, half-chewed it, and spit it onto the floor next to the first.

"You love spit-takes, but you hate my kitchen tile."

She shrugged. "Don't blame me for the state of your kitchen. That floor looked shitty before I got here." She tilted her head as she studied the spots where the jelly beans landed. "They kind of look like nipples."

I would have cleaned the floor, I swear to God, but there just isn't that much time built into my morning schedule. If I wasted a bunch with distractions like that, I'd either have to skip my morning cereal or be even more noticeably late for work.

As it was, I didn't make it in until 9:06, and I ran into Ruth as I was coming off the elevator. "Are you sure you should be back at work?" she asked, shifting the tall stack of documents in her arms as she stopped to talk.

"I'm good," I said. "I got plenty of fluids over the weekend, and I feel fine. I might have to leave a little early, though, to pick up a prescription."

"Okay, just…make sure you wash your hands frequently throughout the day. Those stomach bugs are highly contagious, and the auditors are still here. Oh, and try to get here on time from now on, okay? We're letting that copier situation slide, but you already have two written warnings, so I expect you to be on your best behavior. If I have to give you another warning, I'd have to fire you, and I'd really hate to do that. You're too valuable to us." She moved to give my shoulder a squeeze but thought better of it and wiped her hand on her pants suit, even though it never touched me.

I smiled and nodded, and promised I'd be on my best behavior.

When she was gone, Dee appeared at my side. "I can't believe you treat that woman with respect but heap scorn on me."

I glanced around to make sure we were alone, and said, "She's a jackass, sure. But she doesn't follow me home, and she doesn't screw up my life."

Dee snorted. "Seriously? You don't think she screws up your life? The only difference with me is, I screw with you to make your life more interesting. She screws with you to make it more boring."

I sneered and said in a harsh whisper, "Well, she didn't get some poor woman framed for a fake murder, did she?"

"Oh, come on," she said. "I've made it my personal mission to nag you until you fix that. What more do you want from me?" She glanced at her hand, chewed idly on a hangnail, and added, "Hey, speaking of fixing things, shouldn't you be fixing things?"

"No, I shouldn't be fixing things. I should be doing my job as a government worker."

She shook her head and said, "Reagan wept."

And that's what I did with my morning. Not weeping, I mean. I did my job, in between checking up on that poor framed tweaker woman, making sure my prescriptions from the hospital got filled, and fruitlessly e-mailing psychologist offices, hoping to find one that would consider giving me a letter saying I wasn't hallucinating the devil. I guess it isn't surprising that this is an almost-impossible task. There aren't many psychologists who are willing to go on record saying, "Yeah, the classic signs of psychosis you're exhibiting are totally not indicative of psychosis. I recommend exorcism, and if that doesn't work, come back and you can participate in the scientific paper I'm working on, titled, 'Burning at the Stake as a Last-line Treatment for Schizophrenia: A New Approach to an Old Method.'"

I was growing convinced that even my curdling power wouldn't help me. Having supernatural strength didn't help that girl in the *Exorcist* convince the shrinks, did it? And that was before you considered the shit Dee could pull to thwart my brilliant plan.

As for the poor framed tweaker woman, there wasn't much news. In the eyes of the media, all the sparkle had gone out of that brutal murder. The public eye had since turned toward the latest celebrity to die: some bigshot director who made dumb yet inexplicably popular action films, whose core audience was teenage boys and imbeciles.

As she read the news over my shoulder, Dee let out a pathetic little whine. "Miguel Gulf died? Oh, no, I love his movies."

I rolled my eyes, shut off my monitor, and headed for the break room.

"Going off to cry?" she asked, following me.

"That or grab some cheese curls from the snack machine and maybe make a few phone calls. I'll just have to see how things go."

She put a hand on my shoulder as we walked. "You have to cry, Jordan. You have to cry, or this is going to be your mother's death all over again."

"Yeah, except that I have no use for Miguel Gulf and I don't really give a damn that he's dead." I stopped to reflect for a moment. "Hey, you're right. It is like my mother's death."

Dee nodded solemnly. "That's why you have to cry."

I shrugged. "Maybe if we're out of cheese curls."

As it turned out, there was one packet still in the machine, so I managed to hold back the tears. Leaning against the wall in the corner of the break room, snack in hand, I set to work unburning my bridges.

I called David first, though on the cracked screen of Frankenphone, it took three tries just to tap his entry in my contacts. When I finally managed, he answered on the first ring and asked, "Are you eating cheese curls?"

I'd rehearsed several dozen possible scenarios for this moment, but this one was not among them. "How the hell do you know that? Can you smell my breath through the phone?" Dee, who'd followed me into the break room and was leaning against the counter, shook her head and pinched the bridge of her nose.

"It's a secret agent thing." He was trying to sound sly, but there was a tremor in his voice that betrayed anxiety.

I stood there, grasping for words, until he finally took mercy on me.

"You sent me a close-up picture of your mouth a few seconds before you called. Must have been an accident, though I'm not sure whether that makes me feel relief or disappointment."

"My, ummm, my phone's been acting a little screwy."

"Yes," he said, "your phone too."

"But," I said, resisting the instinct to speak in a voice so low that even I wouldn't be able to hear it, "you knew I was crazy when we started dating, right?"

He sighed with relief. "Oh, good, so we are dating? I was worried you were calling to tell me you'd met Napoleon in the hospital and you were running off with him."

"I was tempted, but he's a little too short for me," I said.

"But you're out now?"

"Yeah, I'm at work." That's when I ran out of rehearsed lines.

"Me too," he said, having run out as well.

"Ask him if he wants to talk about it," Dee hissed a whisper from the other side of the room.

"Do you want to talk about it?" I asked.

"Not really. Do you want to talk about it?"

"Not really."

"Then we should probably talk about it," he said.

"Yeah." I smiled. "Over drinks after work?"

"Yeah, absolutely. If you're allowed to drink."

"I'm allowed to drink. I'm crazy, not pregnant." And in my family, the women drink more when they're pregnant than when they aren't, anyway.

"Right."

"And I'm not actually crazy, anyway."

"Of course," he said, a little too fast and a little too loud. "I was just joking earlier. Trying to lighten the, umm…" He swallowed. "Mood."

I wanted to reassure him, but Ruth chose that moment to walk into the break room. Her eyes moved to me magnetically, and the scowl started to form.

"Okay, so I'll text you," I said. "With the details."

"That sounds good."

"Talk to you later." I hung up and smiled innocently at Ruth.

"Personal call?" she asked.

"A case," I said. "I'm trying to get him into an e-training program, but for some reason, he thinks it's pointless, on account of all the people in his housing project who've been through the same program and still can't find jobs."

"You've got to keep on them, Jordan," she said, perfectly earnest. I'm not sure if she can't understand sarcasm or if she's learned to filter it out. "A lot of these people never learned how to want help." As I was trying to figure out what the fuck that even meant, she went to pour herself a cup of coffee. "But you know what they say: give a man a fish, and he'll eat for a

126

day."

Dee finished the thought with "But if you turn a man into a fish, *you'll* eat for a day."

"That is fitting," I said, looking to one as I answered the other.

Ruth put her coffee down to get cream and sugar, so I took the opportunity to touch the side of her mug and curdle the contents.

Ruth, after adding cream and sugar, stirring, and never noticing the lumps of goo floating in her drink, took an oblivious sip. She spit it back into the cup and said, "Oh, dear God! People have been complaining about their coffee being goopy all morning. Now I see what they're talking about."

Dee smirked as she raised an eyebrow at me. "All morning?" she asked.

So, umm, yeah. Ruth wasn't the first workplace victim of my meager superpower. It may seem crass, but have you ever run into an overbearing TSA agent or a clerk at the DMV, and you get the impression they're deliberately screwing up your day just because they can? That this is the most power they've ever had or will ever have again, so they intend to make the most of it at your expense?

Well, I could curdle beverages.

In my defense, I hadn't had coffee for days, and the crate of caffeinated gum I'd ordered wasn't scheduled to arrive until Wednesday.

"We need a new coffee machine," Ruth said. "Jordan, I'm putting you on this project. Just tread carefully. The auditors are watching everything."

"It's a big responsibility, but I think I'm ready for it."

"I knew you were," she said, perfectly serious. Really, they must not have sarcasm on her planet.

To fortify myself for the mission ahead, I grabbed the yogurt cup from my lunch bag before heading back to my desk. That and, if I didn't eat it now, Dee would probably steal it. I was kind of surprised she hadn't already.

Back at my desk, I understood why. I was making great progress on my special project, which is to say that I'd already typed *american made coffee makers* into Google, when I sampled my yogurt. It tasted like runny, rotten eggs. I spit it out to find that my spoonful of strawberry yogurt now looked like a tweaker's bubble gum. There was a solid mass of congealed pink stuff, veined with dribbles of red, surrounded by thin yellow liquid.

"I thought yogurt was already curdled," I said under my breath.

When I looked up, Dee was there, leaning against my cubicle wall and reading an issue of *Conservative Teen* magazine. "Yeah but," she said, turning a page, "there's curdled and then there's witch-curdled. I've already told you: your powers allow you to achieve the absolute pinnacle of curdling."

"Super," I said, throwing the rest of it into the garbage, spoon and all. "Is there anything I used to enjoy that won't turn to rancid phlegm on my tongue?"

"Non-colloidal foods and beverages, and breast milk."

I just stared at her for a while.

"It's a safety feature."

"I see."

"Otherwise, you could hurt someone."

"No, no, I get it."

"Still kinda weird, huh?"

"Yeah."

She scrunched her lips and looked up, in thought. "You couldn't curdle some of the firmer non-dairy puddings. Kind of a niche item, though. I don't think they even sell them in this country."

I tried to sigh, but I'd run out. "Have I thanked you lately for all you've done for me?" When she didn't answer, I turned back to my work and tried to ignore her. Soon, I could feel her breath on my neck as she leaned in close to look over my shoulder. I whipped around in my seat, but by the time I turned, she was gone. "Good," I said. The ash she left was still settling to the floor and onto my headrest when I got down to comparing the relative merits of drip coffeemakers. Which is to say, I sorted them in order of carafe capacity and picked the biggest one.

As I was busy clicking on a few decoy coffeemakers—so it would seem like I'd made a carefully weighed decision when Ruth checked my web browsing history—Dee reappeared behind me and slapped a pudding cup down on my desk. At least, it looked like a pudding cup. It had a picture of two half-naked Zeuses shooting lightning bolts above the Parthenon, overlaid with big, uneven, multicolored cartoon letters that spelled POUTÍNKABANG!

"You're welcome," she said, laying a silver spoon on top of it. "If you like it, I'll get you a case the next time I'm in Athens."

I picked it up to examine it more carefully, but most of the writing was in Greek. "It doesn't have horse meat or breast milk in it, does it?"

"No, it's all perfectly wholesome. I mean, for something that's mostly carrageenan and artificial flavoring."

I peeled back the foil and sniffed the contents. "Are you sure there's no horse in it?"

"No, Jordan. This is a peace offering. I would never give you horse meat as a peace offering."

I dipped the very tip of the spoon into the gelatinous, caramel-covered substance and scooped out a tiny divot. I tasted it, experimentally, then set it on my tongue. It certainly didn't taste like a dairy product, but compared to facing a lifetime without pudding, it actually tasted pretty good. I took a bigger spoonful and tried it.

"Then again," Dee said, retreating to the entrance to my cube, just outside of punching range, "one is forced to wonder exactly what you put on your breakfast cereal this morning."

*Holy shit.*

I hadn't even thought of that.

I have such a set, mechanical morning routine that I was practically on autopilot when I made myself a bowl of cereal and poured...*something* on top of it. "Soy milk?" I asked, my voice a squeak.

"No, you would have curdled soy milk." She grinned, and by the sheer magnitude of her amusement, I not only knew exactly what I'd put on my breakfast cereal but exactly whose boobs it had come from.

"No," I said in a tiny, squeaking little whisper.

She was giddier than I've ever seen her, wriggling on her feet like an excited puppy.

"No, no, no, no."

"What can I say? I like to use the tools I have at hand." She leaned against one edge of the cubicle entrance and stretched her arm across to the other, so that she seemed to be looming over me from just outside of arm's length.

Which didn't matter, because I was too stunned to take a swing at her. "You are sick! You are beyond sick. You are the most vile, the most disgusting, the most depraved, the most vile..."

"You already said *vile*." She shifted to the side, in a way that would have seemed suspicious if I'd had any faculty for thought left. "But this is one of my better moments. Maybe it deserves two *vile*s."

"There aren't enough curse words in the world to describe you!"

"It's true. Many have tried."

"This is...this is...this is beyond the pale!" I cried. "You've been making my life hell since you met me, but now...but now...now you're violating my body? With your...your...ugh! With your foul devil milk!"

She just laughed. "You liked it fine before you knew." She looked down, her eyes going from one breast to the other. "Don't listen to her, darlings. She's just jealous."

"I have to get it out." I hunched over my trash can and crammed the spoon into the back of my throat. I gagged and made a pretty gross belching sound, but I couldn't manage to vomit.

Dee just smiled.

"Once I've gotten this out of me, I am going to cram this spoon so far up your fetid cunt, the antichrist will be born with it in his mouth."

All the while, Dee was beaming down at me, grinning like an idiot.

"What the hell are you smiling at?" I asked, and then jammed the spoon into the back of my mouth again.

And that was when Dee stepped out of the way, to reveal Ruth standing right behind her.

Ruth, who couldn't see Dee.

Ruth, whose eye level was right at Dee's.

Ruth, who therefore believed that every word I'd said had been directed at her.

Ruth, who had half a dozen auditors standing behind her, their mouths all agape.

"Does this look like a smile?" she asked.

Dee leaned close to her face and examined it minutely. "You know, Jordan, I don't think it does."

I just stared up at her, eyes wide and mouth clamped around the spoon.

"Oh and, by the way," Dee said, "that spoon's been up someone's ass."

I spit the spoon out. It hit Ruth in the crotch.

I must say, I was impressed by how calm she was when she leaned forward and said, simply, "You're fired."

# 24

Since I was never allowed to have personal effects at my desk, I didn't have much to carry out. Silver lining, right?

When I got home, Simon was playing video games on the couch, still wearing the tatty undershirt and boxers he'd slept in. When he saw my dour expression, he put down the controller and, with his usual measure of empathy and understanding, asked, "You don't have any *Call of Duty* games, do you?"

"Not really my thing," I said, dropping a small box of reference books on the floor.

"Did they give you a half-day or something?"

I shook my head on my way to the kitchen. I checked the cabinets for liquor. Nothing. I checked the fridge, but all I found were four packs of weird Greek pudding and a gallon of milk, which I poured down the drain.

"Is everything okay?" Simon asked, leaving open the possibility that I left work early and was desperately seeking alcohol for perfectly sanguine reasons.

"Not really."

I rechecked the cabinets, just in case a miracle had occurred while I had my back turned. When I stopped searching, he said, "You remember that time Johnny Coulson dumped you, and instead of telling anyone, you just moped around for a week, until everyone noticed he wasn't hanging around anymore?"

I avoided his eyes as I said, "Yeah."

"So, you're still doing that shit, huh?"

I couldn't help but chuckle. "I guess so."

"Okay," he said, making a show of thinking. "So, did you break up with What's-His-Name?"

"David. And no." I poured myself a glass of water and tried to pretend it was vodka.

"Did the Red Sox lose again?"

"No. Or, I dunno. Maybe."

He took a deep breath through his nose. "Oh, I know! You've finally realized you want to be a man."

I laughed but felt decently guilty about it. "That's not funny. One of my cases is like that. One of my former cases, I guess."

"Ah, you lost your job." He shrugged his shoulders. "First time getting fired?"

I only nodded.

"It gets easier, the more you do it."

"Thanks. That's real encouraging."

He grinned. "Wanna go to the Irish pub around the corner? They open at twelve, except on Sundays." You know, it may be true that I never talk about what's bothering me, but Simon always manages to reveal more than he wants to. Together, maybe, we average out to a healthy level of communication.

"Perfect," I said. "By the time you're dressed, they'll be open."

He looked down at himself and said, "Right," as if this was the first time it had occurred to him to put on pants before going out.

I had miscalculated, however, because it took him less than a minute to pull on a pair of jeans over those gross boxer shorts and to put on a stained T-shirt that was somehow even more trailer-park than an undershirt alone. So we were a few minutes early.

"Hey," he said, as we waited for the bar to open, "why are there nipples on your kitchen floor?"

"They're jelly beans."

"That raises more questions than it answers."

"You can't even imagine. Thanks for cleaning, by the way, while you're staying rent-free in my apartment."

"But I haven't been clea..." Enlightenment dawned. "Oh. I see what you did. Touché."

Simon leaned close to the bar window and peered through the glass, cupping his hands around his eyes to keep out the glare. I did the same, if only to give myself something to do. Inside, the bartender was stacking glasses and cracking bubble gum. She looked up, saw us, and shook her head—more in pity than admonition. I leaned away and she disappeared into the noonday glare.

"Who is she to judge us?" I asked. "A fucking bartender? Come on."

"Well, she has a job and we don't," Simon replied.

A disembodied voice answered from inside, saying, "I can hear you. It isn't soundproof glass, you retahds."

"We were talking about a different bartender," Simon shouted at the glass. Then he winced as I hit him on the shoulder.

"Should we go to a different bar?"

"Nah," he said. "Jennifer's just teasing."

"You've been in town four days and you're already on a first name basis with the afternoon bartender here?"

He shrugged. "I'm good at making friends."

The bolt slid back on the door lock, and Jennifer stepped outside. Holding the door open and motioning us inside, she said, "Come on, dum-dums." She gnashed down on her bubble gum as we went past, and closed the door behind us. As my eyes were still adjusting to the gloom inside the bar, Jennifer asked Simon, "You dating her? 'Cause you could do better."

He just smirked and said, "This is Jordan."

Jennifer's eyes widened. "Oh! The sister you're stayin' with." She looked at me. "How come I never seen you in here?"

"I prefer to drink alone." I suddenly realized how that sounded. "But, you know, not in a sad way."

"Right," she said. "The not-sad way to drink alone. Gotcha."

My first instinct was to think Jennifer was actually Dee, but I pushed that thought to the back of my mind. It can't be healthy to assume everyone who insults you is literally the devil.

My thoughtfulness seemed to trigger a memory in her, and she suddenly reached out and squeezed my arm just below the shoulder. "Hey, hon," she said, "sorry about your mom."

I felt like I'd just touched a live electrical wire, suddenly panicked and numb. It wasn't the thought of my idiot mother's death that did it. It was the crushing fear that someone might be feeling sorry for me. I hate that feeling, especially because you're supposed to be thankful for their pity. I mean, why the fuck should I thank some patronizing son of a bitch who thinks they know my emotions well enough to play fucking doctor to them? I don't know how most people can stand it, though I have to assume it's just a very common personality flaw that I managed to dodge.

"Thank you," I said. Because, you know, I may think I'm better than everyone else, but I'm not an ass about it.

She gave my arm another squeeze and went behind the bar. "What are you guys having? First one's on the house. Anything you want."

"If I'd realized you had a Free Drinks When Your Mom Dies promotion," I said, "I'd have been in here earlier. You should advertise that."

She stared at me from the other side of the bar for a few seconds, apparently thrown for a loop. She recovered admirably, however, with "We used to advertise it, but we had to stop after a bunch of people killed their moms."

And now I was certain that Jennifer wasn't Dee, because I really liked her. I sat down and said, "I think I'll have an old-fashioned."

"Bourbon or—"

"Rye."

Simon got a frozen daiquiri and was already half finished with it by the time my drink was ready. I held it warily, not sure whether it would curdle in my mouth. It would need oils and colloids and shit to curdle, no matter how powerful the witch is, right?

I took a sip from the glass, then a sip from the straw, and the sweet, muddled nectar at the bottom ran over my tongue and down my throat. Oh, glory be! Not all the joys of life were denied to me. I took another sip and sat to savor it. "Oh, that's good. Thank you, Jennifer. You're an angel."

♦

We had a couple more mixed drinks before we switched to beer—not for the long haul, mind you, but just to cool down a bit before going to shots. You can ruin a good bender by doing too much too fast. But if you do it right, you can maintain a nice, unruly level of drunkenness for days. I had a whole schedule worked out on a bar napkin, designed to optimize inebriation through alcoholic synergies. Ruth would have been so proud of me.

She'd have been less proud if she could hear what I was comparing her to, mind you. Not unless she has a favorable opinion of leprous pustules. Once I was sufficiently buzzed to be a little indiscreet, I complained about Dee, too. I was sober enough to call her "Dee, my new friend" and not "Dee, the literal devil who talks to me," and Simon agreed that I had to get her out of my life as soon as possible.

"So, your new friend got you fired," Simon said, chewing on a pretzel. "What a turd."

"Yeah, but it's not just that," I said. "It's everything. It's the firing, the harassment, the crossbow."

He blinked several times, trying and failing to form a question.

"Oh," I said, "she made me shoot a crossbow inside a church and it hit...something." I decided to leave out the finer details.

"Jesus!" he said. Simon's always been a good guesser.

"She was trying to keep me from talking to the priest."

He put a supportive hand on my shoulder, looked me in the eyes, and asked, "Jordan, does this have something to do with all those demon books? Are you in a cult?"

"It's not a cult!" I cried. "I wish everyone would stop saying it's a cult. It's not a cult."

Two regulars stopped short of the bar and turned to take a table instead.

"I think you should go to the police," he said, lowering his voice to barely audible levels.

I gave a good snort and whispered back, "She's the one who should go to the police. She's the one. Not me. Let her take the rap for this. It's her fault." Yeah, I sort of forgot myself there. It's possible I was a little ahead on my drinking schedule.

Simon was growing more and more concerned, so much so that he'd stopped eating pretzels. When Simon stops eating free food, you know the situation is dire. "Jordan, did she kill someone?"

I probably shouldn't have stopped to think about that question. It's the kind of question you really ought to have a firm and unambiguous answer to. "No, no. I mean, it's her fault about the crossbow thing. Someone could have gotten hurt."

Simon seemed to buy it, thankfully. After that, the hours kind of slipped away from me. In fairness, it takes a long time to learn how to play darts when you're drunk. I don't understand how that's even a bar game. There's math and everything.

Regulars came and went, and the bar gradually filled up. Simon knew half of them and was drawn into conversations that I just had to nod and smile through. He was off at one of the tables, singing the Portuguese national anthem, when Jennifer came by and wiped down the bar top. "Sounds like you had a rough couple a' weeks," she said. "Sorry, didn't mean to eavesdrop. Well, all right, I did, but only outta concern for my customers. Losing your mom, shitty friends, getting locked up in a mental ward, problems with the cops, and then gettin' fired…"

I laughed a little. "Don't tell anyone, but I don't care that I got fired. I'm more pissed at my boss for being an asshole generally. And, see, now I don't have to be around her all day. It's a little like spearing an abscess, you know? It hurts like hell for a minute, but then the pressure goes away and it feels so much better."

Jennifer wiped the same spot on the bar for the tenth time. "So, why are you in here?"

"I don't understand," I said.

"I think you do."

I stared into one of the neon signs on the wall, took a deep breath, and said, "I didn't go to my mom's funeral."

I thought she'd be disgusted with me, but she wasn't. I guessed it came from having to clean customers' puke on a regular basis. "You feel bad about it?" was all she asked.

I shifted my stare to the bar. "Nah," I said, and I meant it. "I don't feel bad about anything I did to her. I was as nice to her as she deserved—which is to say, I treated her like garbage."

She said nothing. She just kept wiping that same spot on the bar.

"Not always, I guess. Until I was about seventeen, I tried to be nice. I tried to save her." I laughed and looked up. "I thought I could do it, too. I thought if I just loved her enough, if I just cared for her enough, she'd get better. If I was a good-enough daughter, she'd get clean. Keep a job. Turn into a loving mother. That's how it always works in the movies, right?"

"Movies are full a' shit. You ever see that *Boondock Saints*? Supposed to be in Boston, but you can see the fuckin' CN Tower half the time." She paused in wiping the bar and cleared her throat. "Sorry. You were sayin' somethin' about your mom?"

"After a while, I just gave up," I said. "I gave up and she died."

She put a hand on my arm and said, "That ain't your fault, hon."

I laughed again. "No, that's not what I mean. I don't blame myself. I just... It just sucks."

"You know, I lost my dad a little while back."

True to form, I refrained from offering sympathy and only gave her a supportive little look.

"And the thing about it," she said, "is I never really got along with my dad. And when he died, my first thought was 'Good.'" She put on a wry smile. "Pretty fucked up, right?"

I shrugged and made a noncommittal sound.

"But the thing is, I was a total wreck for years after. But then you look at my brother, the rabbi. He and Dad got along great, so you'd think he'd be real torn up, right? Would you believe it hardly even fazed him? Sure, he cried for days and he felt like shit for a while, but then he was back to his old self. Turns out it's a lot easier to mourn someone you love than someone you hate."

I nursed my drink while I pondered it. "I guess so," I finally concluded. "I wonder why that is."

She just smiled. "Well, hate's a funny thing, isn't it? It's real easy to hate someone when they're alive, 'cause they keep giving you new reasons. You can forgive them for everything they've ever done to you, and mean it, but the next morning is a new day, with new betrayals. But hatin' someone after they're dead? That's hard. Maybe 'cause they ain't hurtin' no one where they are." Her smile faded for a second, then returned. "There's no one more innocent than someone in the ground. Hating the dead is like hating a child: it's just not natural. Some part of you knows that and rebels; it throws that hate right back in your face. Maybe that's why it feels like you're tearing yourself apart."

And just like in the movies, the wise bartender provided the clarity I needed. That, or she was so goddamn depressing, it brought me to tears.

So, yeah, I cried right there at the bar. Bite me. Just bite my ass, okay?

What really got me was how suddenly it came on. Have you ever had that? Where one second you're fine, and the next you get hit by an emotion so intense, you just start sobbing?

I was worried the bartender wouldn't know what to say, but she handled it with unusual aplomb, putting on a supportive face and squeezing my hand while I cried. Which is, yeah, pretty fucked up, that it took some random bartender to bring this out of me, that I could cry in front of her but not in front of my own brother or my best friends.

Whatever. I direct your attention to my previous instruction as regards biting my ass.

*Anyway*, that kept happening long enough for Simon to finally notice and come over, though he had no idea what to do. He just kept patting me on the shoulder and telling me that this was good for me, over and over until I wanted to punch him in the face just to get him to shut up. Which, I guess, might be why I didn't want to cry in front of him in the first place.

By and by, it all subsided. You never cry as long as you think you will, you know?

And Jennifer, unlike Simon, knew exactly what I needed at that moment. "How 'bout another free drink?" she said, already grabbing bottles. "I'll mix you up a White Russian. It's the perfect drink for a day this bad: cream for comfort, coffee to lift you back up, and alcohol for what ails you."

I snuffled back some snot and said, "I can't have cream or coffee. Anything that can curdle." In answer to Simon's puzzled look, I added, "Stomach problems."

"Then you're in luck," she said, "because nothing curdles above fifteen percent alcohol."

I was skeptical but extremely intrigued. "Are you sure?"

"It's one of the first things they teach you in bartender school," she said. "The alcohol works as a solvent. Look it up if you don't believe me." She mixed it swiftly—there were other patrons trying to get her attention, but she only shook her head at them. "Give me a minute. VIP customer, okay?" She set the drink in front of me and stood by. "In case you need me to put in some extra vodka," she explained.

I took a test sip, and it was absolute heaven. My God, was it heaven. I savored it, drinking slowly, which is to say that it took me just over a minute to finish the glass and ask for another.

But as Jennifer picked a clean glass off the rack, I suddenly remembering something and narrowed my eyes at her. "Wait," I said, steadying myself as the first waves of dizziness preceded the coming tsunami of inebriation. "Did you say your brother is a rabbi? As in your father's son?"

She put the glass down and leaned against the bar, cupping her chin in her hand with one finger pointed up along her cheek. "Did I say that?" she asked, grinning.

"Your brother the rabbi, is he kind of a lanky guy?" I asked. "Long hair, scraggy beard?"

"Depends on the local market," she said. "We call that 'global branding.'"

"You lying sack of shit!" I screamed, diving across the bar with all the coordination I could muster. Which wasn't much, but enough to grab her by the throat.

Simon, having drunk significantly less, got me by the shoulders and pulled me away from her. He dragged me back and held me outside of choking range as my barstool toppled over and bottles rolled off the bar and clinked across the floor. I was still trying to escape his grip for a while, until I finally realized it was futile and signaled my surrender with an aggravated sigh.

Silence fell over the bar, every patron's eyes locked on me.

"So, uh, you two know each other?" Simon asked.

"We go way back," I muttered, eyes still on Dee née Jennifer. "Why are you doing this? What more can you take from me?"

She was still grinning like a disgusting little imp. "I'm doing this because it's what you need. And it took a lot of doing—a *lot* of doing. I had to tiptoe right up to the edge of breaking my own rules, but I finally managed to get through to you, didn't I?"

"So, you engineered all of this, all this pain and misery, you ruined my fucking life, all so I'd cry about my mother?" When she didn't answer right away, I tried to break free of Simon's grip, but he was ready for me and held on to my arms all the tighter.

"Well, yes," she finally said. "I'm not going to pretend I didn't enjoy it. What can I say? Doing good deeds is its own reward."

"I cried the day after we met!" I screamed. "You couldn't have just accepted that and gone home?"

She shook her head and *tsk*ed at me. "No, no, no. Jordan, we both know that was you crying over your own problems. Which is frankly kind of tacky when your mom just died."

"Jordan," Simon said, whispering into my ear, "what the hell is going on?"

"What's going on is 'Jennifer' has done her job and she's going home now. We won't see her again. Right?"

Dee, still looking like Jennifer, seemed to think about this for a moment, then shook her head. "I dunno," she said. "I think this proves that you still need my help. I might have to clear my schedule."

"Are you both insane?" Simon asked, shouting it louder, I think, than he intended to.

Dee smirked. "I've always thought sanity was the most perverse form of peer pressure."

I was on the cusp of finding the perfect biting comment, one that would reduce her to a smoldering pile of emotional wreckage, but Simon dragged me away while I was still formulating. He answered my resistance with "We're leaving. This isn't good for you."

"Listen to your brother," Dee called after us. "He's as smart as he is sexy."

"You stay away from my brother!" I shouted through the door.

It swung closed in front of me and Simon said, "Thanks. I was totally in with that before you ruined it."

"I didn't ruin it!" I protested, as I shrugged off Simon's now-slackened grip. "She's the devil! Metaphorically, I mean."

Nice save, Jordan. Nice save.

We started home in the dying light. "Holy crap, it got dark," I said, looking at the sky and stumbling as soon as my eyes were off my feet.

"Happens most days, around this time," he answered, holding me upright. "I think it's because of global warming."

On the short walk around the corner to my apartment, I occasionally grabbed Simon to keep from falling over, and he occasionally did the same—more to keep me from feeling embarrassed than out of actual need, I think.

When we finally made it to my front door, I fumbled for my keys for a good half a minute before I realized Simon had a set and was standing there, smirking and waiting for me to give up. Which I did, and graciously let him unlock the door.

As soon as I was inside, I remembered that we didn't have any alcohol in the house. "Shit," I said. "I should have grabbed those bottles off the floor before we left."

"Some places have alcohol delivery now," Simon said, flopping down on the couch.

"I'm sure Massachusetts isn't one of them." I pondered our options. "Maybe someone on Craigslist will go to the liquor store for us?"

I took out my phone to look into it and noticed that I had three missed calls from David, and one from my group therapist. "Oh, shit." Either that bar had been too loud to hear it, or Frankenphone had just given up on ringing. "Oh, shit. Shit shit shit shit shit."

"What?" Simon asked, twisting around to look at me over the back of the couch. "Is Craigslist out of vodka?"

"No, I missed therapy and I'm late for my date with David. Shit shit shit."

"Do you want me to…" I think he was about to say *drive you*, but upon reflection, he continued, "Fake a hostage situation?"

I tapped David's entry on my call log and, while it rang, I said to Simon, "No, that won't help."

"Hey," David said, picking up. "Were we supposed to meet at your place?"

"Uhhh, no," I said, unable to come up with anything better.

"Hey," Simon called, shouting through a hand cupped over his hand, to sound farther away. "Where'd you get that phone, hostage?" Then he made a less-than-convincing shotgun cocking sound.

"What's going on?" David asked.

I made an angry face at Simon and waved my free hand so hard at him, I almost lost my balance. "Nothing, I just... It's been a really weird day."

"You sound funny," David said. "Is everything okay?"

"Yes, it's... No. But I just... Can we reschedule?" Yeah, that's the best I could come up with, given the chaotic state of my mind, my little brother trying to distract me, and how drunk I was. It was like being fourteen again.

"I think I should come over."

"David, I... I think you'd hate me if you saw the state I'm in right now."

"Okay, I'm definitely coming over," he said. "You don't have to let me in, but I'm coming over. Whatever's going on, we'll figure it out."

"But..."

"I'm already on my way."

It sounded so final that I hardly thought of not giving in. "Okay" was all I said, and I hung up. Looking to Simon, I said in despair, "He's coming over."

Simon beamed back a smile. "So, the hostage ploy worked? I told you."

I think that's when I passed out.

# 25

I woke to swirling spots of light, the smell of medicated vapor rub, and my brother's annoyed voice saying, "Well, it's the closest thing to smelling salts we have, isn't it?"

My vision was beginning to clear, but Simon was still only a vague shadow looming over me. "What's going on?" I asked.

The shadow shifted and grew larger. "Are you okay?"

"Yeah," I said. "What's going on?"

"You passed out," he said. The shadow shook its head. "You really shouldn't drink so much without eating. That's why they have pretzels at the bar."

"I don't think that's why," said a shape behind him, slowly resolving from a shadow to a blur. I didn't need to see him to recognize David's voice.

I groaned. "Goddamn it. You've already seen me get carted away to an asylum; why did you have to see this, too?"

"Maybe it's fate," David said, and I could hear the wry smile in his voice. "It can't get worse than this, can it?"

"I'm not so sure about that."

"All the more reason to keep dating you," David said, and the relief hit me so hard, I nearly passed out again. "I'd kick myself if I didn't find out what you manage to do next."

"I'm sorry I told you you'd feel better once you cried," Simon said. "I was *way* off on that."

"No, you were right. I do feel better."

I could make out just enough of his face to see his eyes bug out. "Jesus Christ. What did you feel like before? I was about to call 911."

"I wouldn't let him," David said.

"Thank you. Thank you thank you thank you." A visit from the paramedics would have landed me back in the mental ward, and the best lawyers that soup-hate could buy couldn't get me out. I looked from David to Simon. "Hey, do you mind if we talk?"

"Sure," Simon said, almost chipper. Then his face drooped and his shoulders sank. "Oh, you mean with him. Yeah, sure. I'll just…" He looked around the apartment, which was neither large enough nor soundproof enough for privacy. "I'll just hang out on the fire escape."

I gave him a hug. He looked like he needed it.

"I, umm, love you," I said to David when Simon was gone.

He grinned. "I umm-love you too. And also the regular kind."

I shut my eyes and winced. "Can we try that again?"

He only nodded, that same little grin on his lips.

"I love you," I said, opening my eyes and staring deep into his.

He leaned in close, until our noses almost touched. He let the moment linger a while, as his grin turned into a soft smile. "I love—"

"Whoa," Simon's voice rang out from the bedroom, "there are so many cardboard boxes in the alley back here!"

"—you," David said, after he'd waited patiently for Simon to finish talking.

"Oh, did I interrupt something?" Simon called back. After a few seconds without an answer, he continued, "Okay. I'll just be here on the fire escape, then. If you need me."

I was about to ask David to give it another try, when he slowly nodded his head and said, "That was perfect."

I tried not to smirk but failed. "My own personal version of perfect, maybe."

"Why would you settle for anyone else's?"

I answered by kissing him long and deep and hard.

"You thought you lost me, didn't you?"

I swallowed the lump in my throat and looked at my feet. "More than once."

He took my chin gently in his hand and lifted it, until I looked into his eyes. "Wherever you go, I'll be waiting when you get back. I'll even go with you, if you want."

"Even into a psych ward?"

He nodded. "I've been practicing my Napoleon impression, just in case." He stroked my cheek with a finger, and I leaned into it. "This is true love. You think that happens every day?"

"Ah, the wisdom of *The Princess Bride*."

He quirked his eyebrows. "Really? I thought it was Foucault."

"Foucault said it too, but he was talking about his relationship with crypto-normativism."

"I'm going to be completely honest here. I'm not smart enough to get that, but I'll look it up later and record my reaction for you."

I answered with a grin.

"So...are you ready to tell me? Tell me whatever it is you haven't been telling me, that you're worried I'd dump you over."

I looked a question at him, with big saucer eyes for emphasis.

He smiled. "You haven't been hiding it very well. As smart as you are, this thing makes you stupid."

"Okay." I took a deep breath. "The thing is—"

Over his shoulder, I saw Dee pop into existence in a cloud of scattering ash. She waved her hands back and forth in front of each other and said, "Whoa! Whoa! Whoa there! Whatever he says, he's not ready for me. Just let that sit for a while, okay? Trust me!"

Oddly enough, I did. Perhaps it only validated my own anxiety, but I think it was more. I think she meant it. I think she sincerely wanted it to work between David and me.

"Whenever you're ready," David said. "Doesn't have to be tonight, or any particular time."

"My mom died a couple weeks ago," I said, since there wasn't just one thing I wanted to get off my chest. "I didn't go to the funeral. I flew down for it, but I didn't go. I just couldn't, for some reason."

He didn't say anything at first. He just wrapped his arms around me and squeezed, holding me, letting me melt into him. After so long that I wondered if he ever planned to let go, he said, "People grieve in all kinds of strange ways. It doesn't make you a bad person."

And I started to cry, not just because he'd cut to the core of my obsessions over the past two weeks, but because he didn't feel sorry for me while he did it. He was there, he was supportive, he held me and let me feel his warmth, but he didn't slap me with the pity I dreaded so much. He understood, too, that people *need* all kinds of strange things when they're grieving, and he knew my needs without even asking. That was something that Gabby, Michael, or Simon could never seem to manage, as much as they love me.

Dee gave me a thumbs-up and added, "Don't tell him about the woman who'll be in prison for the rest of her life because of you, either. Good-hearted people have the weirdest prejudice against that kind of thing."

I leaned back, looked David in his beautiful brown eyes, and asked, "Would you still love me if I had a horrible, horrible secret, a hundred times worse than not going to my mom's funeral?"

"Yes," he said. I knew he meant it. It was truth absolute. "But that is a hypothetical, isn't it?"

I was a second away from telling him the truth. Every bit of it I knew.

"Don't," Dee said. "He'll stay with you, but he'll never believe you. He'll love you forever, but he'll start to hate you the moment you tell him, and he'll go on hating you until you wise up and go back to lying to him. It doesn't make any sense, but you humans are funny little creatures, aren't you?" And with that, she disappeared in a fine dusting of ash.

"So, how's work?" I asked.

He saw right through me, saw the change of subject for exactly what it was, but he indulged me anyway. He heaved a big sigh and said, "Not great. I had a talk with Debby about her performance lately, and she quit on the spot. Everyone else thinks I fired her."

"She probably told them you did. That's the problem with Debbys. They used to care a lot, so when you point out to them how little they care now, they take it real personally." Shut up, okay? Just don't even. "How's everyone else dealing with it?"

He looked away, guilt written on his face. "They're working harder than ever. They think I'm five minutes from firing all of them."

"Fantastic!"

He looked back to me, one eyebrow arching up.

"See, now you get all the benefits of being a hardass monster of a boss without the stain of actually being one. It's like you got it for free."

He chuckled, obviously unconvinced. "Do you want me to stay tonight?"

"Yes, but it would be weird for Simon." Beside which, if he stayed, I would tell him everything. I knew it.

"I guess so," he said. "But I'd rather stay."

"I'd rather you stay, but there are things that need to be worked out first."

"I understand," he said, and though of course he didn't, the earnest sentiment jabbed at me.

Because I love him, I feel like we're a part of each other even now, and yet I kept a part of me hidden, locked away from him, because to unlock it would destroy us. There was a tourniquet around one of the limbs of our shared being, and behind it the flesh was dead and rotten.

I had to cut it away.

My thoughts weren't quite as coherent in that exact moment, of course. I was still sitting on the couch, staring into space and piecing them together, long after David left me with a kiss and a wan smile cast over his shoulder.

It took, I think, another twenty minutes for Simon to peek around the bedroom door and ask, "Is he gone or what?" His face was reddened, his palms ghostly pale, and he was shivering so hard, I could hear it in his voice.

"Oh, my God," I said, hopping up and rubbing his hands between mine. "Did you not take your coat?"

"I was gonna come back in for it, but after the box incident, it seemed too awkward."

I put an arm around him. "Come on, you beautiful idiot. Let's get you warmed up. How late is that bar open?"

He tried to make a sour face, but the muscles were numb from the cold and he only ended up looking constipated. "I dunno if Jennifer will let us back in," he said.

"She will."

♦

"I haven't been entirely honest with you," I said when we were back at the bar and settled in.

Simon looked at me across the table and burst into giddy, snorting laughter. "Oh, no," he said, and gulped a breath before succumbing to another bout of laughter. "How can I cope with this unprecedented turn of events?"

I took a sip from my old-fashioned and imagined myself stone-faced and impassive. Though, considering how much I'd drunk already, I probably just looked droopy.

"'I haven't been entirely honest with you,'" he said, imitating my voice as he wiped away laughter tears. "Jordan, maybe you should just start every sentence like that?"

"Ha!" Dee said from behind the bar, a good ten feet outside ordinary human earshot. If Simon noticed the peculiarity, he didn't comment on it.

The bar was beginning to bustle at this time of night, so I leaned down to join Simon, close to the tabletop. I asked, "Are you prepared to be shocked?"

"If I was, I wouldn't be. By definition." Simon is the only person I know who becomes smarter when he's drunk. It's fucking irritating.

"Okay, then, shithead. I'll just come out with it. The reason I'm so mad at Jennifer is, she's the devil."

Simon blinked slowly, three times. "Like, literally the devil? Or like Mom?"

"Literally the devil."

Simon glanced at Jennifer née Dee, stuck his lower lip out, and said, "Fuck. I almost hit that."

"Don't sleep with her, whatever you do. Take my word on this." And then my brain caught up. "Wait, you believe me?"

Simon nodded without even reflecting on it. "You have a tell when you're being truthful. The corners of your mouth relax."

"Yeah, but...you believe me?"

He was more annoyed than confused by the question. "Yeah, I do." His annoyance softened into a goofy little smile. "I always believe you when you're telling the truth."

"Okay, but…about *this*?"

He shrugged. "Sis, I've lived in Florida my whole life. This is the weirdest thing I've ever heard, but only just barely. Like, there's a snowbird from Wisconsin in my trailer park who gets abducted by aliens every time he comes down for the winter, but he *keeps coming down for the winter.*"

I don't believe in aliens, but it felt like hypocrisy to turn skeptical all of a sudden. "Do they anal-probe him?" I asked.

"He says they don't, but I wonder."

Dee came over, set another old-fashioned in front of me, another beer in front of Simon, and sat down at the head of the table, right between us. She pulled a bottle of Maker's Mark from her jeans and set it in the middle.

After a moment of uncomfortable silence, the kind that seems to stretch out to minutes of subjective time, Simon asked, "So, you're the devil, huh?"

"Yep," Dee said.

"Can you make fire from your fingertips?"

"Yes," she said, and let pass another uncomfortable silence. "But I won't, because it's tacky." He just kept staring at her, until she sighed and said, "Okay, fine. But you can't let anyone know, okay?"

She glanced around the bar to make sure no one was watching, then set her hand in a fist on the table. A little tongue of flame came out of her thumb, about the size of a cigarette lighter. Simon looked more skeptical of this than he had been of my word on the matter. He examined her hand, and she opened it for his perusal. Once satisfied that the flame couldn't possibly be coming from anywhere, and had to be supernatural, he gave her a nod and asked, "So, what is this? Some kind of Faust thing?" In response to my surprised and impressed expression, he added, "You have to watch the movie if you want to be an admin on the *Ghost Rider* wiki."

Dee scooted her chair over and managed to put an arm around me, because I wasn't fast enough to get away from her. "Jordan and I are friends with benefits," she said.

Simon's eyes opened very wide, just as his face contorted in equal parts horror and discomfort. "Oh," he said.

She shot him a gleaming smile. "But that doesn't mean the two of us can't, you know, have a good time too. Powerful, evil people are invariably bisexual, but I guess you already knew that from television."

"Don't sleep with her," I warned again. "Not even in the same bed. She's very big on technicalities. She'll make you a witch."

"Warlock," Dee corrected. "And I'll tell you what. I'll suspend that rule if your sister joins us. I love threesomes with siblings. It's a back door to outright incest."

"Well, I don't think I have to worry about sleeping with you and becoming a warlock. In fact, that may have ruined sex for me forever." Simon scrunched his nose and unfocused his eyes, as if studying his own soul. "Yeah. Yeah. I'm pretty sure I can never have sex again. And it's not even like I was having much up to now."

"If it helps," I said, "we are *not* friends with benefits. It's closer to babysitting, but babysitting that kid from the *Twilight Zone* who wishes people into the corn."

"That kid had real moxie," Dee said. "He knew what he wanted and he didn't let anyone shame him into accepting less. That's the American dream, right there."

"See? This is what she does." I uncapped the whiskey and refilled my old-fashioned to the top. "She just hangs around, making stupid comments and getting me into trouble. And the worst of it is—"

Simon finished my sentence for me. "You *can't* tell David, but you *have* to tell David." His face fell. "Aw, shit, that's horrible."

I would have leapt up and wrapped him in a ten-minute-long bear hug if Dee hadn't been talking about incest a minute earlier. Instead, I held his off hand in mine—so neither of us would have to stop drinking—and squeezed it tight. No matter how bad things were, at least there was one person in the world who *got* me, who believed me in the face of absolute madness, who understood, who loved and respected me no matter what I did.

"So," Dee said, "do you want to tell him about the innocent woman who's in jail because of you, or should I?"

"Goddamn it."

# 26

Dee became progressively drunker as the night went on.

"Listen, I'mma tell you the thing about God," she said, hours later. She'd just broken down in tears of regret after beating the bar's high score in *Deer Hunter*, and now we were back at our table. I don't know how legitimate her inebriation was—I suspect not very—but I could find no flaw in the act, as she became convincingly maudlin and lurched from topic to topic.

I mentioned as much to Simon, who lifted his head from the table, where he'd set it a moment before, and shouted in a slurred voice, "I'm awake!" He'd gotten sloshed after I told him about the innocent woman's confession, and though he hadn't had a drink in hours, the lingering effects and the lateness of the hour left him more inert than not.

"Shut up!" Dee cried, reaching out to poke his cheek for emphasis but missing. "Shut up! I'mma tell you the thing about God. Lessay God's really real." At this point, she burped up a mouthful of vomit and swallowed it back down. She proceeded to speak with breath so foul, I wondered how a loving God could allow it. "If'n God is real, then the thing you gotta understan' about God is, he just is not very fuckin' bright, is he?"

"Example," Simon said.

"Shut up! Shut up!" After shouting at him, Dee started to cry again, and reached out to pat both his cheeks. "Ah'm sorry. Yer great. I'mma give you an example. Just shut up and I will. I'll give you an example." She stared into space for so long that Simon put his head back down on the table and closed his eyes. "I got it! Tree inna garden. You know about the tree inna garden?"

"You mean the Tree of Knowledge of Good and Evil, in the Garden of Eden?" I'd cut myself off earlier in the night, so I was a little sharper than my drinking companions.

She stared at me with awe and lust. "You so smart and beautiful, Jordan. Okay, okay, shut up. So, here's this tree right? An', an', an' it conveys knowledge of the good and the evil, right? So, so, there's no murder, no war, no genocide, no cheatin' at chess. An' this tree, eatin' a' this tree makes all suffering possible. It's, like, the most dangerous thing God ever created. If ya eat it, it turns paradise into Hell on Earth."

Simon began to snore.

"Shut up!" Dee shouted, waking him. "So, so, first question, right? Why did he even make the damn thing in the first fuckin' place?" She threw her hands dramatically into the air, hitting both me and Simon by accident. "Who the fuck even knows, right? Maybe, maybe he was jus' fuckin' bored one day, an' he was like, 'Oh, there's nothin' on the fuckin'...television, or whatever. I think I'll make, like, a fuckin' doomsday tree with the power to corrupt every good thing I've ever created.' Because, what? Is that fun? How fuckin' drunk did God hafta get, before that seemed like a good idea? Fuckin' drunker than me. 'Cause I'm the motherfuckin' devil, and I'm drunk as shit right now, an' that *still* sounds like the worst idea I ever heard.

"Okay, okay. So, God wakes up the next morning, right? Shut up. God wakes up the next morning with a headache, an' he's like, 'Aw, shit. What, whaddid I do last night? Why is this tree wit' the power to corrupt all a' creation here? Did, did I do that?'"

At those words, Simon perked up and looked at me. Together, we cried out in our best Urkel impressions, "Did I do that?"

"Yeah," Dee said. "'Cept, that was fuckin' God talkin'. So, shut up. So, God's, like, havin' breakfast, an' he keeps lookin' at the tree over his cereal bowl, like, 'Oh, man. What the fuck am I gonna do with this fuckin'...with this fuckin' doomsday tree I made?' So, is he gonna destroy it? No. Is he, is he gonna sink it to the deepest, darkes' depths a' the fuckin' ocean? Nuh-o. Is he gonna seal it inna impenetrable vault and shoot it inta the depths of space? Noooo. He's like... Instead a' that, he's like, 'Oh, fuck, I know. I'll put it in the kids' room.'

"So, he puts it in the fuckin', in the fuckin' garden where his children live, an' he's like, 'Just don't eat the fruit off it.' Can you fuckin' believe that? That's like, if you stuck candy in, like, a hand grenade, an' you handed it to your lil' kids and you were, like, 'Okay, I'mma go to work now an' leave you here alone with this hand grenade. Don't, don't pull the pin out to get the delicious candy, okay?'"

She went silent, as if waiting for agreement.

"Yeah, but," Simon said, sluggishly, "you can't hold God to modern standards of parenting. Those were different times."

"True," I said. "If you left your kids home alone with a doomsday device today, I'm pretty sure you'd get child protective services called on you. That's how we got taken away from Mom."

"She left us with a doomsday device?" Simon said, and blinked several times. "I musta been too young to remember that." He blinked several more times. "What's goin' on outside?"

I looked over my shoulder, at the grey haze hanging in the street. "Sunrise," I said.

"Coffee?" Dee asked, looking infinitely grumpy, as if we'd missed the point of her drunken ramblings.

"Fuck, yes," Simon said.

"I'll take mine with just enough whiskey to keep it from curdling."

As Dee rose and stumbled toward the bar, Simon looked at me strangely.

I shrugged. "Curdling is a side effect of being a witch."

"Oh," he said. "Is it reversible?"

"The curdling, or the being a witch?"

He seemed to reconsider his first answer, then said, "The witch thing. Is there, like, a ceremony?"

"I've been trying to get an exorcism," I said. "That might do it."

He found this confusing, and I don't think that reflects poorly on him. "So, why don't you just get one? Are they booked through the spring or something?"

Dee set a pot of coffee and a third bottle of whiskey on the table, and sat down. I spoke without looking directly at her. "*Someone* keeps interfering. Plus, you need a letter from a psychiatric professional saying it's not the result of a hallucination. That's…tricky, you know? And even if I could find a shrink willing to write that letter, Dee would fuck things up somehow. She always fucks things up."

"So, you're just giving up?"

"No, but…" I trailed off, at a loss for words to describe what I was doing. Mostly because, yeah, I'd pretty much given up.

Simon looked between Dee and me. "So, I just want to be extra, extra clear on this. The real reason you've lost hope is *her*?"

I shrugged but, after some moments' consideration, added, "Yeah."

The word hardly had time to leave my mouth before my brother threw a pot of boiling hot coffee into the devil's face and shouted, "Run!"

♦

I obeyed without thinking, so forceful was my brother's voice and so authoritative the tone. I dashed for the door, a step behind him, as my chair skittered away and fell over from the force of launching myself from it.

I don't remember hearing screams behind me, but that doesn't mean there weren't any. My memory of those seconds has a peculiar hyperfocus to it. I remember every single detail that's physically related to my escape, and absolutely nothing else, with one single exception. As we stepped into the morning light, and as Simon slammed his shoulder back against the door to speed its closing, I caught sight of Dee for just a moment. Half of her face was mottled with bloody red patches, the skin seared and sloughing away in sickening, discolored lumps of dead flesh.

There was pain there. I don't know if it was physical pain, or the pain of anger, or the pain of betrayal, or if it was just another act—a joke in terrible taste, to cap off a week and a half of them.

And then the door was shut, and the reflected morning light blocked the view inside. I tried my best not to feel sympathy for her, if you'll forgive the expression. I really did. I stood there, frozen, doing my best to believe that it was all an act—that she wasn't really in pain.

I think I would have started crying if Simon hadn't grabbed me by the arm and yanked me away. I guess that means there's something wrong with me, huh? Well, shit. You already knew that.

We ran down the street together. I almost stopped at the bus stop, out of reflex born of a hundred hurry-up-and-wait races to work. "Where are we going?" I asked as we crossed the street against the light and were nearly run over by an angry driver.

"Just keep running!" he cried, already out of breath but moving no slower because of it. "We can't stay ahead of her, but we can stay ahead of the fallout from any of the shit she pulls. *TAXI!* Come on, come on, come on!"

The cab pulled up fast but not fast enough for Simon's taste. He threw the door open, stuffed me inside, leapt in after, and slammed it shut. This was so unlike my brother that I thought he might be Dee. But I'd been with him continuously since the day before, so it couldn't be her. But what the hell had gotten into him?

"Start driving!" he said. I don't know if cab drivers get that very often, but this one had at least seen a movie, because he put the gas to the floor and peeled out along Mt. Auburn Street. Of course, he had to slam his foot on the brake a second later when we hit the back end of a traffic jam—because Boston.

"What the hell are we doing?" I asked as I was alternately slammed against the front and back seats, fumbling for the seatbelt.

"Start heading for the West End," he said to the driver. "And stay off the freeways. If I spot you heading for an on-ramp, we're bailing, got it?"

"Simon!" I grabbed him by the shoulder. "What are you doing?"

"We have to stick to surface roads," he whispered, "so we're going slow enough to get out of here if it turns out he's actually Dee. Then we can start running again, or hail a rideshare, or steal a bicycle, or whatever. The critical thing is to stay on the move, and stay ahead of her tricks, and not let her corner us anywhere the cops can catch us, until we've made it to that priest of yours."

I blinked several times, but was otherwise frozen.

"Once we've made it to him," he explained, "you can declare him your spiritual leader or guider or whatever. Then, when the authorities show up—"

"*When* the authorities show up?"

"Jordan," he said, patiently, "I just threw boiling hot coffee in the devil's face."

My eyes grew wider, between blinks, as the full implications of the devil's anger settled onto me.

"It's fine, it's fine. I have a plan." When he said it out loud, he seemed as surprised as I was.

"When the hell have you ever had a plan for anything?"

"I dunno," he said. "Maybe I've been saving it up?" He shook the confusion out of his head and went on, rattling off points like he was the male lead of an Aaron Sorkin drama. "Once we make it to that priest and you declare him your spiritual leader, even if Dee keeps us from doing the exorcism today, he's our advocate, officially. That's the First Amendment, right? He can vouch for us to the authorities. He can get private visits with you in the psych hospital, which means sooner or later, we'll manage to get you an exorcism. Once that's done, once Dee is out of the picture, it's just a matter of being on your best behavior for a few months and they'll have to let you out, right?"

"But Father Cunningham won't do the exorcism without a letter from a shrink. That's a hard rule, and it comes straight from the Vatican. Even if I showed him I could curdle milk, I'd still need that letter!"

Simon grinned a little. "So, show him the documents from your hearing at the hospital. They're in your e-mail on your phone, right? They clear you from needing in-patient treatment."

I blinked several times. "That's not the same thing!"

He grinned more. "So what? He's a priest. What the fuck does he know about this?"

"Holy shit, you're right. That's brilliant! Simon, when did you work all this out?"

"When Dee was telling that stupid story about the Garden of Eden. I was only pretending to be drunk." He wobbled a little. "Well, half-pretending."

I wrapped him up in my arms and squeezed tight. I started crying, I was so touched that he'd thought of all this, and so proud that he *could* think of all this. "I love you," I said.

"Shut up," he said. He started to tear up, too. "Shit. I love you too, *I guess.*"

◆

On the way, I called ahead, while Simon kept his phone open to a rideshare app, in case a Dee-related emergency forced us to switch vehicles. Father Cunningham was already awake, even at this early hour, and if anything, he was more alert than usual. He agreed to meet us in his office, with everything we'd need for an exorcism, and he agreed—way too enthusiastically, really—to stop at nothing until that exorcism was complete, even if social workers, mental hospitals, and the cops got involved.

Traffic was completely stalled on Storrow Drive, and even though we could literally see the spire of the church from there, the driver got lost trying to find an alternate route—because Boston. So, we paid him, got out, and resorted to running straight through a building and out the back door. We got to Cambridge Street, cut across to New Chardon, then realized we were farther from the church than when we'd started running—because Boston. We did, however, have a straight shot to our destination, so we hailed another cab and were about to climb in when I noticed a peculiar pattern of coffee stains on the driver's top.

"Stop!" I cried. "It's Dee!"

"Shit," the driver said, the image of him changing to Dee's in a moment. Her face was untouched and perfect.

Something was still wrong. I narrowed my eyes at her coffee-stained Metallica T-shirt. She'd been wearing something else back at the bar—a blouse, I think.

Noticing my attention, she snorted. "What? You think you're the only assholes who ever threw hot coffee in my face?" She picked at the shirt, shaking her head. "And on laundry day, too."

We ran for it. Simon hailed a rideshare, but we moved so fast, we were only a block from the church by the time the car was there. The driver figured out it was us just as we reached the church. He rolled alongside with the window down, making rude gestures and screaming something about a one-star rating.

Dee was waiting for us on the steps of the church. She stood with her arms crossed over her chest, making a stern expression at me. "You're not going to get away with this," she said. "That old shit may start an exorcism, but he won't finish it. Not again."

Simon and I were both exhausted, but hearing those last two words put fresh energy into us. We pounded up the steps.

"In fact," Dee said, and got no farther before Simon slammed into her. Even tired, even going up steps, he rallied enough strength to push her bodily off the ground and slam her into a stone column.

Dee, as near as I could tell, was taken entirely by surprise. She let out a windy gasp and crumpled, wheezing, to roll down the steps to the sidewalk.

And, even though the coffee attack had invoked sympathy in me, this one made me smile. Maybe she'd pissed me off that much in the interim, or maybe television has just desensitized me to blunt-force injuries.

Father Cunningham was waiting on the other side of the doors. He locked them after we were in, for all the good that would do. "What was the commotion out there?" he asked.

Simon, grinning despite the sweat pouring off of him, smiled and said, "I body-checked the devil."

The priest's face went blank as he said, "Okay."

"This is my brother, Simon," I said.

"Okay."

"Simon, this is Father Cunningham."

"Okay," Simon said.

As much as that failed to fill me with confidence, I looked the priest hard in the eyes and said, "Father, I know I ran out before, but that's because the devil tricked me, messed with my head. She'll do it again. She might even send social workers to cart me away. Please, don't give up on me until it's done."

Dee appeared behind him, and spoke in perfect synchronicity with his "Okay." She smirked. "I love, by the way, that I've got you believing the social workers are on my side. There's an ironic beauty to that, isn't there?"

"Is the demon here?" the priest asked, apparently noticing my attention.

"Right behind you," I said.

"Then we must hurry." He began shuffling out of the narthex and down a hallway, at a pace I wouldn't exactly describe as hurried. "I have everything ready. You have the proof that it's not a hallucination?"

"Right here," I said, digging out my phone.

"Okay, good," he said, as we went down a hallway. I brought the documents up and he perused them as we walked. He seemed only interested in confirming that my name and the name of a psychiatric professional were there, and that the gist of the report didn't tend toward me being irredeemably insane. Simon was right. He was a priest, not a psychologist.

I lost track of Dee, then saw her waiting ahead, leaning inside a doorway along the hall. She said, "Somewhere deep inside of you, you know this isn't going to happen—now or ever."

"I'm not going to let you sabotage me again," I said, as I passed her.

She was at the next doorway, too. "I'm not going to sabotage anything." She pronounced "sabotage" as "sabotaaazh," like in that outtake where William Shatner is yelling at some poor sound engineer because he's insecure about his weird Canadian pronunciation. "I didn't do anything to sabotage you the last time. I didn't make your boyfriend call you, Jordan. I only told you the consequences of ignoring him." A sly and truly devilish smile formed on her lips. "Besides, I don't have to sabotage this exorcism. Know why? Because you're going to sabotage it yourself."

Father Cunningham, to his credit or detriment, was unfazed by my conversation with someone he couldn't see or hear. He didn't even look up when I screamed down the corridor, "For God's sake, stop saying *sabotage!*" He just kept walking, and scanning my documents.

Dee shook her head and answered, "Racist."

We went down a set of narrow stairs, to a basement stuffed with boxes of candles, feast day banners, vestments, and other Catholic paraphernalia. The priest led us through a gap between piles of boxes, to another, smaller basement room.

There was a window high on the wall that would have looked out at ankle level to the sidewalk outside if it hadn't been bricked up and painted over. There was one chair, one lightbulb on a wire overhead, and a portable cabinet in the corner—Father Cunningham's exorcism kit, I thought.

"What an excellent day for an exorcism," Dee said, already in the room. She frowned as she looked around. "Terrible place, though." She pointed at the bricked-up window. "How's that supposed to work when he jumps out of it?"

Father Cunningham looked at Simon and said, "Close the door. No one will hear us in here."

Simon obeyed, albeit hesitantly. "What does that mean?" he asked.

"It means I have to suffer to rid myself of her." I smiled reassuringly and put a hand on his shoulder. "We have to make me an undesirable host so she'll *want* to leave."

Simon gulped. "Does that mean…"

"Your sister is fertile soil for the devil and all his demons," Father Cunningham said, less reassuringly. "We must turn that soil bitter. It's a painful process, okay? She has to want it enough to suffer for it."

"I want it that much and more."

"We'll see about that," Dee said.

"Sit," the priest said. When I complied, his inevitable "Okay" was strangely comforting. And I sure needed the comfort, because he handed back my phone and walked behind me, and the next thing I heard was the cabinet opening. I'd done my research, so I knew what might be in there. Traditionally, making a person's soil unfertile involved many of the same implements the Inquisition used to extract confessions.

I clutched the handrests on the chair, knowing that in a minute I might be tied to it. I heard the clinking of metallic instruments behind me. If I turned my head far enough, I might get a look at them, but I didn't want to. I closed my eyes instead and braced myself for the ordeal to come.

I winced as my face was peppered with the icy, sharp touch of…water? I opened my eyes to see Father Cunningham, holding a Bible in one hand

and an aspergillum—you know, one of those little holy-water maracas—in the other. He splashed me again and said, "Confess your sins."

"What?" I asked, incredulous.

Dee laughed. "Fucking Catholics, am I right?"

Father Cunningham repeated himself, screaming the words now, "Confess your sins! Cleanse yourself of evil so that the Lord may take root in your heart, and your soul become unfertile soil for the evil one!"

I stared blankly. "And…then after that we do the pincers and the red-hot pokers?"

"Why would you ask for them?" Simon cried.

The priest looked aghast and more than a little insulted. "No, child. Pain won't purify you. Your soul can't be redeemed with pain. Some terrible sin weighs on you. That is why the devil can abuse you, manipulate you, come inside you."

Dee snorted. "I wish." She looked at the priest and pointed a thumb at me, though he couldn't see it. "This one's ice-cold."

"Ew," Simon said.

"Shit!" I slumped my shoulders and shook my head. "You mean, all this time, all I had to do was confess that I didn't go to my mother's funeral?"

Dee was still looking at the priest. She turned to me and said, nonchalantly, "Oh, sorry, did you say something?"

Simon scrunched his lips up. "I don't think that was it."

"But that's when she showed up! That's when she first appeared to me! That has to be it!"

"Okay," Father Cunningham said, in a tone that belied the answer.

"Are you sure you don't have a set of pincers in there?" I asked. "Maybe at the bottom of a drawer?"

He shook his head.

I growled. "I'll lend you my tweezers, then! For God's sake, man, this confession thing isn't working!"

Dee's lips parted into a wide, toothy smile as she knelt down next to me and put an arm around my shoulders. "That's because you haven't made the confession. I already told you. I came to you after the funeral because you needed me. If I'd wanted to, if you'd needed it, I could have appeared long, long before that."

"Oh, God." My skin prickled with goosebumps, and not because of the renewed splash of holy water Father Cunningham was throwing at me. "No, no, no, no," I said, staring straight at Dee with pleading eyes.

"Yes, yes, yes, yes," she answered.

I swallowed hard and looked at Simon. "Leave the room."

"Nooooooope," Dee said.

The priest, too, shook his head. "That won't do. Not if it's weighing so heavily on your soul, okay? I can take your confession in private, if you wish, but the deeper stain won't come out if you're hiding it from those you love most."

"Listen!" I barked, lashing out reflexively against the stinging pain of what I had to do. "Is the thing on my soul a root, a weight, a stain, or what? This metaphor is just sloppy! Very, very sloppy! Jesus wouldn't stand for this kind of sloppiness. Because there's a guy who knew his parables, goddamn it! While we're confessing shit, why don't you confess that you can't stick to one fucking analogy?"

Father Cunningham recoiled at the ferocity of my voice. But he steeled himself and leaned in to splash more holy water in my face. "Okay," he said. "I think we're close."

Dee started to laugh.

"What?" I asked, whipping my head round to stare daggers at her.

"I just realized," she said, speaking between guffaws. "I just realized! You told this old bat to keep trying to exorcise you, no matter what. So, after you sabo… Sorry. After you fail yourself—eh, ya hoser, for sure—he's going to keep bugging you for the rest of his life!" Her laughter intensified until she doubled over with it.

# 27

So, the thing is, I haven't been entirely honest with you.

I know, I know.

What I mean is, I haven't been honest with you for a long time. In fact, I think it's impossible for me to be honest about this. I don't have it in me. So let's do it this way: let me tell you a story about a girl named Jordan.

Jordan was young and stupid, and her mother was also young and stupid. Jordan's mother was a drug addict. Her father was a drug dealer. He was her mother's drug dealer, in fact, and when Jordan's mother had been short of cash, she'd offered him payment in other ways. And that's the story of how Jordan came along.

So far, none of this is very unusual by the standards of Central Florida, where Jordan and her mother lived. And maybe what comes next isn't so unusual either. I don't know. I can't look into the souls of other people. I can't tell you what's in their hearts. For all I know, everyone on Earth might be the same kind of monster Jordan is. Perhaps that's why people are so mistrusting of each other: because they know what kind of evil shit their fellow humans might *also* be hiding inside themselves.

Sorry. I got off track. This is a story about Jordan.

Jordan was seventeen. Her mother was thirty-two. The story begins at the end of a bad week for Jordan's mom and everyone around her. She'd lost her job as a bartender. The owners caught her accepting shots in lieu of cash tips—which was against bar policy—and taking free shots on top of that—which was, you know, theft.

With her primary source of both money and alcohol gone, Jordan's mother was starved for downers. The first couple days, she dealt with this by sleeping most of the time and begging Jordan for money. By midweek, however, she couldn't sleep at all, so she dealt with it by sitting in front of the television and begging Jordan for money. By Friday, she was so desperate, she started begging Simon for money, but of course he didn't have any, and Jordan's mother had already pawned Simon's PlayStation a few months earlier.

On Saturday, Jordan was worn down by her mother's constant, annoying pleas for money. She gave in, because she was young and stupid. Despite being informed enough to quote you the exact definition of *enabler*, she didn't have the true appreciation for its meaning that she'd gain in the years to come.

So, Jordan cashed her paycheck from the grocery store instead of putting it into the special account where she was saving money for college. She offered her mother fifty dollars of it but ended up giving her the entire thing, right down to the cent, as she'd somehow known she would all along, deep in her heart.

Which is not to say that Jordan *planned* her mother's overdose. Not...exactly. But then, it didn't come as very much of a surprise, did it? Put an addict into the deepest throes of withdrawal, keep her there for a week, then give her nearly two hundred dollars, and the result is predictable.

Jordan had to work Saturday night, so she never found out what her mother bought with the money. There would have been pills, of course, but their exact makeup would depend on what was on tap across town. And there'd be vodka. Cheap vodka was always in the mix. Whether her mother shot up, Jordan didn't know, because her mother had a tiny grain of common sense hidden away in some corner of her brain, and she always injected herself where an employer couldn't see the marks.

When Jordan came home, she didn't know if her mother was alive or dead. In the pale light of the television, her body was stretched out and motionless in her ratty old recliner. Jordan crept in and put down her backpack. Her quiet, slow steps might have been mistaken for politeness— as if she was trying not to wake her mother—but, in truth, they were born of trepidation. She knelt next to her and couldn't see any sign that she was breathing.

Tears were already forming in Jordan's eyes. She worked up the nerve to reach out and shake her mother's shoulder.

She woke with a snort, then a cry of alarm. At first, Jordan's mother thought she was somewhere else, and it terrified her. It terrified her all the more because she was too heavily drugged to get up from the recliner. "Jordan, get me out of here!" she screamed, her voice distorted and slurred. More so than usual, even.

"Mom, you're safe, you're safe!" Jordan shook her. She didn't even have to grab on, because her mother was already clutching at her arms. "You're safe. Chill the fuck out. Jesus. Calm down."

"Oh, God," she said. "I was dreaming I fell asleep at your dad's house." Jordan was at real risk of feeling sympathy for her mother at that moment.

But then her mother went and ruined it. "You know you lived there for a while, when you were little," she said.

Sympathy gone. "I thought I lived with Grandma when I was little," Jordan said, carefully modulating the tone of her voice so it wouldn't reveal her feelings on the matter and so give her mother advance warning of how unwise it was to keep talking.

Jordan's mother wore a goofy grin, unaware of what she was doing. "This was before that. Grandma wanted you, but I wouldn't give you to her, because she was being such a bitch about it. She didn't take you until you were, I dunno, at least a year old."

"Uh-huh," Jordan said. "That makes sense. So, you lived with a baby at Dad's house." In the vernacular of the time, *house* wasn't an accurate description of the structure in question. *Den* would have been the more common usage.

"No, we just left you there," Jordan's mother said, then laughed like a maniac. She pawed at Jordan's face and added, "Don't be mad. Don't be mad, sweetie. Don't be mad at me, baby doll."

"I'm not mad," Jordan said, doing her best to smile.

In the faint light, with her mother half-comatose, it was enough to convince her. She patted Jordan on the cheek and slumped deeper into the recliner. She closed her eyes but kept on talking. "Nobody liked you," she said, her voice a slurred babble. "*Nobody* liked you. You cried all the time. All the fucking time. You never stopped crying. I tried everything to make you stop—*everything*—but nothing worked. Everyone in the house complained. Goddamn, why didn't you ever stop crying?"

"I can't imagine," Jordan said. "Maybe I was teething?"

"Nah, your teeth didn't start to come in until you'd been at Grandma's a while."

"Uh-huh." Jordan was no expert in pediatrics, but she suspected that this was a very late age for a baby to start teething.

"You never stopped crying, and I hated you for it. I got so angry. *I hated you so much.*"

Jordan fell backward, tripping over her own legs to land in the carpet. Her mother opened her eyes again. She didn't look away from the television, however, and so didn't appreciate the effect her confession had on her daughter. Jordan, however, had learned much about suppressing sadness and rage in her seventeen years, and she recovered herself admirably. In a voice so flat you would never guess it was so much as perturbed, she said, "Tell me more."

"Like what, baby doll?"

Jordan shrugged. "How long did you leave me there?"

Her mother blew a breath between her lips, flapping them. "I dunno," she said. She said it with so much mockery. She said it like it was a stupid question, and stupider still to expect her to have the slightest idea how long she left a baby, alone, inside a drug den. "We just wanted to have fun, you know?" She slumped even deeper into the chair. "We just wanted to have fun. You understand."

"I understand," Jordan said, her voice wavering as she shivered. "You said you tried everything to make me stop crying. What all did you try?"

Her mother was strangely silent, having been so forthcoming until now.

"Mom? What did you try to make me stop crying?"

Her mother winced. "I...I dunno," she said. "I think maybe you had a rash or something." Her composure shifted instantly, and she gave a hooting laugh. "We maybe didn't change your diaper as much as we should have. We didn't know, sweetie. We didn't know how to take care of a baby."

"So, that's when Grandma took me?"

Jordan's mother laughed again. "No. That's a funny story. Did I not ever tell you this one?"

"Not that I recall."

"Oh, God," Jordan's mother said, barely able to start for the sputtering laughter she couldn't contain. "She kept askin' to see you. Like, every day she called, so we'd get back home and everyone would be like, 'Hey, get your mom to stop calling here.' So, I finally took you over to see her, and she's...she's so negative, you know? She's like, 'Oh, this is wrong. And that's wrong. And everything you're doing is wrong.' I can never do anything right in her eyes."

"She sets unreasonable standards," Jordan said.

"So, I was asleep on her couch, and your grandma, your bitch grandma, she *took you*. She took you and went to a goddamn doctor."

"What a thoughtless woman."

"And she came back, and I woke up, and I was so mad. And she's just saying nothing but nasty things about me, and telling me I'm worthless, and yelling at me, and stuff like, 'The doctor said Jordan's gonna die if she stays with you.' Like the doctor would even say that, right? Like he'd say it in those words?"

"How absurd."

"An' I'm gettin' ready to leave, and I go to take you, and she looks me in the eye, and she's so ice-cold, she's so angry, and she says, 'You are not leaving here with that baby.' That's what she said. She said, 'You are not leaving here with that baby.' What a bitch, right?"

"Bless you, Grandma."

"Wha'?"

"I said, 'Fuck you, Grandma.'"

The hilarity of that was too much for Jordan's mother. She fell back into peals of laughter, unable to go on. Jordan took the opportunity to retrieve the remote from her mother's fingers. She turned off the television, then sat back on the carpet.

"Turn the TV back on, sweetie," her mother said.

Jordan didn't move.

"Baby doll, are you there? I wanna see the end. That guy was about to eat Ray Liotta's brain."

Jordan didn't say a word. She sat in the dark, waiting.

And sure enough, her mother fell asleep. Removing the stimulus of the television was all it took. And as the vodka and the pills—and maybe more—worked their downer magic, her breathing grew slower and shallower. With the TV off, Jordan could hear each breath quite clearly. Though, as the time ticked by, she had to creep closer and closer to the recliner to detect the faint wheeze that still rattled through her mother's windpipe.

Finally, it was gone, and no sound was apparent even with Jordan's ear nearly touching her mother's lips. That's when Simon walked out of his bedroom and turned on the light. He stood in his boxer shorts, looking between Jordan and their mother. "What the hell's happening?" he asked, his adolescent voice breaking into a croak on the last word.

Jordan blinked away the dazzling brightness of the sudden light, leapt to her feet, and said, "Mom isn't breathing. Call 911! Quick!"

# 28

"Good God in Heaven," Dee said. "I can't believe you actually did it."

The priest was as unfazed as ever. He takes confessions in Boston, so I guess he's used to this kind of thing.

Simon, on the other hand, bore the confused resentment of a kicked puppy. "You saved her life that night," he said. "You gave her CPR until the ambulance came. I wouldn't have known what to do if you weren't there."

"What a hero," Dee said. "It's a wonder you didn't get your picture in the newspaper. Then again, I suppose they only do that for people who save accountants or airline pilots."

"You're babbling," I said. "Nervous?"

As the priest yammered in Latin, Dee crossed her arms and looked hard at me. "Yes, actually. I'm nervous you're about to do something very, very stupid. *Again.*"

I didn't answer, not because I didn't have a quip to throw back at her but because I thought it impolite to ignore the priest. It wasn't because I didn't have a quip.

The priest switched to English. "Do you have true regret for your sin?"

I was silent a while as I searched myself for the answer. It's not that I was unsure. I just wanted to be honest. I didn't want to give an automatic reply, which on reflection I might doubt. And it wasn't because I was worried the magic hokum wouldn't work without sincerity. I just really, truly wanted to regret it. Moreover, I wanted to be the kind of person who'd regret it.

I found, to my surprise, that I was. I think I'd gradually come to regret what I did that night, over the years—so slowly I didn't even notice. The very fact that I had to think about it, however, was another crushing blow to Simon. That was when he started to cry.

"I do," I finally said. "I do regret it."

Father Cunningham, who had been standing patiently through my self-reflection, nodded and said, "Okay."

Dee pantomimed strangling him.

"And there must be penance," the priest said.

I nodded, imagining myself saying about a billion Hail Marys for the rest of my life.

"You must be baptized, come to Mass, confess your sins, and receive the sacred Communion."

"Ha!" Dee cried. "Told you!"

The priest went on, "Every week, for the rest of your days."

*Oh, come on!* What was this shit? But other people did it and survived, so I guessed I could. "I will."

"Okay," he said. He went back into Latin for a while, before cutting in with "I absolve you from your sins in the name of the Father, and of the Son, and of the Holy Spirit!" He crossed himself.

I glanced at Dee, who did not look happy, but who was still as annoying as she was visible.

"Okay," Father Cunningham said, and took a deep breath. He took a crucifix from his portable cabinet and refilled the aspergillum with holy water.

He stood in front of me and stared hard into my eyes—harder than I'd imagined he was capable of. The fucker brought his A game. He shoved the crucifix into my face, splashed holy water on me, and began to chant. His prayer switched from Latin to English without interruption, perhaps for emphasis, or perhaps because he'd forgotten some of his Latin over the years.

"Behold the cross of the Lord!" he said, shoving it closer to my face, until my nose was against Jesus's crotch. Always with Jesus's crotch.

"In the name and by the power of our Lord Jesus Christ!" He made the sign of the cross in front of me with the crucifix and threw more holy water. "May you be snatched away and driven from this Church of God, and from this woman who was made to the image and likeness of God!"

At this point, I was expecting another comment about my weight from Dee. But when I looked, she wasn't saying anything. She was just staring at me and looking...uncomfortable. It was unnerving, because while I'd seen her angry, and I'd seen her in pain, I'd never seen this.

"Most cunning serpent! You shall no longer..." His voice turned to a croak. When I looked back to him, he was staring straight at Dee, as if he could see her. The terror in his eyes confirmed it. She was visible to him. He swallowed hard and, though shaking with fear, steeled himself at the sight of her. "You shall no longer dare to deceive us!" he screamed.

There was more Latin as he turned toward her and advanced, crucifix held before him like a shield. Dee stood her ground, though she eyed him with trepidation.

"God the Father commands you!" cried the priest. "God the Son commands you!" He made the sign of the cross in front of her, and she recoiled. "God the Holy Ghost commands you!" Another sign of the cross.

Dee took a step back.

"Christ, God's word made flesh, commands you!" Another two signs of the cross, and another two steps. Now Dee was standing in the corner. I could see sweat glistening on her face.

More Latin. "The Sacred Sign of the Cross commands you!" She pushed herself back against the walls and covered her face with her hands when next he shot a sign of the cross at her. He followed it up with a volley of holy water, which made her hiss in pain. I thought I saw a faint light shining from somewhere in the room.

"Jordan, tell him to stop!" she said in a whimper. "It hurts!"

I didn't dare say anything. I'm not sure I'd have been able to, even if I had the courage. Simon, however, gave a snort and answered her with "Like hell."

"The Glorious Mother of God, the Virgin Mary, commands you!"

More Latin, more holy water, more signs of the cross, and now Dee was screaming.

"The faith of Holy Apostles Peter and Paul commands you!"

Shit, she sure had a lot of people commanding her. And now I was certain of that light. It was coming from the old priest's crucifix. Dee pressed herself tighter and tighter into the corner.

"The blood of the Martyrs commands you!"

He was all up in her grill now, holy water flying.

"BEGONE, SATAN!" he cried, and shoved the crucifix right against her face. The flesh there didn't sizzle. Yeah, I'd been expecting it to sizzle, too, but it didn't. She reacted like it had, though. She screamed in agony and crumpled to the floor, curling herself into a ball.

"Give place to Christ!" the priest said, and pressed the crucifix against the back of her neck. "Stoop beneath the all-powerful hand of God!"

Stoop she did, and the light from the crucifix increased until it dazzled the eyes and hid every detail around it. I had to turn away, but as I did, I saw that the old priest had his face turned firmly toward her, enduring the brilliant light with a will that I couldn't muster.

I could still hear him. His voice was clear as day, even over Dee's screams. "O Lord, hear my prayer! God of heaven, hear my prayer! Deliver us by thy power from all the tyranny of the evil one! From her snares and her furious wickedness! Grant us thy powerful protection, that we may serve thee in peace and crush all enemies of the church!"

And suddenly, the light was gone. When I looked, so was Dee. No hellfire rising from above, no smoke, not even her customary dusting of ash was left behind to show she'd ever been there.

Father Cunningham turned to look at me, panting for breath. I know what he was thinking. He was wondering if that really just happened or if it was all some kind of hallucination. Well, it wasn't. I knew it was real. Waffles, remember?

Finally, Simon broke the silence with "Amen."

I echoed him, and so did the priest, albeit a little numbly. "Okay," he said, after a few more seconds. Simon and I echoed, "Okay," as if it were part of the rite.

◆

"You really gonna go to church every Sunday?" They were the first words Simon had spoken since boarding the bus.

"Sure," I said, trying to get comfortable in the plastic seat. "That was the penance, right? I'm not going to risk Dee coming back."

He was silent for an entire block, then his face quirked. "Is that the rule, though? Fail the penance, lose the forgiveness? Or is there wiggle room?"

"I should look into that," I said. "Maybe I just have to do my best. If I miss a week here and there due to unavoidable circumstances…"

"Like a hangover?"

"Or, you know, whatever."

Silence again, all the way to Harvard Station, and halfway down Mt. Auburn Street. On the way to the exorcism, we'd been buzzing with energy, making plans and working out every possible contingency. What we'd do if it worked. What we'd do if it didn't work. What we'd do if it was interrupted by the authorities. We stood poised for every possibility, ready to leap into action and set right everything that had gone wrong. Now all of those plans, and all the energy behind them, had turned to dust and blown away. I didn't know what I was going to do about that tweaker woman rotting in jail, what I was going to do for a job, how I was going to follow the regimen that kept me out of the mental hospital—I'd already missed a group therapy session. We'd made plans to deal with all of that, but now I couldn't remember any of the details.

They were all lost in the shadow of the plan I'd never made and didn't know how to begin: the plan that would get Simon to forgive me.

When the bus stopped to drop off passengers at Arsenal Street, I noticed white flakes drifting on the breeze. "Hey, look," I said, nudging Simon. "First snow of the year."

He twisted in his seat to look out the window, his eyes widening for just a few seconds. Then he slumped back down.

"Is this the first time you've seen snow?"

"Yeah," he said.

He said nothing more until we reached Watertown. "This is our stop," I said, getting up.

We got out, crossed Mt. Auburn, and walked slowly along the sidewalk to my apartment. Simon made a sullen, listless attempt at catching a snowflake on his tongue and was hardly disappointed when he failed.

Back home, I turned on the heat while he turned on the television and fell into the couch. He put the volume all the way up to drown out the semi-regular squeaks, thumps, and moans coming from the ceiling. It seemed that my upright, moral Christian neighbor upstairs was having some of the wildest and most energetic sex I'd ever heard.

"Well, at least someone's having a good day," I said, sitting at the edge of the couch's arm rest. I didn't want to commit to sitting down next to Simon, in case it made him uncomfortable. "Do you hate me?"

"Yes," he said, with no real force but with so much conviction, and with so little need for reflection, that I nearly fell over.

"Listen," I said, "I'm, like, eighty percent sure Mom was trying to kill herself that night, anyway. It's not like I gave her those pills. It's not like I made her take them."

"You didn't do anything to stop her," he said, staring hard at the television. I didn't notice what was on, and I'm not sure he did either. "By the time I was your age, I was stopping her from doing that."

I wanted to have sympathy, but that was too much. "Oh, were you?"

He sniffed. "Sometimes. When I could. When I found her stash. I definitely wasn't giving her money to overdose, then sitting there, doing nothing while her lungs stopped working. I was trying to help. I *tried*, at least."

"I tried too, until that night," I said.

It wasn't a lie. I really did try. I always try. I try with every goddamn ounce of strength I've got. I chain myself to hope, and for a while I'll do just about anything in pursuit of that hope. It's only that, after a while— after I've lost hope—I stop trying altogether and wait for the refreshing freedom that failure brings. If it's hope that chains me, it's failure that sets me free.

I wish I'd said that to Simon.

I didn't, of course. I didn't have the words then. Only now, when it's too late, have I managed to put it all into something that, I think, sort of makes sense.

At the time, I expressed those thoughts thus: "I really, really, really tried, Simon. You have to believe me."

"I don't," he said.

"Why not?"

If that question accomplished nothing else, it at least gave him a laugh.

"Ha! Where do you get off asking that? You lie about everything, Jordan! When the fuck are you not lying?"

"You have to believe me about this," I said, clinging once again to hope if not to any sort of eloquence.

"You know, Jordan, there was one time when I thought I saw the real you."

*Aw, fuck.*

"That night, you were perfect. You were pushing on her chest so hard, it broke three of her ribs, and I thought you were doing it too hard, I thought you were hurting her, but then the paramedic got there and he said that was what saved her. You had these little stick arms, you needed help lifting a bag of groceries, but somehow you pushed hard enough to break her ribs, and that's what saved her."

"Simon…"

"And I thought that was the real you. I thought I finally saw past all the layers of bullshit you wrapped yourself up in, to the real Jordan Liang."

"Simon…"

"Shut up!" It was the first time he raised his voice since leaving the church, and the sound pierced me. "It was all a show." He finally turned his eyes on me, and they finished the job his words had started. I wanted to drop dead right there. "All a show so I wouldn't know what a fucking monster you are—so I wouldn't know that you're bullshit all the way to the core."

He took some time to catch his breath, blow his nose, recover from his shaking.

"So, yeah," he said. "I hate you. And I'll always hate you. That doesn't mean I don't love you, but I definitely hate you." He turned his eyes back on the television. "It's all very confusing, okay? Could you give me some time to figure it out?"

"Yeah, sure," I said, and retreated to my bedroom.

I knew exactly what he meant, by loving me and hating me at the same time. They're not mutually exclusive, you know. They're not exclusive at all. I didn't know that at seventeen, but I know it now.

# 29

I tried to sleep. God knows I needed it.

Of course, I couldn't. Not with Simon's words buzzing through my head, and the sounds of carnal debauchery coming through the ceiling.

At least it gave me time to think, lying there in fitful unrest. I wondered if Simon was right. Did anyone really know me? Or did they just know the layers of lies I'd built up to hide myself? Was there anything left of me under them, or was I just one big shit golem?

Whatever I was, I had to come clean about Dee. Because there was either something left of Jordan or there wasn't. If there was, then perhaps I could find her by getting into the habit of telling the truth. And if there wasn't? Well, in that case, what did it matter?

So, I chained myself to hope again, maybe for the last time, and texted David, Gabby, and Michael, asking them to come over after work. I told them to bring lots of alcohol. This was going to be a confession, not a fucking intervention, right?

As the hour approached, I made coffee, poured myself a cup, and took a hesitant sip. It was perfect. It was over-roasted and the beans were stale from being in my cabinet so long, but it was perfect. I drank it down by gulps, not even waiting for it to cool, then poured another cup.

With coffee on my side, I could do this.

I stepped into the living room, where Simon was still on the couch, playing a mindless beat-'em-up video game—the one I played when I was too stressed to think and just needed to mash buttons and thrash thousands of mooks so I could chill out.

He looked up as I entered, leaving his well-muscled hero to be ganged up on and overwhelmed. "Hey," he said.

"Hey," I said back. "Wanna play co-op?"

"Not really."

"Okay." I looked at my feet. "David and Gabby and Michael are coming over. I'm going to tell them about Dee."

He arched an eyebrow, his forehead wrinkling right up to his hairline, halfway across his scalp.

"I'll tell them the truth. Most of it. That I was talking to the devil for a while, but that I'm taking something to keep the voice away, and it's working."

"A weekly pill?"

I laughed softly. "Yeah, I guess. Better to not go into details, or Gabby will have a fit."

"Don't you think they're going to notice where you go every Sunday morning?"

"David will," I said. "But he's cool."

"Okay," Simon said, and went back to the game.

It was David who got there first. He must have left work early, to make such good time from downtown Boston. As soon as I opened the door, he wrapped me up in his arms, held me tight, and kissed me deep and hard.

"You okay?" he said when we finally separated.

I smiled. "I am now."

"This is Simon? Hey, Simon."

Simon didn't respond. He was fixated on the screen, ignoring both of us. It was as if, because of his trauma that morning, he'd experienced some reversion to childhood, and now he was the little kid who sat, playing video games and making an awkward nuisance of himself whenever I had friends over.

Not half as much of an awkward nuisance as what was going on upstairs, mind you. "Is there a limit to the number of orgasms a woman can have in a day?" Michael asked when he and Gabby arrived together, and I told them how long it had been going on.

I smirked. "I think that might be exactly what she's trying to find out. You know, for science."

"We should have been scientists," Gabby said.

"Isn't a sociologist a type of scientist?" David asked.

"God, I hope so," Michael answered, staring contemplatively at the ceiling.

"You both brought booze?" I asked them.

Gabby and Michael held up their bottles.

"Good. Start drinking. You'll be glad you did."

"So, what about you?" Michael asked, with his usual concern. Bless him.

I held up my coffee cup. "David already took care of me."

Gabby waggled her eyebrows.

"In terms of, you know, alcohol." In fact, I think there was as much whiskey as coffee in my mug. He'd asked me to say *when*, and I hadn't until the cup was near to overflowing.

"Ugh," Simon grunted from the couch. He made it sound like a reaction to something in the game, but I'd learned to see through that many years earlier.

"Let's, uh, talk in the kitchen."

Talk we did. I spilled almost everything. I filled Gabby and Michael in on everything about my mom and the funeral, and almost suffocated in all the supportive hugs I got.

And then, the main event. I let them know I talked to the devil, that I'd sincerely believed that I'd talked to the devil, and that I *still* sincerely believed that I had talked to the devil. Pretty ballsy of me, right? Of course, I went on to explain that I wasn't *currently* talking to the devil, nor did I currently believe I could talk to the devil, nor did I believe that it was rationally possible to talk to the devil. When this was met with confusion, I explained that such contradictory patterns of belief are a common element of psychosis. All of which is absolutely true, so you can hardly accuse me of lying to them.

You can maybe accuse me of leaving them with the wrong impression, since they all left believing that, somewhere deep down, in the most rational parts of my mind, part of me knew it was all a hallucination. If they'd seen the waffles, maybe it would be different, you know?

Which, come on, even if you're committed to the whole and honest truth, it just makes sense to maintain at least a small nucleus of prudent lies. Plus, it led them to the conclusion that I wasn't currently psychotic, which *was* the truth. So, in a way, the lie was more honest than the truth. You follow me? At any rate, this whole "being honest" thing was turning out to be a lot more complicated than I'd ever realized.

I don't know. Fuck. Maybe I'm still wrapped up in layers of bullshit. But I'm trying to be honest with you. I'm really trying, and that is the truth.

So, we talked and we drank. We were honest with each other, if not entirely truthful, late into the night. Simon kept playing his video game, long after he'd stopped enjoying it—if, indeed, he'd ever been enjoying it. He must have killed about a million mooks before, finally, he gave in to our entreaties to come over and drink with us.

We gathered in the kitchen. The living room was open now, of course, but we were already too drunk to appreciate the fact. By his third drink, Simon was crying on my shoulder, sobbing his forgiveness. I knew his forgiveness wouldn't survive the sunrise, but it felt good anyway.

At around three in the morning, Simon and I packed my friends into a cab and sent them home. David too, since he had to work in the morning and I didn't want to fuck up his life the way I'd fucked up mine.

I kissed him through the open window of the cab as Michael snored and Gabby yelled at him to close it against the cold and the blowing snow. As I leaned back, he remained there, head in the window, eyes closed and lips puckered.

Simon gave him a sloppy kiss, and we all erupted in laughter. Even Michael woke up and started laughing, though he hadn't seen it happen. The cab driver must have gotten tired of us at this point, since he pulled away from the curb without even glancing in his mirror. I could still hear them laughing until they were fifty yards down the street.

Simon returned to the warmth of the apartment, but I just stood there a while longer, watching the snow come down. It's that first snowfall that's always the most beautiful, you know? By January, it's been churned into a shit Slurpee, but you never seem to think of that during the first snow of the season. That first snow is pure beauty, swirling through the streetlamps and coating everything in a thin, sparkling layer.

It was a while before the cold drove me back inside. I was in the shared hallway, just about to return to my apartment, when I saw her coming down the stairs.

"Miss me?" she asked.

♦

I didn't say anything. I just slumped against the wall outside my apartment and put my head between my knees. I didn't even cry. I didn't have it in me anymore.

Dee squatted beside me and tilted her head. "You okay?"

I looked at her over the curve of my knee. "Allow me to answer your question with a question: I hate you. Question mark."

She patted me on the head and smiled. "Oh, Jordan. That's all I ever wanted."

"So, all that cowering before the power of the Lord, that was just an act?"

She smirked. "Yeah. Pretty good, though, huh? And appropriate. The lesson you've learned today has implications beyond religion, to lies in general."

"Well," I said, "I've definitely learned an important lesson about the futility of ever telling the truth."

"Aw, sweetie pie," she said, stroking my hair. "You already knew that. You just forgot it for a while. I'm glad I was here to help you re-center yourself."

I was thinking of going back to the priest and asking for a do-over. In the moment, I decided against it not because I thought it was a useless effort, but because I was too embarrassed to admit it hadn't worked the first time.

I pushed myself to my feet, leaning against the wall for support as I rose.

When I was up, I got out my phone and hailed a rideshare. It took a few tries, given the screen's condition, but I got it eventually.

"We going to a club?" Dee said, peering over the jagged edge of my Frankenphone. "I wish you'd picked any other night, Jordan. I am totes sore down there."

I followed her eyes to her groin, then whipped my eyes away in repulsion. "Are you shitting me? That was *you* upstairs? With my Bible-thumping neighbor?"

Dee rolled her eyes. "Oh, please. She's bi but intensely closeted because of her upbringing. But I got her to agree to go to a local LGBT meet-up. She has a crush on you, by the way. That's why she's always so angry. Repressed feelings."

I shook my head, more in wonder than denial. "Huh. Okay, that kind of makes sense. Closeted bi chicks always seem to glom onto me, for some reason."

"Probably because you look so much like a man. You're like training wheels."

"Thanks."

She smiled brightly in answer.

"I told David about you."

Her smile disappeared, and she held up her hands in a defensive posture. "Hey, that was your decision, not mine. You could have gone your whole life lying to him and been perfectly happy doing it."

I shook my head.

"Bullshit," she said. "Maybe you *want* to be the kind of person who couldn't be happy lying to your soulmate, but wanting doesn't make it so. Ironically, if you were more true to yourself, you'd be happy lying to the people you love, like a normal person."

I said nothing. I only lowered my head.

My phone rattled, jabbing a sharp piece of screen into my palm. Outside, my rideshare was pulling up. I was starting toward the front door when Dee brought me up short with a hand across my chest. "You're not going to tell Simon where you're going?"

I shook my head. "I don't want to admit that you're still here."

She laughed, without humor but with a lot of mockery. "It doesn't reflect badly on you, you know, that I'm still here. It only reflects badly that you thought I wouldn't be. You may not get another chance to talk to him without a lawyer and two cops in the room."

So, she knew where I was headed. "I just can't, okay?"

She obviously didn't want to accept that answer, but her arm dropped to her side and she said, "Okay."

She said nothing through the entire ride to the police station in Wellesley. She just sat next to me in the back of the car. The only annoyance was that, once, she tried to hold my hand supportively.

When I got out, the driver took a look at the distinctly indoor clothes I was wearing, passed me a hand warmer through the window, and said, "You'll give me a five-star rating, yes?" I nodded, not thinking until later that a five-star rating from a soon-to-be confessed murderer might not be the best thing for him.

Inside the station, there was one guy on duty, sitting at a desk behind a wall of glass. When he saw me come in, he put his phone down and started writing in a ledger. He didn't look up from it as I approached, but only sat there pretending to work, until I leaned close to the little circle of holes in the glass and said, "I'd like to turn myself in and confess to the murder of that woman you found buried out in the woods."

I believe I've never seen a human being more annoyed than the police officer at that moment. "Oh, come on, lady," he said, in a Southie accent so thick that the word "on" had about eight syllables in it. "Gimme a break."

"I'm serious," I said, with as serious a face as I could muster. "The woman you caught is innocent. I know, because I did it."

"Lady, listen," he said, putting his pen down, "why don't you go home, sober up, and if ya still think yah murdered someone in the mahning... Well, ya can always come back then. No rush."

"I'm not leaving," I said. "I'm going to stand right here until I get the chance to make a confession."

He let out a tortured sigh, stood up from his chair, and disappeared around the corner. A full minute later, he emerged from the door adjacent to the glass and said, "Ya sure about this, lady?"

I said nothing.

He sighed again, even more dramatically. "Fine." He didn't even cuff me. He just waved me through the door as he recited my Miranda rights. He had a female officer frisk me and put me in an interrogation room.

"I never doubted you," Dee said, appearing in the room. She looked at herself in the two-way mirror and adjusted her bra. "Well, maybe for the all of the past week and a half, but that's all."

I just grunted and slumped in the plastic chair.

She turned to me. "Don't worry; you can speak freely. There's a camera back there, but that cop didn't even turn it on. In fact, he didn't bother to call the investigator in charge of the case. I hope you like sleeping on metal tables, because no one's going to bother checking on you in here until morning."

I grunted again and slumped further.

Dee hopped onto the table and lay across it like a lounge singer on a piano. "So," she said, "why'd you do it?"

"Isn't that what the interrogator is supposed to ask?" I wasn't sure she was telling the truth about the camera not being on, but at this point, what did it matter?

She waved her hand at me, playfully. "Not that, silly. Why did you finally decide to confess?"

I shrugged. "Got nothing left to lose, do I?"

Dee recoiled, her playful attitude ceasing instantly. "Ugh," she said. "Really? Setting aside how entirely wrong that comment is, what a shitty reason to save a girl's life."

"I don't care," I said, falling forward, against the edge of the table, with my head buried in my arms. "She still goes free, right? Her life still gets saved. So what?"

I could feel her breath on my head as she leaned in close to me. "It's the wrong reason."

I groaned. "I don't care. The result is the same. What does it matter if I do it for the right reason or the wrong reason?"

"If, in your whole life, you only had to make this one decision, that would be reasonable," she said. "But your life is a string of decisions, each one leading into the next, bending the entire course of your existence one way or the other. So, sure, you can do the right thing for the wrong reason, but how long do you think you can keep it up?"

"At least until I get to prison," I said. "And then I'll see about changing my evil ways."

Dee was unusually silent. If she hadn't been stroking my hair very gently, I'm not sure I would have known she was there.

"I tell myself that I did the right thing in the end," I said, after a lengthy silence. "I tell myself that, in the end, I didn't let my mom die. But I did, didn't I? It just took longer than I thought."

"You're a deeply stupid person," Dee said, but by her tone, she didn't mean it as an insult. Somehow, I didn't take it as one.

"I keep thinking she's going to show up, and it'll turn out to be a big misunderstanding."

She said nothing for the entire rest of the night. She just lay there, silently, until I fell asleep.

# 30

"It was a frying pan."

The inspector didn't look up from his newspaper. "You killed her with a frying pan?"

"No, I killed her with a boning knife, thrust through the abdomen, below the ribs."

That seemed to get his attention. He looked at me over the Marmaduke comic.

"I dug the hole with a frying pan."

He lowered the paper an inch.

"Hey, I live in an apartment, okay? Then I buried her wrapped up in cling film and a throw rug. I'm sure you'll be able to match up the fibers to the ones left in my apartment. I don't clean very often."

He put his newspaper down, pulled a notepad out of his pocket, and started writing.

"Let's see, what else? I was driving a green Ford Fiesta I rented from Zipcar. The body was wearing a red skirt and red blouse. Oh! And I dropped the murder weapon into the Charles, over the west side of the Galen Street Bridge."

"And what was your relationship to the victim?"

"I thought she was the devil."

"Why did you do it?"

"Same answer."

The investigator looked over his notes, his face tightening with anxiety. "I'll, uh, be right back," he said.

"Right back" turned out to be several hours later, but Dee showed up to chat, and the time passed surprisingly fast. She was civil with me, I think because she knew she'd won. I'm sure the cops were recording me, but talking to people they couldn't see wasn't going to hurt my case at this point.

The investigator returned while Dee was explaining why the movie version of *Faust* had a terrible ending. He held records from the auto rental company in one hand—I recognized their logo—and what I assumed was a forensics report in the other. "Listen," he said, "we got divers ready to go, and a search warrant for your apartment. Are you sure about all this?"

"If I say no, what are you going to do? Let me go and keep that woman in jail?"

"Don't go confusin' the issue. All I want to know is if you're sure about this." I think his mind must have blocked out the implications of my question, in the interest of preserving his self-respect.

"So sorry I'm putting you guys out, but yes. I'm sure."

He heaved a deep sigh and left the room.

Dee shook her head. "You *literally* can't get arrested in this town. I always thought that was just an expression."

"They know how bad it'll look if they have to let that tweaker lady go." I looked at the mirror. "I think they're hoping I'll just get tired and leave so everyone can pretend this never happened and get on with their lives. Except for, you know, *her*."

◆

Confessing to murder is more like buying a used car than it really ought to be. Just when I thought we were done, and we'd arrived at a story I could sign my name to, the investigator would leave the room for a few minutes to talk to his manager, then come back with a change. The written confession went through a dozen versions, and each time he'd try to sneak in some minor detail that I didn't actually recall, or an event that didn't actually happen. I think he was trying to insert enough wiggle room to nab the tweaker lady as an accomplice, but I dunno. Maybe he just sucked at being a cop.

Eventually, the confession was signed and I was booked into holding.

The booking officer listed my possessions on a voice recorder as he put them into a baggie. "Wallet," he said. "Inside, seven dollars. Subway pass. Massachusetts driver's license. Health insurance card. BevMo Saver's Club Card. Liquor World Saver's Club Card. Watertown Whiskey and Wine Saver's Club Card. Credit cards, five."

"I guess I should have cleaned that out before I came here, huh?"

Dee shrugged beside me. "Next time you confess to murder, you'll know."

"I don't even use most of those. It's not what it looks like."

The booking officer was impassive. He didn't even make eye contact as he took the next item. "Cell phone, broken."

The phone began to ring, and even being proved wrong didn't evoke the slightest surprise or resentment in him.

I glanced at the screen. It was Simon. "Can, uh, can I just answer that?"

He looked me in the eyes and made a stern, callous face that expressed *no* better than words possibly could.

Once they had all my stuff, I was chained to a bench in an empty room for several more hours. I tried to start a conversation with Dee, but she kept getting down on all fours and clawing at the corner of the room like a terrier.

"I got you into this," she said with nervous energy, "but I'll get you out, too. Here, eat this plaster dust so they won't know we're tunneling." She stuck her open palm under my mouth.

"Ew, no! That's not even plaster dust. It's just dirt off the floor."

"Admittedly, the tunneling operation is going slower than I'd hoped. But that's no reason to give up." She started whistling the tune from *The Great Escape*.

She hadn't made any progress when they came for me again, this time to load me on a shuttle van and take me to the county lockup, where I'd have to wait for the district attorney to get their charges in order before I could appear at an arraignment.

Word must have gotten out about my confession, because there was a crowd of people outside the gate. As I was loaded in the van, I saw news crews, bloggers, rowdy Bostonians, and what looked like the tweaker lady's entire extended family, all screaming bloody murder at me. I tried to flip them off, purely out of habit, but only bruised my wrist on my manacles.

"Good, they kept the cuffs loose," Dee said from the back seat.

I turned back to see her dressed as a police officer, plus sunglasses, a cowboy hat, and a mustache. She looked out at the crowd and said, "My, my, my. What a mess."

I shook my head. "*The Fugitive*, right? Tommy Lee Jones didn't have a mustache in that one."

The cop next to me shrugged at the driver, who was staring at me in the rearview. He said, "She's been talking to herself all day. Just ignore her."

Dee was still stuck on the subject of where her mustache was from. "So, what movie am I thinking of?"

"Uh, *Lonesome Dove? The Hunted?*"

"*The Hunted!* Thank you! That would have bugged me until I remembered it."

While I'm good at remembering Tommy Lee Jones movies, I'm apparently not so great at putting two and two together, because we were already near MIT in Cambridge before I twisted in my seat and asked, "Wait, why *The Fugitive?*"

She had just enough time to wink before the bus hit.

◆

It's funny, the things you do and don't remember.

I don't remember the crash. I do remember seeing the bus just before the crash, blowing through a red light on its way toward us. That memory is so clear, I could recite its fleet number and tell you which passenger the driver was yelling at.

My next memory is of the aftermath. My shackles were gone, my ribs ached, and I was reaching into the front half of the van to pull the driver out. Dee stepped out from behind the wreck, thumbs tucked into her waistband. "Now that's what I call a Dee-us ex machina." As she stepped over to me, she added, "Leave him. Unless the van's on fire, he's safer inside."

I felt particularly indignant about that advice, because I already knew it. I'd just forgotten in the chaos, or maybe I'd mistaken steam for smoke. I put one hand on his head, keeping his neck stable while I checked his pulse, as if that had been my plan all along.

"Come on," Dee said. "He'll be fine."

It did seem that way, so I ran across broken glass and shattered plastic, with the thought of checking the victims on the bus.

Dee grabbed me by the arm before I could get to it, hurting a bruise I hadn't noticed was there. "Jordan! Everyone is going to be fine. I made sure of it. There are actual professionals coming right now to treat them and arrest you."

I stopped and studied her face, looking for signs of deception. Her Tommy Lee Jones mustache was missing, but at the time that didn't seem strange, because I remembered her losing it in the accident. Sadly, that remembrance of a memory is all I can recall now, which sucks, because it sounds pretty awesome. Even without the mustache, she seemed to be sincere, and I remember thinking that everyone I'd checked so far had been stable.

"Now, Jordan!"

I'd love to tell you that I was completely convinced she was telling the truth, but really, I was only about three-quarters convinced, and self-interest filled in the rest. Dee pointed down Third Street, so I ran, with her leading the way.

She stopped short when we got to the Museum of Science, and peered at the street sign on the corner that read CHARLES RIVER DAM ROAD. Even as I urged her on, she only looked up and down the street, searching for something.

"What?" I asked.

"Where's the dam?"

I blinked several times. "What dam? You're not going to make me jump off a dam, are you?"

"Oh, come on!" she cried. "It'll be fun. And how else are you going to get away from the cops? But where is it?"

"The Charles River Dam is three streets down. There, past I-93." I pointed to the locks and pumping station of the dam, barely visible around a bend in the river.

Her eyes went from Charles River Dam Road, which we were standing on, to Charles River Dam, about a mile away. She blinked several times, then threw her arms into the air and screamed, "But that doesn't make any sense!"

"It's Boston," I said. "What do you expect?"

"I expect that I, the devil, the omnipresent master of deceit, ought to be able—"

I cut her off with "Babe, you got nothing on Boston where deceit is concerned. This town could give you lessons."

"Fuck, and there are the cops. Would you mind jumping off the railing when they get here?"

I followed her eyes along the road to where a trio of staties were running toward us, shouting at curious onlookers, telling them to get back into the Science Museum. I looked over the railing, to the river. "It's only, like, five feet down," I said, more in disappointment than relief. If I had to jump into freezing water, it seemed a shame to cheapen the spectacle.

"I'll make it up to you later," Dee said.

I climbed onto the railing and stood there, unsteady, hands on my head.

As the staties approached, Dee shot me a grin and said, "Say it."

I wrinkled my nose at her.

"Saaaaaay iiiiiiit!"

I sighed and said, "I didn't kill my wife!"

She doubled over in glee, but the staties only pointed their guns and screamed commands, telling me to get on the ground and lie flat. Disappointing, I know, but in their own way, they were telling me they didn't care.

I stepped off the railing.

# 31

*Fuck*, that water was cold.

I'm not a terrible swimmer, but the freezing shock turned me into one. I flailed and doggy-paddled in a pathetic little circle, while the cops tried to shout commands between bouts of laughter.

Dee, now wearing a skimpy bathing suit, swam in a wider circle outside mine, doing an elegant backstroke.

"What now?" I asked, then inhaled a spray of water and started coughing.

"I was going to have you swim to Mass General Hospital and become a janitor." She looked up at the staties, who were calling for a boat. "But I don't know if that will work now. I think we have to switch movies. You ever see *Waterworld?*"

I spit out a mouthful of the Charles River and said, "More times than I want to admit."

She wrapped me in her arms, looked deep into my eyes, and said in a husky voice, "I'll breathe for both of us."

I had just enough time to say "Aw, shit" before she dragged me under. She clamped her lips over mine—more like a lamprey than Kevin Costner, truth be told—and exhaled hot devil breath into my mouth. As she pulled me down to the murky bottom of the Charles, I kept my eyes closed, to protect them from the sediment and pollution. I only opened them when I felt some slimy bottom dweller wriggle out of the way of my foot.

It was then that I took a moment to reflect on how badly my life had gone astray.

As my legs sank into goop that erupted in streams of tiny methane bubbles, I concluded that things could be worse. More of the methane bubbles could be going up my nose, for example, or Dee's breath could be cold. I guess what I'm saying is, recent events had taught me to look for silver linings.

Up above, I thought I caught one of the staties saying, "Like hell Ah'm gettin' in that wahtah."

The depth muffled the rest of their conversation, but I can only conclude that the recalcitrant statie won out, because nothing more than a handful of glowsticks were tossed into the water. And that was another thing that could be worse, because they were actually quite beautiful, their pale green light shimmering through the murk as they floated downriver.

Hashtag blessed.

A minute later, a line was lowered to within a foot of us, and Dee reached for it with mischief in her soggy eyes. I slapped her hand away. It was hard to see clearly, but I think she looked abashed.

I started to swim—one-handed, with the other arm wrapped around my diabolical breathing apparatus—toward what I figured was the Cambridge shore. Dee resisted me, and won out in the end because I needed her cooperation a lot more than she needed mine.

So, by the veto power of the Costner, we remained in place. Despite her hot breath, the cold was beginning to seep into me, starting with pain in my fingers and toes, then proceeding to numbness. Dee seemed to notice this, and a look of concentration passed her face. The water around us became pleasantly warm, and though I could see no change in its color, I grimaced to let her know that I knew the origin. She giggled into my mouth, and I heaved a defeated sigh back into hers.

Weird fucking day, huh?

When the boat arrived, I understood her plan. Its outboard motor kicked up the river bottom and left a cloud of silt in its wake—perfect cover for the trail of silt we left as we swam and pawed our way through the mud. The harbor patrol cops were still busy raking and poking the river bottom at the spot where I'd gone in, when we came ashore at North Point Park.

Getting out was colder than going in. The air was below freezing, and its chill cut straight through me. By reflex, I recoiled from it, trying to stay in the water, and Dee had to drag me through the mud of the bank to get me out.

She didn't have to keep her mouth clamped to mine, of course, but she kept it there anyway. We came out of the river like a couple of conjoined swamp things, fused at the lips. I pushed at her, but my hands slipped on layers of slime, gliding over her body in a way that she took as an invitation to grope me.

When she stuck her tongue down my throat, I found the strength and the leverage to throw her off—kind of like one of those mothers who can lift cars to save their kids. Following Newton's Second Law of Slapstick, I tumbled back with equal and opposite force, lost my footing, and landed with a wet *plop* in the snow.

I wiped the slime out of my eyes and looked around for cops. There were none, only a couple of kids sitting idle on a nearby swing set, staring at us. They were perhaps seven years old, a boy and a girl, bundled to excess in adorable winter clothes.

The little girl shook her head and said, "That's Boston for you."

The boy pulled several layers of scarf away from his mouth and replied, "Must be something in the water."

Even Dee was embarrassed. She got up, pulled me to my feet, and led me away at a brisk pace. Behind us, parents were already gathering together and pulling out their cell phones.

"They're calling the police," I said.

"How is that my fault?" Dee replied.

"You dragged me out of the river and Frenched me in front of a children's playground!"

"It's nothing those kids haven't seen on the internet. Come on. This way. There's a Sears nearby." She turned a corner down a side street toward Lechmere, a route that kept us away from too many gawkers.

The warming effect of the slime layer was starting to wear out, and I was getting grumpy. "Listen," I said, even though the freezing air was like a shiv to my lungs every time I talked, "if we're going to hang out, you have to stop sexually assaulting me."

"I'm the *devil.*"

"So?"

She stopped and looked back at me. "So, you should feel honored that I'm sexually assaulting you, and lucky that I'm *only* sexually assaulting you."

I just stood there, unable to find words.

They must have been written on my face, though, and visible even through the slime, because she snorted and said, "What part of 'the devil' are you still not understanding?"

I didn't have an answer for that, so I made an annoyed grunt and continued on.

Dee's voice came from behind me. "You know, maybe if you communicated more, I wouldn't get confused about your intentions and have to sexually assault you so often."

I responded with an annoyed growl.

"See?" she said. "I can't tell whether you want me to shut up or pinch your ass. It could be either one."

"Shut up!"

She was quiet for only a few moments. "Still getting mixed signals. Your mouth says 'shut up,' but your ass says 'pinch me,' and your ass carries a lot more weight—in every sense of the word."

"Argh!" I cried. "I am a perfectly healthy weight! My blood triglyceride levels are low normal! My doctor says my HDL cholesterol is the best she's ever seen! I'm at minimal risk for diabetes! How many thin people can say all that? Plus, big butts are in!"

"*Devil*" was all Dee replied.

We slipped into the store with surprising ease and made our way to the bathroom despite being covered in river slime. *Sears: Our employees are well past giving a shit.* I cleaned myself off with blessedly warm water from the sink, while Dee sat on the counter and watched, dripping mud everywhere.

I got about 99 percent of the mud off, which still left me filthy by any ordinary standard, but I figured I'd pass with little notice in Boston. Dee made no effort to clean herself, but when I looked away and back, she was pristine, wearing a spotless, snug little burgundy evening dress.

"You couldn't have done the same for me? Like, back at North Point, maybe?"

She only shrugged. "Charity is just theft that the victim agrees to. If you want a dress like this, you can go down to Ann Taylor and steal one for yourself."

"But that would be theft the victim didn't agree to."

"You lost me," she said.

I did not go down to Ann Taylor. Instead, I stole a warm, plaid flannel shirt and work pants from the men's section, which offered the convenience of being right outside the bathroom door. I had to put my own sneakers back on, squelchy as they were, because there was an employee on duty in the shoe department.

On my way out, a girl at the register said, "Have a nice day."

"You too," I answered.

♦

"You look like a lumberjack," Dee said.

I was looking out a top floor window of Building 90 at MIT. At MIT, you can go pretty much anywhere if you're a woman dressed like a lumberjack, because people mistake you for an engineering postdoc.

"Thank you," I said. The thick clouds blowing in from the west had darkened the city, though evening was still hours away. That only made it easier to spot the flashing lights of the police as they canvassed the city.

They'd given up on looking for my body in the river and were now cordoning off bridges and roads to catch me as I fled the area.

"Trying to figure out how you can get to MGH and become a janitor?" Dee asked.

"Not exactly. If I catch a train to New York, though, I have friends who will probably take me in. And if not, I can just keep pushing on to Florida and cash in a favor from the bikers."

"That would be surprisingly coherent logic, for you, if the staties weren't checking everyone who gets on a train at South Station and Back Bay. They caught hell from the local police for letting you get away, so they're strongly motivated."

"Okay," I said, closing my eyes and imagining the Boston transit system. "So, I'll have to cut across Cambridge to Brookline, cross to Boston—I don't think they'll expect me on that side, so far upriver—and take the Orange Line to the commuter rail. I get off at Islington and catch the Amtrak from there."

I opened my eyes to find Dee staring at me, impressed. I didn't bother to tell her I'd worked this out, alongside a bunch of other contingencies, back when she first framed me for murder.

Her expression turned from impressed to curious. "And how are you planning to pay the fares?"

"Shit."

"You could sell your body," Dee suggested.

I snorted. "How much would you give me for it?"

She looked me up and down. "In its current condition?"

I was just about to return the most withering comment anyone has ever unleashed when I spotted flashing lights down First Street. The police were sweeping the campus. I ran for the elevator to get out of the building before they cordoned it off.

Dee shouted, "But...but...what about selling your body?"

"Later!"

Getting out of the building was easy, but getting out of MIT was more difficult. The Cambridge police had surrounded the campus, with cops at every intersection. I had to creep through buildings and courtyards until I reached the athletic fields, where I crossed the road between intersections, hoping the cops would mistake me for a softball player.

It worked like a charm—God bless the plaid flannel shirt industry—and it was just a few blocks from there to Brookline Street. The bridge presented a new problem. It was only a hundred yards or so to the other side, but there was a police cordon backing up traffic all the way to Mass Ave, a mile down the road. I checked out the scene from under the Memorial Drive overpass. Boston police were shining flashlights into every car and waving some off the road for inspection by an adorable German shepherd with a long, narrow nose and a goofy flop to one of its ears.

"If you try to pet that dog, don't expect help from me," Dee said, peeking over my shoulder.

"I make no promises," I said. "Did you see its—"

"One floppy ear. Yes, I saw it. You know that would disqualify her from competition in a dog show, don't you?"

"Okay, Ms. Suddenly-So-Serious, what do you suggest?"

She stared down the street, at the bridge. "The only sure way is to pull another *Waterworld*. We go over the bank, then follow the train tracks as they go under the bridge to hide any silt we kick up."

"Nooope," I said. "I'd rather take my chances on the bridge." Apart from the implied promise of sexual assault, I was still shivering from the last time I'd gone into that damn river.

"Oh, come on," Dee said. She had concern in her voice, as if she was genuinely worried about my safety. "I promise, no tongue this time." I sized her up and was just about to agree when she added, "Or, at least, the minimum amount of tongue necessary to satisfy my social awkwardness."

I eyeballed her.

"I understand your hesitation. That tongue *has* been up someone's ass, but it's the only way to ensure—"

"Nope!"

"Jordan…"

"No more *Waterworld*!"

"What about *Thelma and Louise*?"

"They die at the end."

"Right," she said, and stroked her chin, thoughtfully. "*Natural Born Killers* it is. I know where you can find a gun, and there are only a few cops. You can take them by surprise."

"No!"

"Well, then, I don't know what to tell you, except that I can't guarantee your safety."

"I'll take my chances. Anyway, I have an idea. Every time they wave a car to the side, they get distracted searching it. They give less attention to the cars going by, and they practically ignore the pedestrians."

"And you think they won't notice you, because you're dressed like a lumberjack?"

Okay, yeah, it sounds stupid when you put it like that, but hadn't it already worked twice? "If I get into trouble, I can jump over the side again. It's a much higher bridge, so you'll get the scene you wanted, anyway."

Dee replied with a disapproving rumble from the back of her throat, like Marge Simpson with a side of badger.

"Are you just mad that this plan doesn't involve the possibility of sexual assault?"

"Jordan, there's always a possibility of sexual assault. Have you seen the statistics? They're troubling, to say the least."

I opened my strategic sigh reserves and heaved one out. "I meant sexual assault by you."

"Yeah, so did I."

A big furniture truck was being waved over for a search. Perfect. It was bulky, obscured the cops' view, and would take a while to look through, so

I started down the sidewalk toward the bridge. Though, honestly, I might have made my move even if it was a scooter, just to end that conversation with Dee.

My timing was perfect, or so I thought, stepping onto the bridge just as the truck driver got into an argument with the police about his constitutional right to due process. I looked over my shoulder to gloat at Dee but couldn't find her. When I looked back at the truck driver, he gave me a wink and started haranguing the cops because they were hassling him instead of stopping sexual assaults. "Have you seen the statistics?" he cried. He flailed his arms, which instantly earned him the full attention of the half dozen police officers on the bridge.

I hurried my pace, to take full advantage of the diversion. As I passed the stopped truck on the opposite side of the road, I didn't look over at it, nor did I look back once I was past. I just kept my head high and my eyes forward, walking with the kind of swagger and entitlement that would make you think I owned the sidewalk, just like a Massachusetts native.

Someone else was coming the other way—a real native, I think. She walked the same way and gave me a nasty look as we passed each other.

I tried to ignore it. This was Boston, after all. Somehow, though, her expression was more than just run-of-the mill Massachusetts assholery. On a hunch, I dared to look back, and saw her crossing the street, walking confidently in front of moving cars as she made her way to the police checkpoint. She shot a look back at me for just a moment, then cast her eyes anxiously away.

I walked as fast as I could without being blatantly obvious about it. I hadn't expected random people on the street to recognize me. Panic was growing in my gut, and I knew it, so I forced myself to chill out, to walk slower, to breathe in a regular pattern. After all, I had my backup plan, even if everything else went sideways.

I looked over the railing to reassure myself with the calming sight of the river, where for the price of a cold plunge and some petty sexual assault, I could escape. I saw only railroad tracks.

This was where the railroad bridge ran under the traffic bridge, at such an oblique angle that you couldn't jump without hitting it. In fact, the angle was such that you couldn't jump into the river anywhere between me and the far shore. Why couldn't the railroad just run parallel to the bridge, like any sensible railroad would? Because Boston.

Now I really started to panic. I looked back at the woman crossing the road. I looked several more times than I should have—which was zero. She made it to the other side without being flattened, demanded the attention of a cop despite the best efforts of Dee-as-truck-driver, and pointed toward me just as I whipped my head away.

I finally reined in my panic enough to not look back again, knowing that my restraint might have come too late. I waited until I was across the bridge, turning as if to cross the road there, and only then cast a surreptitious glance toward the checkpoint. One officer was on his radio, while the other five were making their way toward me.

I ran for it, hopped a guard rail, fell farther than I thought I would, and landed in a BU parking lot. From there, I dashed across Commonwealth Avenue, and nearly got hit by a bicyclist, two cars, and a Green Line train. I knew Boston University well, so I should have been able to lose the cops in some alley or hiding spot. Unfortunately, BU doesn't have much depth—I bet you could make a joke about that if you were smarter. It clings to the river, so it's much longer than it is wide.

I made a snap decision to head for the science buildings, to try to lose the cops amid them, then cross I-90 at Brookline. That's, uhh, a completely different Brookline from the one I mentioned earlier, by the way. In the interest of maximum confusion, the two streets are maybe a mile away from each other. Boston will eat your GPS for breakfast and spit the bones at Rhode Island.

If I could make it across I-90, I'd be in the tangled mess of the Fenway. The Fenway has streets that abruptly change their names as you go, connect to each other at bizarre angles, and together form a warren of loops and dead ends. It's like Boston's Boston.

I was just ducking around the Photonics Center and heading for the Math and Computer Building—unlike those Bynars at MIT, we have actual fucking names for our buildings—when a couple of students spotted me. My photo must have been everywhere by now, because one of them took one look and ran for the nearest entrance to the Science Center. The other pulled a phone from his pocket and a selfie stick from his backpack.

He caught up to me in the dingy, covered walkway between the Math Building and Warren Towers, held the camera way out in front of him, and started snapping pictures. I'm not going to lie, I was pretty proud of my school. You think some Harvard shit would have the balls to pull that?

My admiration, however, didn't stop me from grabbing the selfie stick, phone and all, and pummeling him about the head with it. After a few dozen feet of this, we both tumbled to the ground in the courtyard in front of the College of Communication.

That courtyard opens right onto Commonwealth Avenue, where the police had apparently been concentrating their search. So, now I was staring down the radiators of three police cruisers, all of them digging up the snow-covered turf as they sped across the courtyard, right at me.

I made one last sprint for the bio and physics buildings, but one of the cruisers skidded down the sidewalk, its right wheels on grass and the left on concrete, sliding sideways like a crab. It cut in front of me and careened into a tree but stopped in time for the two officers to get out and block my path. The other cops were already forming a perimeter around me, cutting off every avenue of escape.

I was nicked.

I stopped where I was, shoulders slumped. Dee appeared next to me, shaking her head. "I did my best. We should have gone with *Waterworld*."

"I guess so."

She looked more disappointed than angry, but also more angry than mischievous. "Don't expect another chance like this. It would be suspicious if you were involved in two freak escapes."

"Yeah, I figured." I looked around as the police tightened their circle. "Hey, Dee."

"Yeah?"

"Do you figure my friends will visit me in prison?"

She smiled a genuine-seeming smile and said, "Yeah, I think they will. They're just the right kind of idiots."

"Hands up!" one of the cops shouted.

I complied, and only then realized I still had that guy's selfie stick.

Somewhere behind me, another cop shouted, "She has an ax!"

"Like a lumberjack?" I asked, reflexively turning my head toward him.

"Like a lumberjack!" Dee said, clapping her hands with mirth. She began to laugh—a giggly, tittering laugh like the ringing of silver bells.

And then her laugh caught in her throat and turned to a gasp.

It's strange, because I can remember the sound of that gasp with perfect clarity, even though I never heard the gunshot.

# 32

Luckily, my ninja training kicked in immediately. I have mentioned that I minored in Ninja Studies, right? Yeah, I'm pretty sure I mentioned that.

Anyway, with my instinctive situational awareness, I was able to predict the bullet's path without seeing or hearing where it came from. I dodged it just in time. It passed by my eyebrow so close that it shaved off a few of the lower hairs, giving me the exact sort of arch I could never achieve by plucking alone.

I did a back handspring, dodging more bullets and coming down on the roof of a cop car. With a series of spinning dragon kicks, I knocked out the officers who were crouched behind it, without doing any kind of permanent neurological harm or even giving them a concussion—thank you for teaching me that technique, Professor Kosugi.

I did a somersault off the car roof and landed behind it in a really cool position with both feet and one hand on the ground, just as bullets ricocheted off the frame. I stuck my head up for a fraction of a second—all I needed to get a complete tactical picture of the situation. Two more police cars were on the other side of the courtyard, at my ten and two o'clock. Dee was still standing where I last saw her, and she was flickering. *Curious.*

I ducked down as bullets whizzed over my head, close enough to disturb the part in my hair. Following a hunch, I sprang from a crouched position and did a shoulder roll on the sidewalk, coming out of it behind a nearby tree. Above me, a point of light sparkled atop a foot-thick branch. I reached up and karate-chopped it, breaking it without hurting my hand. When it fell, Dee disappeared and was replaced by a tiny image in the snow, right at my feet. It was being projected from a small device that had been carefully hidden in the tree.

"Hologram!" I said, biting back my unquenchable thirst for vengeance.

The other cops, hearing me and seeing what had happened, immediately understood the situation and stopped shooting. I came out with my hands up, and they let me explain the situation peacefully. A little digging on their part confirmed it.

Ruth, the boss from hell, had been playing an elaborate and cruel prank on me the whole time. In the days to come, she was exposed and went to jail. I hired Gabby's soup lawyer, and we were able to sue Ruth for ten million dollars and the intellectual property rights to the hologram technology she'd invented.

Hard to believe that was a whole year ago. It seems like yesterday.

In the time since, David and I got married, and now we live in a big house on Beacon Hill, with Gus the cat and a brand-new, perfect little baby girl that we named Dee, in honor of that strange and extraordinary ordeal.

So, I guess that's the end of my story.

Bye.

# 33

I sense that you're maybe not buying this. Yeah. I guess I wouldn't either, in your shoes—so to speak.

The truth is, I have practically zero situational awareness, Dee was not a hologram, and I didn't take Ninja Studies in college. Not even as an elective.

That cop's bullet entered low on the right side of my chest, hit a rib, and sprayed fragments of bone and metal into my lung, gall bladder, and liver. I wasn't knocked down by the force of it, nor did I fall after losing control of my body. I went down from the pain. It brought me to my knees first, my hands pressed tight to the wound, and from there I fell sideways into the snow, splattering its pristine surface with crimson.

"Roll onto the other side before you pass out," Dee said frantically. She knelt down next to me. "That's your best chance." Then she looked at the cops and screamed so loud that flecks of spittle flew from her mouth, "That is if these trigger-happy shitheads don't shoot you again!"

I obeyed, as much as it hurt to do it, leaving a deep and disconcertingly dark puddle of red in the spot where I'd fallen. When she saw that, Dee held her eyes on my torso, assessing the situation on a level I couldn't comprehend.

She was silent for a few seconds, during which I could hear the police still shouting commands at me from behind the safety of their cars. Then Dee shook her head and said, with tears in her eyes, "Goddamn it, Jordan. If you'd listened to me, this wouldn't have happened."

Beyond her, I could see the personification of death.

It was blurry, but it was him. "Hey, you're not gonna be needing your blender, right?" he asked. Yeah, definitely him.

Dee wiped her eyes, her face turning from somber to angry as she looked at me.

"Bad time?" Death asked.

"No, it's a perfect time," Dee said. She gave her nose a wipe and stood up. "Let's get back to her apartment. That stuff will just get auctioned off, otherwise."

As they were walking away, I held my hand out to Dee, prompting a new round of shouted commands from the police. "Please stay," I said.

She looked back at me with fire in her eyes, shook her head, and said, "No. You can manage dying on your own."

"Ouch," Death said. "Pretty harsh, don't you think?"

"That's life," Dee said, and then added, "no offense."

"Please," I said, using the last of my strength to utter that single word. I could taste blood bubbling on my breath, though I couldn't feel it anymore.

"Dude," Death said. She kept walking, but he held his ground and said again, "*Dude*." She stopped and looked back, at which point Death pulled out his most potent argument yet, saying, "*DUDE!*"

Dee sighed and, without another word, came back to me. She crouched in the snow, lifted one hand from where it had fallen, and squeezed it tight.

"See ya in Hell," Death said.

◆

So, I died.

If you didn't see that coming, you may want to consider the possibility that you're not as smart as you think you are.

◆

It wasn't some pansy hallucination or anything, either, because I'm pretty sure that's not a side effect of liver trauma. So, the moral of the story is simple. It's the same moral I should have learned from network television: if you're a woman who tries to have it all, you'll be tormented by wacky hijinks and get shot to death by the police. I never watched it, but I'm pretty sure that's how the *Mary Tyler Moore Show* ended.

I didn't so much wake as my mind came back into existence, piece by mental piece, in the bottom of a boat. I looked at myself and saw that I was still dressed like a lumberjack. Death stood at the prow, grunting with effort as he pushed a gondolier's pole.

I sat and looked at the inky waters of what could only be the River Styx. I looked up and asked, "Is the sky bloodier than usual?"

Death glanced at it. "Nah. About normal."

The far bank was perhaps a quarter mile away. On it gathered a teeming multitude of humanity. "So, you're Charon, too?" I asked.

"Karen? Oh, *Charon.* Yeah, yeah." He stared at the shores of death. "Shitty job, if you ask me."

"How are the benefits?" Idle conversation was all that kept me from freaking the hell out—if you'll excuse the expression.

"Oh, the bennies are great. Thanks for that blender, by the way."

"Don't mention it."

We hit the bank hard, and Death stumbled forward as the boat lurched onto shore. "Shit," he said. "Sorry. I get distracted real easy." He held out a hand to help me out. "Thanks for being brave, by the way. Most of the people I meet are total pussies. 'Wah wah, I have unfinished business, it's not my time, I have so much to live for, and who'll take care of my cats?' Fucking douchebags." He handed me a slip of paper. "Don't lose that. It tells you which line you need to get in."

"Thanks," I said as he pushed off and headed out into the river. I couldn't see the other side from where I was.

All around me were hundreds of dazed people holding slips of paper like mine, bumping into each other, and generally getting nowhere. They only moved inland when more dazed travelers were disembarked behind them by a whole fleet of Deaths—who came in a variety of shapes and sizes and degrees of scariness. The Deaths steered ferryboats, escorted the dead over bridges, or simply dropped them from above and flew away on great black wings. My Death had said something about a line, but there were no lines, so I pushed my way inland with the rest.

And pushed my way inland. And pushed my way inland. And pushed my way inland.

The ground was desert sand, not hot or cold to the touch, nor anything in between. It had no temperature, and neither did the air I breathed.

The sands never seemed to end, just like the masses of the dead. As far as I walked, all I met were my fellow shades, all going nowhere. I couldn't see the end of them, in any direction.

A strange sort of timelessness pervaded those shores. I don't know how long I walked. Hours, at least. Days, maybe—insofar as a day means anything in a sky without a sun, only a red glow that gives no warmth.

Suddenly, one of them grabbed my collar and yanked me back in the direction I'd come, saying, "No cutting in line!"

"This is a line?" I asked, seeing no evidence of it, even when I was made aware.

She gave me a cold look. She was taller and looked stronger than me—not that I knew whether that mattered here—and I retreated with my hands in the air.

"It's line 218," she said. "It starts directly behind me."

"Okay, okay, sorry." I examined my ticket, trying to remember my Roman numerals and figure out which line I was supposed to be in.

"I thought this was line 219," someone said, well out in front of the line monitor.

"Wait, these are the lines?" asked a voice from behind.

"Will you idiots in 219 please leave some space?"

"Is there a line for five dash one dash, umm, four hundred, I think?" I asked. "Because mine doesn't really make sense."

"Here, let me help you, love," a British man in a bowler hat said, reaching for my ticket. He seemed to come straight out of the 1800s, which made him an odd fit among the modern, recently deceased shades around me. Maybe he died while cosplaying, but I was wary, because I knew from history classes that the British of that era were famously good at stealing shit—you know, like subcontinents.

I flicked my ticket back, and someone behind me tried to grab it. "Here, I'll help you find your line," a woman said.

A third shade, and a fourth, were now approaching me, all smiling and far too eager to help.

The woman who'd first grabbed me pushed her way into the fracas of helpfulness, saying, "Away, vultures!" She shot a particularly acid look at the British guy, and as I took a good look at her, I realized from her dress, appearance, and accent that she might have died in India in the '50s. Whether this was her version of Hell or if she just saw a job that needed doing and decided to do it, I never found out, but she took me by the hand and said, "The VIP line is that way. The one on the very edge."

"Wait, VIP? Does that mean I..." I hesitated to say it, not wanting to sound foolish.

"Get to go to heaven? No one knows. But it can't be much worse than waiting here with these tossers. Now go, before anyone else decides to 'help' you."

So, I walked, skirting the edge of what could be called "lines" if one were feeling very generous. After another timeless space of hours or days, I arrived at the edge of the mass of shades. There, holding them back on their left flank, was a velvet rope with a sign on it that directed VIPs to the left and OTHERS to the right. A man with a barrel chest and cherry-red skin stood just behind the sign. He wore sunglasses and a shirt that read STAFF.

When I approached, I flashed my ticket, and he hooked his thumb toward the left line. "Thank you," I said. He returned only a grunt, and I caught a glimpse of yellow eyes behind his glasses as I passed.

I hurried on, passing lined-up shades to my right. Their line stretched forward as far as I could see, for as far as my vision could resolve in the crystal-clear, hazeless air. I walked until I lost track of time again. I began to pass shades that displayed the casual chic of the Oughts, then the grunge look of the Nineties, then the mega-hair of the Eighties.

It just kept going, an archeological record of the dead that stretched back through the decades. I came across a group of hundreds wearing a mix of sailor suits and early twentieth-century attire. I had just opened my mouth to ask when several of them shouted at once, "We ain't from the bloody *Titanic!*"

A sailor in a spiffy, double-breasted outfit added, "They're two years ahead of us, up there. We're the *Empress of Ireland.*"

I shut my mouth, swallowed, and nodded politely.

"You know, *Empress of Ireland?*" He shook his head at my ignorance. "Sank in the Saint Lawrence River? A thousand people drowned? A thousand dead, and you've never heard of it? Oh, but you know aaaall about the goddamn *Titanic!*"

"Read a fookin' history book!" one of the passengers shouted, making a rude gesture at me. The other victims joined in, and I hurried past them.

Two years down the line—measured by the time of their deaths, I reached the *Titanic* victims, who also made rude gestures as I passed them.

I walked on. On and on and on, passing a seemingly endless parade of the dead. And then, one day, one week, one month—I really don't know—I could see the lines disappear into an unmoving bank of mist ahead. I quickened my pace. I don't know why I hadn't before, since my legs never got tired.

On the other side of the velvet rope, a group of Chinese people waited at the front of their line, wearing attire ranging from hemp pants to Tang suits to silk robes. A few even wore blue cotton suits with a distinct maritime style to them. "Let me guess," I said to one of them, "you're from the *Titanic?*"

Come on, it was a joke! Something to lighten the mood.

"*Tek Sing,*" he said, without a trace of amusement. And when it was clear I had no idea what he was talking about, he threw his arms in the air and said, "More people died than on your stupid *Titanic*—piece of crap boat!—but you don't know about it because no one made a movie with sexy white people. You're a disgrace!"

"How do you even know about that movie?"

"I hear things!" the sailor said, then crossed his arms and turned away.

I kept going. I stepped into the mist and walked straight into a bank of counters. It didn't hurt, but it was still embarrassing. The counters ended at the edge of a precipice to my left, and stretched out into the mist to my right, interspersed with turnstiles. I could see two or three demons—let's not be coy about who the people with STAFF shirts were—interrogating exasperated shades.

"Did you visit a country with infectious diseases within ninety days of your death?" the demon asked some poor woman, who looked like she just wanted to get this over with so she could finally get to Hell and have some peace.

"Yes," she said.

The demon checked a box on a sheet of paper, the topmost in a stack of hundreds. He pulled another from under the counter, placed it on top, and licked his pen. "Are you travelling with the intent of violating the national or regional laws of your destination?"

"What? I don't even know what the laws are! None of us know where we're going!"

"Hey, take this seriously or I'll send you to the back of the line." The demon glanced at me, then flashed a smile full of shark teeth at the poor woman. "Just a moment. I have to attend to a VIP."

"But we're almost finished!"

His shark smile never wavering, the demon slid his hand forward over the counter, pushing the hundreds of completed pages onto the sand, where they promptly burst into flames. The lady managed to save exactly one of them. He turned to me. "How can I help you, miss?"

I flashed an apologetic grin at the woman in line, but she just cursed and made two-hundred-year-old rude gestures at me.

"Miss?" the demon asked again, his lips forming a tight but warm smile. "What can I do for you?"

"Uhh... Checking in?"

"Ticket?" the demon asked.

I showed it to him without handing it over. "Oh, you're Jordan Liang," he said. "Or, at least, you're whoever mugged her and took her ticket. Right this way." He indicated the nearest turnstile with a flourish.

I stepped through, and the lady at the next counter absolutely lost her shit. She flailed around, shaking her fists and screaming curses at everyone within earshot. The demon made a beckoning motion toward the sky, and two men floated down on either side of the unruly woman—one with the head of an ox, the other with the face of a horse.

I watched from the other side of the turnstile, even as the mist closed around me, slowly cutting off my view. The men grabbed her by either arm and dragged her back through the crowd. "No! No! I'm sorry! Don't put me in line for two hundred years again!"

"Two hundred years was the wait time when you first got in line," Ox-Head said.

Horse-Face blew a fluttering snort through his nostrils and said, in a calm and pleasant voice, "Current estimated wait time is three hundred and forty-seven years. Thank you for your patience. Your business is important to us."

The last thing I heard, before the mist closed around me, was, "Fuck you, you wicked bitch! Fuck your mother! Fuck your ancestors!"

"Sorry!" I called back, though I'm not sure she heard it.

"People can get pretty angry in that line," said a calming voice from behind me.

I turned to see an old white guy in a bright white robe, with white hair. I didn't know his face, and yet I seemed to recognize him somehow.

◆

He beamed a welcoming smile.

I swallowed hard and asked, "Are...are you God?"

He put a hand on my shoulder and squeezed. "Some call me that."

He squeezed harder, then started squeezing down my arm. I jumped back when he went for my boobs.

"You know," he said, "I might have a place for you here if you lost forty pounds."

I was wary of my first instinct, which was to punch him in the face. Instead, I stepped forward to get a better look. His white hair was an illusion of the mist. It was actually sandy blond, and his white garment was apparently a tan bathrobe. But I was certain I recognized him from somewhere. "Wait...are you Miguel Gulf?"

"Guilty," he said, holding his hands out in an exaggerated gesture of surrender. He flashed a pearl-white grin at me. "Seriously, though, I'm not sure if you can lose weight down here, but you could be smoking hot if you were a little lighter. Turn around."

"No!" I stormed past him, ignoring the cat sound he made as I went by and the other, more sexual cat sound he made once I'd passed. He followed me as I emerged from the mist into something like a hotel lobby. There was a concierge desk, a bank of elevators, and a sign on the wall that read VIP LOUNGE.

"Hey," Michael Gulf shouted at the concierge demon, "can she lose weight down here?"

The demon's upper eyelids drooped as he sighed. "Neither of you are made up of massive particles."

As Miguel Gulf tried to wrap his brain around that answer, I asked, "Why are you here, anyway?"

He smirked—just about the smirkiest smirk I'd ever seen—and said, "Sold my soul to the devil. Thirteen-movie deal, with an option for thirteen more under...certain conditions."

The concierge demon cut in with "He had to 'show the potential to destroy every vestige of self-respect left in American cinema.'"

"Yeah, well, I made the VIP line, so I must have done something right, eh?"

I held my hand up, palm flattened, and pushed him away by the face. "I want to see Dee," I said to the concierge.

"Elevators," the demon said, "but not many people get in to see her.

Since you're new, you might want to consider taking the VIP bus tour."

I blinked twice. "Bus tour?"

"We call it Hell on Wheels. Ha ha ha. It goes through every level and sublevel. They point out the sights, show you where celebrities are being tortured—that kind of thing. It takes a while, but there's a prize for whoever spots the most popes."

"Thanks," I said, and headed for the elevators, trying to ignore the discussion between Miguel Gulf and the concierge demon about the technical definition of the word *weight*.

I approached one of the elevators. A demon stood next to the doors, a red phone behind him. Above him, a sign said EXPRESS ELEVATOR TO HELL.

"Shouldn't that be 'Intra-Hell Express Elevator?" I asked.

He nodded. "Yeah, but marketing liked this better. Level?"

"All the way down," I said. "I want to see her."

He looked at me skeptically.

"Please?"

With a long-suffering sigh, he picked up the red phone and said, "Yeah, I've got a VIP asking to see the big man." I could hear some conversation on the other side of the line. Whatever it was, it surprised the elevator demon, who looked more optimistic as the discussion went on. Someone on the other end asked a question, and the demon looked me up and down. "I don't know if I'd call it a pot roast, exactly." He cupped a hand over the receiver. "Are you Jordan Liang?"

I nodded.

"Yeah, it's her." He quirked his brow at whatever the other party said. "Shit. It's all about who you know, isn't it?" He hung up as the doors opened to a magnificent glass elevator.

I stepped aboard and looked out, and all of Hell stretched before me. It was Hell as Dante envisioned it, down to the very last circle. "Is this real?" I asked, as the doors closed and the elevator began its descent.

"*Real* is one of those squirmy, wriggly words that's hard to pin down," the demon said. "It's all 'real' insofar as your perception of it maps accurately to reality via a—how to put this in terms that your puny ape brain can understand?—complicated web of…things."

I turned to find him looking quite proud at his explanation. "'Complicated web of things'?"

He only nodded.

"Got it. Thanks."

The elevator was accelerating now, descending past the fields of Limbo, to be buffeted by the winds of the Second Circle. It emerged from the bottom of the storm and promptly plopped into muck. We sank past suspended bodies, which I could only see as hands clutching toward the glass. Another plop, and we were through the muck, accelerating again. Just enough mud had fallen from the glass for me to catch a glimpse of shades pushing boulders before we descended into a tunnel that opened above a river. We plunged through it, and in the newly washed glass, I could see hundreds of people fighting each other underwater, like in a James Bond movie.

I'm not going to lie: it was pretty cool. If I wasn't a VIP, I'd want to end up there.

I caught a glimpse of the flaming tombs of Circle Six as we went through a sinkhole in the riverbed, then I looked away. I asked the demon, "So, Dante really did come through here?"

"Absolutely," the demon said, then seemed to reconsider his answer. "But, you know, after he was dead. He wasn't nearly as flattered as we expected."

"Right."

I kept my back to the window and my eyes on the marble floor until the doors opened and the demon said, "Level Nine, Center Stop."

I looked out and saw nothing but blackness outside the door. Without hesitation—well, okay, with a little hesitation—I stepped into the Ninth Circle of Hell. The doors closed behind me, cutting off the only light.

Or so I thought. In time, my eyes adjusted and I saw a vast lake of twilight ice marred with crevasses and surrounded by glassy cliff face. Dee was standing in front of me, hardly a foot away. Perhaps she'd been there since I stepped off the elevator. In appearance, she looked perfectly human, dressed in the same burgundy dress I last saw her in.

"You colossal shithead," she said, and smacked me across the face. It didn't hurt, but I recoiled by reflex. "Why did you go and get yourself killed? We were having so much fun. It's almost impossible to have fun down here, you know, because you people stop taking yourselves so seriously as soon as you're dead."

"I don't see how that stops me having fun."

She looked genuinely confused. "What? No, I meant *my* fun. It's harder for *me* to have fun."

I gave the barest shrug, to show how thoroughly I didn't care. "Maybe you take yourself too seriously when you're down here?"

"Maybe." She rolled her eyes while she said it, but after a few moments' reflection, she added in a softer, more thoughtful, and acquiescent voice, "Maybe."

"Hey, aren't you supposed to be chewing on Judas, Brutus, and..." I snapped my fingers, trying to remember the name. "That... other guy."

"Cassius," she said. "But I only bring them out for special occasions." She broke eye contact on the excuse of picking at one of her fingernails. It reminded me of myself nervously trying to gauge the right level of familiarity with someone. "So, how's your day going?"

"I'm in Hell. How do you think it's going?"

She laughed at me, and pointed to make sure I knew it was mocking and not humorous laughter. "It could always be worse, Jordan."

"Sure, but why am I in Hell?"

That brought her laughter to a trailing close. She looked at me, seeming to contemplate not the answer itself but how to properly express it. "Well, there are a lot of reasons, really." She started ticking off on her fingers. "You slept with the devil."

"In the same bed as!"

She ignored me and went on. "You lusted. You lied. You're sullen. You're a hypocrite. You flattered. You took oaths thoughtlessly. You wore linen clothing with mildew on it. You had a rash and didn't show it to anyone. You didn't respect your mother." She'd run out of fingers at this point, and started over. "You doubted the word of a truthful man. You gossiped. You slandered. You bore grudges. You wore clothing made from two types of material. You failed to respect your elders. You had pride. You had pique. You had vanity. You took intoxicants. You were gluttonous in the taking of intoxicants. You were gluttonous in the taking of pudding cups. You failed to get a receipt when shopping. You showed transilience. You were cynical. You laid with a woman as if with a man. You knocked out a guy's tooth without paying him two shekels of silver. You made people cry. You eavesdropped. You grieved uselessly. You were angry without cause."

I stood patiently through the whole list, unwavering even as she abandoned her fingers and instead leaned closer to me after every item. When she finished, I asked, "Those are all sins in somebody's religion, huh?"

"A few of them I made up," Dee said. "Bet you can't tell which."

I didn't bother trying.

"But there's a simpler reason you're not in heaven, Jordan. Let me ask you this: what do you suppose heaven is?"

Is it weird that this was the first time I'd considered that question since I died? Yeah, I think it is. "I dunno," I said. "Clouds, harps. Maybe endless bliss? Communing with God? Getting to sleep in every morning?"

She smirked. "That last one, you can do here. You're not going to get fired, except literally. As for the others, how long do you suppose it would take you to get bored of them?"

"Point taken," I said. "But there has to be something."

"Not for you, toots. I could grant you your wildest dreams and desires, and you'd be bored in a week. Because nothing satisfies you. People like you think you can find eternal happiness for the same reason you think a house in the suburbs will make you stop cutting yourselves: because you're so good at lying, you've even got you fooled."

"Sorry," I said, and I didn't even mean it sarcastically, "I'm not quite cynical enough to believe that."

"But you're close? Well, let's give it a few centuries and reexamine the matter. I'm patient, you know."

I arched an eyebrow at her. "Are you? I thought patience was a virtue."

She smiled back. "Hey, I have lots of virtues. Fortitude. Hope. Faith."

"Faith? Really?"

She smiled a little wider. "You'd be surprised." Something seemed to occur to her. "Speaking of which, I was at your funeral. Ruth was there. She cried."

For the faintest glimmer of a second, I was moved. Then I thought about it and said, "No, she didn't."

"Okay, you got me. But she did get pretty emotional at the eulogy, when she lamented that you'd been failed by yourself. Of course, at the wake, she went around telling everyone how productivity increased across the board after you were fired, and then again after you were shot by the police."

"Oh, good. So, it wasn't a useless end, after all. What about the others?"

She took a deep breath. "They're getting there. It's been three weeks, and David still cries every day. I can't believe you fell in love with that pansy. Simon, on the other hand, still hasn't cried, because apparently your entire family is as emotionally stupid as you are. Gabby and Michael are…well, they're starting to cope. It's a process, you know. In spite of your best efforts—and their best interests—a lot of good people were very attached to you. You left big holes in big hearts."

I couldn't help but snort at that, dislodging some grief snot from my nose. "Don't ask me how. What about my mom? Does she know? Is she in one of those lines?"

The devil shook her head. "No, I expedited her case."

"Why?"

"Because I like you, you fucking idiot." She smiled fondly, even as she slapped me in the face again. This time, I didn't recoil. "She doesn't know you're down here, though. Best if she remains ignorant, if you ask me."

"I want to see her." I got the request out just in time to not think better of it.

Dee *ts*ked. "That's an awful idea. That's possibly your most awful idea ever, and I'm including every idea in the chain that led to your death. That's the kind of idea that's so awful, I'd make you sign a waiver."

"Fine," I said.

She arched an eyebrow at me.

"I'll sign a waiver, but I want to see her."

Dee deflated, her shoulders slumping and her gaze falling to the ice at her feet. She reached up and pinched the bridge of her nose. "Jordan, why must you be so contrary?"

"I'm a product of my environment."

With a deep sigh, she pulled a document from behind her back and produced a stiletto dagger with the other hand. "Fine. Hold out your finger."

"It has to be signed in blood?"

"No, but…I don't have a pen. Do you?"

I held out my finger. "Do I even have actual blood down here?"

"It's complicated," Dee said, pricking my finger.

I examined the contract, which read, in its entirety:

> I, Jordan Liang, acknowledge that I have been a complete idiot, and I will finally start taking responsibility for my bad decisions.

I signed with no more hesitation than you'd expect from such a frightening promise. I handed the document to Dee.

"You may not like what you find," she said.

"I'm sure I won't," I said, and turned back to the elevator. The doors were open. The elevator demon waited patiently, his hands folded together at his waist.

Dee spoke from behind me. "She's in Circle—"

"I know where she is," I said.

♦

And so, with a demon elevator attendant at my side, I came to Circle Seven, crossed a river of blood, and entered the Harpies' Wood. The harpies kept their distance, and the sinners guilty of profligacy steered wide of us, pursued as they were by ferocious bitches—most of whom were literal dogs but one of whom I definitely recognized from *Real Housewives of New Jersey*. No joke. The trees, as you know, were stuck in place, no matter how much they wailed.

Somehow, I knew exactly where I was going. I walked through the woods, being extra careful when I had to push aside the gnarled branches of a tree that barred my way. Even with the lightest touch, however, I still caused the trees to break, to bleed, and to wail all the louder. Even the trees I managed to get past without harm were promptly attacked by harpies—as if they were paying those poor souls back for the pain I'd failed to cause them.

I guess that's Hell for you, huh?

I apologized to the trees I harmed, and to those who would be swarmed by harpies after I passed. After a while, it seemed a useless effort, so instead I simply talked to them. I told them about recent events on Earth, about the price of bread and the progress of society in not driving souls such as themselves to this end.

Finally, I arrived here. Well, okay. No use lying about it. I arrived at the tree next to you, and my demon friend had to gently nudge me until I got the message.

In fairness, you're a fucking tree. You don't exactly have a ton of distinguishing features.

So, I guess, that's my story. That's how I came to be here, spilling my guts to a bleeding, wailing tree.

You know what the real hell of it is? You're the only goddamn person I could ever talk to, and we spent most of our lives not talking to each other. In a strange way, you were the only person I could trust with the truth—the only one who could handle it, the only one who could hear it and still respect me.

I dunno. Maybe that's bullshit. Or maybe it's just a mom thing.

The hell of it for you, maybe, is that I was the only person you could ever talk to, and now you can't even talk. Well, okay, I guess the hell of it for you is being a bleeding tree getting attacked by harpies. But the not-being-able-to-talk-to-your-daughter thing is at least kind of ironic, right?

Right?

Wail once for yes, twice for no.

*Fuck.*

I don't even know if you can hear me.

Do you even know I'm here?

This isn't going the way I thought it would.

But hey, when did it ever?

So, I guess I'll just say what I came to say.

Mom, I'm sorry. I'm sorry I didn't go to your funeral. I'm sorry I cut you out of my life. I'm sorry I was going to let you die. You're not a good person, but you deserved better than me.

The thing is? When I was seventeen, I thought I was the sort of person that the intervening years have proven I'm not. I thought that if I couldn't fix you, there had to be something unfixable about you—that you were broken beyond repair. So, I stopped trying, and I hated you instead. After all, how worthless did a person have to be that they couldn't be fixed by my brilliant interventions and advice and monologues? How broken and vile did you have to be that even my snow-white virtue couldn't fix you?

Yeah, I was a real shithead.

More of a shithead than you, even. You, at least, had the decency to be an inert shithead. I was a shithead with a mission. I think there are few things more dangerous than a smart, self-righteous crusader on a mission to fix people, especially when they've never bothered to fix themselves. Mote, meet eye, right?

Fuck, now I sound like Dee.

I hate when that happens.

Let's get back to the point.

I forgive you. I forgive you for being a drug-addled mess and terrible mother, and I hope you'll see your way to forgive me for my shortcomings.

Wail once for forgiveness.

You know what? I choose to believe that was a forgiveness wail. So, thank you.

I'll be on my way now.

Goodbye, Mom.

♦

Oh, and that night in the mental hospital? I haven't been entirely honest with you.

We did fuck, and it was outstanding. For all her faults, Dee is a genius with her fingers.

Hey, I was lonely and I thought David was going to leave, so sue me.

Okay, bye for real now.

# ABOUT THE AUTHOR

Robyn Bennis is a writer and biologist living in Madison, WI where she has one cat, two careers, and an apartment full of dreams.

She has done research and development involving human gene expression, neural connectomics, cancer diagnostics, rapid flu testing, gene synthesis, genome sequencing, being so preoccupied with whether she could that she never stopped to think if she should, and systems integration. She is the author of the Signal Airship Series from Tor Books and wrote her debut novel, The Guns Above, within sight of the historic Hangar One at Moffett Airfield.

http://www.robynbennis.com/

Made in the USA
Middletown, DE
19 August 2019